JUSTICE DELAYED, IS JUSTICE DENIED

A JON WILLARD NOVEL

#1 Best Selling Amazon Author

HENRY MARK HOLZER

JUSTICE DELAYED, IS JUSTICE DENIED
A Jon Willard Novel
Henry Mark Holzer

www.henrymarkholzer.com
www.henrymarkholzer.blogspot.com
hank@henrymarkholzer.com

JON WILLARD NOVELS

The Paladin Curse

A Fool for a Client?

Justice Delayed, is Justice Denied

. . . Abuse of Power . . . .
(Forthcoming 2022)

To Alyson Thal

Justice Delayed, is Justice Denied

— William E. Gladstone,
Nineteenth Century British Prime Minister

PREFACE

In late 1989, a Manhattan criminal defense lawyer was justifiably outraged because a New Orleans federal judge had recently been complicit in the near-certain murder of the lawyer's client.

The lawyer was also justifiably outraged because the former Brooklyn District Attorney — whom the lawyer had sent to prison for trying to frame an innocent man with a double homicide — was falsely making it appear that the DA was the real victim in that case.

The lawyer decided to use a prominent syndicated talk radio show to set the record straight, by revealing to listeners throughout the country what the federal judge and the former DA had done. The lawyer's intent was to expose and disparage them.

That is exactly what he did!

The lawyer's name was Jon Willard.

CHAPTER 1

IT WAS SAID OF WILLARD that he had combined in his character and law practice a Paladin's fealty to truth and justice with Don Quixote's idealistic quests as the means to achieve those noble ends.

Willard was a lawyer at the top of his game, and not to be trifled with.

Most recently, Exhibit "A" was three New York lawyers, including the State's Chief Judge, Robert Jackson, who had tried unethically, illegally, and unsuccessfully to have Willard disbarred. In turning the tables, Willard had gotten them disbarred, and Jackson imprisoned.

Exhibit "B," demonstrating what Willard was capable of, was the New Orleans federal judge, Amos Deveroux, who was successfully impeached, convicted, and then incarcerated for taking bribes from mobsters.

Exhibit "C" was the former district attorney, Michael Quade, whose disbarment and four-year prison sentence destroyed his career and his life.

In the last several years, Willard's criminal defense practice had boomed, largely because of the notoriety of his cases and his ability to win acquittals for those defendants who righteously deserved them. "Truth and justice" was the mantra by which Jon Willard lived and practiced law. Despite the cynicism that pervaded his personal and professional lives, existentially he usually obtained the legal results truth and justice demanded. Willard's internal and external conflicts, however, remained unresolved.

The accumulation of his cases in the last few years — especially Willard's unsuccessful attempt to save a defecting Chinese seaman, and the conspiracy of New York legal elites that was trying to disbar him — had taken a crushing toll on the lawyer. He was more tired mentally and physically than ever before.

Soon after their engagement party, Jon and his fiancé, Andrea Vardas, had agreed that he would go to his second home in Santa Fe for indefinite recuperation and cogitation, while hopefully writing a book he had been putting off since attending college in Albuquerque nearly two decades earlier. Willard had no cases pending, and his secretary would hold the fort in Manhattan. Andrea would wrap up her *pro bono* legal work at the Innocence Project in Boston and join him in New Mexico as soon as possible.

Aside from missing Andrea the moment he started loading his new Cadillac Escalade, Jon looked forward to being alone during the two-thousand mile, thirty-hour drive to Santa Fe. He intended to use some of the time to review the epiphany he had experienced during his recent battle with the disbarment conspiracy, and his successful counterstrike that had crushed the conspirators and vindicated him. Jon's time in Santa Fe would be a civilian version of military R&R—Rest and Recuperation—when he and Andrea could try to put his life in order and plan their future together.

CHAPTER 2

T*HERE IS NO DOUBT,* JON thought as soon as he left New York, *that during the disbarment litigation with help from Miles and Andrea — and Ayn Rand's ideas — I had a bona fide epiphany, facing the empty glass demon and eventually accepting that it always began full. No longer would I start with the iron-clad assumption that the game is fixed and that I cannot win. I finally accepted that most likely in the end truth would be told and justice done. I am convinced that I was not rationalizing. But if that is true, why since the disbarment case ended have I been wondering if I can sustain the epiphany? Was it real, or illusory? Does the glass always start full, or am I kidding myself?*

The first leg of Jon's journey was from Manhattan to Washington D.C., some two hundred miles straight down I-95. With pit stops, Jon allowed about six hours. Senator and Mrs. Thomason had invited him for dinner and to stay overnight on his way to Santa Fe, but before getting to their home in Maryland Jon had two stops to make.

His first was at the Vietnam Veterans Memorial, the "Wall," where again he visited memories of men he had served with at Firebase Ripper.

Jon's second stop was at the Korean War Veterans Memorial.

Although Jon had not served with anyone who fought in that "police action," as President Harry S. Truman and his sycophants had labeled it, his MIA father disappeared forever into that conflict's jaws.

At his last visit several months earlier, Jon had promised his father he would fight with honor the disbarment war about to engulf him. At this visit, Jon reported that he had. And won.

CHAPTER 3

ARRIVING PUNCTUALLY AT 6:00 P.M. for pre-dinner cocktails, Jon was greeted warmly by Jim and Ava Thomason. The men had agreed in advance not to resurrect their Vietnam War stories. But the recently concluded disbarment case was not off limits because, as Jon had explained, he was trying to understand his psychology, emotions, and ultimate epiphany.

But despite the men's agreement, as soon as the three were comfortably seated in the living room, Ava Thomason said, "I know what you two promised about war stories, but there's something a once near-widow has to say." From Ava's tone and look, the two combat veterans knew better than to argue with her.

Ava seized Jon with her eyes across the coffee table. "Jon, I know the Firebase Ripper story, every cruel word of it, but I will not repeat even a syllable now. The best and worst of what happened there is buried with the good and bad men who died there, and others whose wounds later killed them."

"Understood," Jon replied solemnly.

Ava Thomason continued, "Before you wonder why I didn't say anything when Jim and I were recently in New York for your and Andrea's engagement party, I want to tell you now. What happened in Vietnam was beyond ugly and immoral, and any mention of it at your wonderful party would have rained on everyone's parade. That is why when we were leaving, I said softly, 'We will speak again'."

"I realized that," Jon said, "and I was grateful for your considerateness."

"Okay," Ava said, "so I'll say now what I didn't then. Lieutenant Jon Willard not only risked your life to save Jim's, but in doing so you saved our future children, their children, and the children of uncountable generations yet to be born. Think of that, Jon, literally an infinite number of human beings have had lives because of a single act of generosity you rendered to a man you hardly knew. And, no small thing, you gave me the life I've had these many years with Jim."

Ava Thomason stood up, walked around the coffee table, bent down, and kissed Jon on the forehead. She offered no further words. None were necessary.

While silence reigned, Jon flashed back to the wider picture of Vietnam, a largely conceived and fought political war. Nearly sixty thousand American military dead, uncountable wounded, ample deferments resulting in draftees averaging age nineteen mostly from minority and working class-backgrounds. Thanks to the loud, active anti-war movement, many returning drafted veterans were treated like criminals, exacerbating their suffering from post-traumatic stress disorder.

Through an act of will, Jon pushed Vietnam out of his mind and dinner passed with conversation about Jon's disbarment case, and associated events.

Jim had a few questions. He had become a prime player in that case by giving Jon most of the Senate Judiciary Committee files, and later convening a Judiciary Committee hearing to investigate Deveroux's appointment to the federal bench, all of which contributed to the destruction of some of the conspirators who were trying to have Jon disbarred.

"First," Jim asked, "how sure were you that Quade's testimony would be what you hoped for?"

"I knew Mike Quade from law school onward, so I knew his weaknesses. He would save himself, whatever he had to do. Everyone other than Quade goes under the bus. Mike Quade is not immoral, he is amoral. Worse than simply a bad guy. For him, morality does not exist. As to the three New York lawyers, Quade had instigated the conspiracy, and I expected him to sacrifice them along with the federal judge. That's exactly what he did."

Thomason also wanted to know what Jon would have done if Jim had not convened a Senate Judiciary Committee hearing to expose Quade and Deveroux.

"I would have gone public with what I already knew, which was enough to sink the conspirators. But I never doubted you would hold a Judiciary Committee Hearing."

"Why?" Ava interrupted.

"Because he is the man you and I know," Jon said, with admiration. "Jim had no choice. There were not only legal, constitutional, and political issues involved, but a moral one as well. Quade and Deveroux had lied to the Senate Committee and thus to the United States Senate. The reputation of each body had been sullied and had to be redeemed. There had been a criminal conspiracy, a prominent member having been a United States Senator."

CHAPTER 4

AN HOUR LATER, THEY CALLED it a night, and after breakfast the next morning the three close friends said goodbye as Jon drove away. To what, he did not know.

As soon as Jon left the Thomason's home, he began subjecting himself to no-holds-barred introspection, which he would continue during his two-thousand-mile journey. He scrupulously examined the facts of the *Vardas-Quade* and *Chow* cases; his first and subsequent appearances on the radio; stoking the legal fires he had started; the ultimately unsuccessful disbarment conspiracy; his successful counterstrike, which ruined the conspirators. Jon went over and over the facts, making sure he remembered all the relevant ones.

Then, trying to be ruthlessly honest with his answers, he asked himself hard questions.

Could not Chow, the Chinese defector, have gotten a different lawyer? Sure, but Freddy Kim begged me for help, and I owed him from Vietnam. And I had previously saved the Ukrainian boy who defected, and those two Romanian acrobats who defected from the circus, so I had some experience with religious and political asylum cases.

But the Chinese defector's case was assigned to a federal district judge who resented me, probably because I am white and because I had been too good to him in law school and after. What possessed me not only to take the case, but to bait Deveroux in his own courtroom and chambers? And why did I just now use the word "possessed?" Was I, am I, and if so, why? I told Miles I thought I could handle Deveroux, so was I looking for a fight? If so, why?

Nick Vardas was innocent of murdering Mr. and Mrs. Jimmy Valente. But should I have let some other lawyer represent Vardas and allow Nick to be framed as penance for his actual crimes. That way, Mike Quade's life wouldn't be ruined? But did not Quade deserve to be disbarred and sent to prison. If so, by me, his former friend?

Was I just showing off when I went on Barry Farber's radio show, threatened Quade, and excoriated Judge Deveroux?

Should I have negotiated a settlement with the conspirators who were trying to disbar me, instead of rejecting their offer out-of-hand. And then publicly vowing to destroy them, counterstriking, guns blazing, with a federal constitutional lawsuit of my own?

Why did I do, or not do, any of it? No one knows better than me how the rotten judicial system works. But seaman Chow had a right to his freedom. Judge Deveroux was everything I said about him. Vardas was innocent. Quade was guilty. Truth and justice. No choice. Step up to the plate, Willard.

Jon thought of his late friend, Soviet dissident and GULAG prisoner, Vladimir Bukovsky's immortal words: *"If not me, then who?" Or is this all a rationalization, because of my apparent inability — or is it unwillingness — to cure myself of the Paladin Curse and Quixotic quests for truth and justice?*

Around and around it went in Jon's head, questions, and answers, and then more. Often, they distracted him from driving, so he would try to quit thinking until his subconscious raised the questions again and he could continue his search for answers which eluded him.

I don't have the answers, he would often say aloud, *but before Andrea and I leave New Mexico, I will,* Jon promised himself. *I finally beat the Malevolent Universe glass-always-empty premise, and next will be my old, not-so-dear, companions, Paladin and Don Quixote.*

CHAPTER 5

J ON PLANNED TO MAKE THE drive from Maryland to Santa Fe in no more than six days.

After driving about five hundred miles in seven hours on Day 2, he had reached Knoxville, Tennessee, where he filled his Escalade's gas tank, found a hotel, and stayed the night. Days 3 and 4 were spent on the road, arriving in Memphis, local sightseeing, and unwinding. On Day 5, Jon was on the road again. At the end of Day 6, he pulled up to his house on Juniper Drive in Santa Fe, New Mexico.

It was one of four traditional adobe homes in a family compound on a dirt road at the edge of Santa Fe's business district, owned by and resided in by the Romero family. A small two-bedroom typical house, with vigas, corbels, latillas and brown stucco, he had bought it years ago with a full-price offer when a Romero daughter married and moved to Albuquerque. Although Jon was a gringo lawyer from New York who drove an expensive car, then a Jaguar convertible, the Romero family treated him as one of their own, forwarding mail and caring for his house while Jon was absent.

When the senior Romero, Emiliano, saw Jon pull up, he stopped washing his truck and walked over. He was a short, wiry Hispanic with long black hair and a dark complexion from genes and a lifetime of too much sun. The men embraced.

"Seis días?" Emiliano asked.

"*Sí, pero dos mil millas,*" Jon replied. *Yes, two thousand miles.*

"I see you've picked up some Spanish," Emiliano said.

"I had to," Jon said, smiling. "Your English is so bad."

They laughed.

"You don't look so good, Jon. Your weight is down, no color in your face, bags under your eyes. What's up?"

"It's the last couple of years. Pushing myself too hard. That's why I'm here."

"I'm not surprised," Emiliano said, "we heard you on the radio, and then watched the senate hearing. Then we read about those three lawyers in New York who got disbarred, and the big shot judge who went to prison. No wonder you ditched New York and came out here. How long are you staying?"

"Indefinitely."

"What about Andrea?"

"She's wrapping up some legal work in Boston. Probably get out here in a couple of weeks."

"Well, better get that big New York car into the garage, and park your beat-up truck in front of the house," Emiliano said, "before the Escalade finds its way to Mexico."

When Jon bought the house, he had gotten an old Ford Ranger pick-up truck to leave in Santa Fe for when he flew out from New York. By now, with its faded red paint, scratches, and dents, it looked right at home in New Mexico. He would use it locally instead of the Escalade. If Andrea needed a car, she could use it and they could use it for long trips.

After Emiliano helped move the truck and car, he invited Jon to dinner. "Lorraine's looking forward to seeing you. We'll get some of the kids, too."

"Thanks, but tomorrow. I'm shot," Willard said. "*Que hora?*" What time?

"Five," Emiliano said, as he returned to washing his truck.

CHAPTER 6

EVER SINCE JON OWNED THE house, he had provisioned it with everything needed for a quick move-in, and recently added Andrea's necessaries. It was a turn-key operation in every respect. Clothes, ammo and guns, books, cable service, diesel generator, pantry items and more. This trip, he had stopped at nearby De Vargas Center and stocked up on groceries. Once that was done and everything put away, Jon set a wood fire, poured a glass of Chardonnay, kicked back, and reviewed his thinking during the last thirty hours. Still, there were more questions than answers.

The next morning, Jon's first stop was at Tia Sophia's restaurant on West San Francisco, favored for breakfast by the notables of Santa Fe. It was there he had agreed to represent Bill Richardson in a free speech case. Willard had won it 2-1 in the United States Court of Appeals for the Tenth Circuit. *Memories.*

After a sumptuous, albeit vegan, meal, Jon walked up the street to First National Bank of Santa Fe where for years he had maintained his New Mexico financial accounts. A few minutes early for his 9:30 appointment at the private banking branch, which had once been a small adobe residence, he stood outside soaking in the sun and realizing how glad he was to be back in town.

As Jon entered the bank through an antique door that looked like it had been there since the Pueblo Revolt of 1680, Private Banking manager Tomas Ramirez bolted out of his office. Taller and heavier than Jon, Tomas grabbed him in a bear hug. Jon returned the gesture, not squeezing as hard.

"How the hell are you?" Tomas asked, as they walked into his office.

"OK," Jon replied. "Considering."

"Well, 'considering' is right. All over TV lately, and especially that senate hearing. If you will be here long enough, let's have lunch and you can tell me as much as you can."

"Sure, Andrea will be here in a couple of weeks, and then we're here for the duration."

"That could be a long time."

"Part of me hopes so."

"What about your law practice?" Tomas asked.

"I have that covered, at least for a couple of months. Did you receive that wire transfer I sent last week?" Jon asked.

"I did, already in your account, don't spend it all in one place."

They laughed, with a familiarity born of a long friendship. About the same age, they shared the Vietnam experience where Jon had lost part of a leg, and Tomas one eye. They never talked about it, or even alluded to the painful subject.

As Jon was about to leave, he asked, "Do you ever see Stan Horden?"

"I do. He was in a few weeks ago. Interesting guy. Why do you ask?"

"He's my next stop," Jon said.

"Give him my regards."

They hugged, Jon left, and walked down West San Francisco to his beat-up Ford Ranger.

Because of Jon's long-standing interest in the 'Converso' phenomenon, several years earlier he had become acquainted with Stan Horden, Ph.D., then, as now, New Mexico State Historian.

Years earlier, Horden began to learn of Hispanic Americans in New Mexico who, some knowingly, some not, engaged in traditional Jewish observances: placing six-point stars on gravestones, covering mirrors when grieving a death, not eating pork, lighting candles on the sabbath, and giving their newborn such typically Jewish names as Israel, Deborah, Jacob, and Abraham. Horden had done extensive research and conducted countless interviews, particularly in northern New Mexico, concluding that in the Southwest and New Mexico there were still many crypto-Jews whose ancestors went back hundreds of years.

Horden greeted Jon warmly and updated him on the historian's current Converso research, although that was not the primary purpose for the visit. As they sat opposite each other on comfortable couches drinking coffee with the amenities over, Jon said, "Well, Stan, you may finally get your wish."

Surprised, Horden asked, "You're finally going to get into the judicial aspects of the Reies Lopez Tijerina affair in Tierra Amarilla?"

Although the name Tijerina and the place, Tierra Amarilla, were no longer well-known to many New Mexicans except for some elderly living in the north, they had been the subject of many long conversations between Horden and Willard.

In June 1967, Tijerina and his small band of locals staged an armed raid on the Rio Arriba County courthouse in the village of Tierra Amarilla, north central New Mexico. The raid was unsuccessful in obtaining relief for those who claimed their historical land grants had been stolen. Still, its audacity resulted in national publicity for a cause which, while festering for decades, had never been abandoned by those who claimed their ancestors' land had been stolen, and whose complaints and resistance had spawned complicated and largely unresolved legal problems for the United States, New Mexico, and the farmers and ranchers who considered themselves victims.

Answering Horden's question, Jon said, "I'm going to take a close look at the entire affair, not so much politically, but rather whether land was 'grabbed' as some say, or whether the true ownership was so clouded that no one could know who owned what legally, or how."

"You're questioning whether Spain or Mexico had any legal right to make the grants in the first place," Horden asked, somewhat tendentiously. The historian's sympathy for the victims was well-known throughout north central New Mexico.

"Not 'questioning'," Jon said. "Wondering. Just wondering, Stan."

To avoid acrimony between friends, Jon soon left.

But his discussion about land grants was not over for the day.

* * *

Promptly at five, Jon walked next door to the Romero's house carrying a shopping bag containing three bottles of champagne. Ringing a brass bell instead of a modern electric chime, Lorraine Romero opened the door, hugged Jon, took the bag, and said, "Welcome."

Already there was son Jack Romero, a professional guitarist, and his wife Mercedes, an intensive care nurse at St. Vincent's hospital. Son Renaldo Romero, a late-blooming student at UNM's school of liberal arts, arrived just behind Jon. The Romeros' daughter, Esperanza—a social worker—and her life-partner could not attend.

When Emiliano saw the three bottles of champagne on the dining room table, he said, "Might as well ditch that French bubbly water, I'll have a Corona."

"It's not French," Jon responded, "it's from California. I bought it at De Vargas Center yesterday."

"Well, that's different. American made, American sold, American consumed," Emiliano said, smiling.

The six diners toasted to everything they could think of while eating and finishing the champagne. The conversation consisted mostly of Jon relating everything he could legally say about what he had been doing in New York and Washington. Sort of a behind-the-scenes report of what the Romeros had read and seen on TV. And, of course, of what they heard on the Farber show.

When Lorraine asked how Jon had spent the day, he dutifully told them. When he mentioned Stan Horden, Emiliano said, "I remember you introduced us to him years ago. An historian, about the Converso Jews."

Before Emiliano could say anything more, Mercedes said, "Dr. Horden was also interested in land grants."

That was a red flag for Jon, who responded neutrally, "There are some interesting legal questions about that, which I'm going to look at in connection with the Tijerina affair. To see if he and the farmers and ranchers were treated fairly by the New Mexico and federal judicial systems."

Mercedes said, also neutrally, "A lot of people up north, and even here in Santa Fe, think not."

While there was not yet a problem with his hosts and their children, to avoid one Jon said, "I'm going to do some research at the Espanola library and see what's what. I don't know much about any of it."

"Why Espanola?" Emiliano asked, deliberately diverting the conversation.

"It's the closest to the Rio Arriba County land grants, and to the Santa Fe and Albuquerque libraries, which may have what I need. There is one in Chama, but it is not large enough to have what I'm looking for."

"Buena fortuna," Emiliano said.

"Muchas gracias," Jon replied, in the best Spanish accent he could muster, which was not great.

Everyone laughed, ending the evening on that cordial note.

CHAPTER 7

S TILL BUSHED FROM HIS CROSS-COUNTRY trip, Jon rose about 9:15 a.m. and managed to walk a half-mile up the dirt road outside his house before his left leg began to ache. Downhill was easier. By 10:15, he had showered, dressed casually, eaten breakfast, put his .38 Special Smith & Wesson revolver and some ammo in his truck's glove compartment, and headed for U.S. Route 84. It was not so much that the drive to Espanola during the day was dangerous, but rational concern increased after dark.

For about a half-hour, Route 84 would take him northwest thirty miles to the small city of Espanola. Some of the central and eastern part of it was in Santa Fe County, the northern part of Espanola was Rio Arriba County whose county seat was Tierra Amarilla, a village notorious as the site of Tijerina's 1967 raid.

Several miles out of town, Jon began to feel a wobble in his right front tire. He knew instantly it was going flat, the inner tube would quickly puncture, and he would have a flat. Reducing his speed from about 60 to 25, he drifted to the road's shoulder and coasted to a stop. Jon calculated the tire had lost close to half its air, but he had prepared for the problem of old tires with inner tubes. Turning on the truck's safety blinkers, he removed a can of compressed air from the Ranger's toolbox and emptied it into the tire, restoring about seventy percent of the lost air. As he was stashing the empty can, a banged-up four-seat roofless jeep pulled up behind him occupied by six Mexicans, including the driver. One walked over to Jon, who quickly realized his revolver was in the truck, and said in Spanish, *"Necesita ayuda?"*

Well, Jon thought quickly, "necesita," like "necessary" *probably means "Do I need," and "ayuda" must mean "help." So, here goes, with a smile on my face.*

"Gracias, yo no hablo Espanol. Yo necesita una gas station." The Mexican guy and the other Mexicans in the jeep laughed.

"Okay," the Mexican guy said in English, pointing at the Ranger's gas tank and then down the road. *"Milla y media milles."*

Jon got it. *Mile and a half down the road. I must learn more Spanish words*, he thought.

Even though Jon had a spare tire, with some air restored to the front right tire and apparently holding, he decided that rather than trying to change the tire and abusing his bad leg, he would risk reaching the gas station. After shaking the Mexican's hand and waving to the others, who waved back, Jon climbed into the truck's cab, let the jeep follow him at 25 mph, and in a few minutes drove into a dilapidated one-pump gas station. The jeep and Jon's benefactors roared down Route 84.

After more fractured Spanish from Jon and a lot of broken English from the gas station guy, yes, he could remove the weakened tire, patch the inner tube, and reinstall the tire. *Una hora. Diez dólares.*

Encouraged by his linguistic success with the jeep and gas station guy and faced with an hour wait, Willard said, *"Yo quiero comida y una Corona. Talves dos. Donde esta?"*

The gas station guy got it. The gringo wanted something to eat and a beer, maybe two. He took Jon outside the general store, stood behind him, grabbed his shoulders, and pointed the New York lawyer north on the highway. *"Dos calles y giro a la derecha." Two streets, turn right.*

Jon knew Spanish for left and right, said "thanks," in English, and started walking.

CHAPTER 8

THE SALOON — "PABLO'S LA Taberna" — was in an old
ramshackle one-story adobe house.

Jon Willard entered through authentic swinging
doors, thinking for a moment he had stumbled onto a
movie set. A twenty-foot-long bar with only six stools,
several decrepit tables stained from years of use, garish
neon signs promoting varieties of Mexican beer, two tough-
looking Hispanic men shooting pool, dense cigarette smoke
hanging heavy under the pool table's plastic Corona beer
lamp shades, the overweight bartender wearing what was
once a white apron speaking machine-gun Spanish into the
telephone. In his faded jeans, denim shirt, and work boots,
Willard did not look out of place. Instead, he felt as though
he had entered another world. In one sense, he had.

Willard walked up to the bar, studied the bottles arranged
behind the talkative bartender, and waited.

And waited, while the large bald man in the soiled apron
kept exploding Spanish into the telephone, his back half
turned to Willard. Jon could understand every fifth word or
so. The bartender seemed to be talking to a woman about
a car. *"La Machina." "El battery." "Muerto."* Apparently, the
car's battery had died.

When there were no more bottle labels behind the bar
to examine, Willard looked at the bartender and said, *"Por
favor*, I'd like a beer and something to eat."

The bartender kept talking.

Okay, Willard thought, *when in Rome . . . , or New*

Mexico . . . , here we go again. "Por favor," he said, *"Yo quiero una cerveza y comida."*

That did it.

One of the pool-playing Hispanics laughed out loud. The other one shook his head and swallowed the dregs from his bottle of Corona.

The bartender said something into the telephone that ended with *"adios,"* and turned to Willard. "Your Spanish is not great," he said with a faint smile and in perfect English.

At least the ice was broken.

"Can I get something cold, and something to eat," Willard asked, looking toward a small kitchen in the back room.

"The beer's easy," said the bartender prying the cap off a Corona and pushing it in front of Willard. No glass. *"La comida,"* he said. *The food.* "That's not so easy. All I have is frozen pizza and a microwave."

Willard looked at his watch — noon — and asked how long the pizza would take. "More or less, ten minutes," the bartender answered.

"Okay," said Willard, still unable fully to accept where he was, and what he was doing there. *"Gracias."*

This is, he thought, *one hell of a long way from my condo and law office in Manhattan. And the Four Seasons restaurant.*

Seated at one of the taberna's tables, Jon was working on his second Corona and examining various initials carved into its long-ago defaced top when his pizza arrived. The bartender placed it in front of Jon, sat in the opposite chair, and stuck out his right hand. Jon shook it and said "Jon Willard."

"Pablo Gallegos," the bartender replied. "What are you doing in Espanola? You don't live here." It was not a question.

"I live in Santa Fe. Really in New York."

Pablo helped himself to a slice of Jon's pizza, some of the sauce ending up on his already blotched, once-white apron.

I guess he is also the chef, Jon thought.

"Both?" Pablo managed to say as he took a large bite from the pointed end of the slice.

"Well, you're right. I was not clear. I live and practice law in New York, but for a long time I've had a second home in Santa Fe, near De Vargas Center, close to the military cemetery. Back in the day, way back, I went to UNM."

"So," Pablo picked up the earlier conversation, "if you live and work in New York and have a second home in Santa Fe, what are you doing in the garden spot of New Mexico, Espanola?"

"Well," Jon said, "it is a long story, so here is the short version. I'm a lawyer. Had some tough cases for a year or two, and I am badly in need of some R&R to get back in shape mentally and physically. Santa Fe is a good place for that, New York is not."

"A lawyer. *Abogado*?"

Not wanting to say too much, Jon replied by saying, "Yes. I do trials."

"Physically back in shape, I get," Pablo said, "but how do you get in shape mentally?"

"By tuning out everything to do with practicing law, and instead researching and probably writing a book."

"Fiction or nonfiction?" the bartender asked, with interest.

There is more to this guy than meets the eye, Jon thought. *His English is good, he asks questions.*

"Nonfiction."

"Contemporary, politics, economics, what?" Gallegos asked, with apparent authentic interest.

Well, here goes, let's see if I hit a nerve.

"If the research pans out, it will be a nonfiction book I've been thinking about since law school," Jon said, still trying to be cagey.

"What about?" Gallegos persisted, politely.

"Not 'what,' 'who.' It will be about a certain person."

"OK, who?"

"Reies Lopez Tijerina."

Pablo Gallegos was visibly surprised, but asked, "Why him? If you are talking about the raid on the Tierra Amarilla courthouse, that was a quarter-century ago. Ancient history. Even if you write a book, who will read it? Besides me, maybe."

"That is not the point, Pablo. For one thing, there are only three published books that discuss the raid, and only one of them covers some of the legal aspects. You ever hear about the Englishman who climbed Mt. Everest in Tibet, the highest mountain in the world?"

"Can't say I have."

"Well, he was asked why he did it, when so many climbers before him had tried, failed, and died."

"What was his answer?" Pablo asked, clearly interested.

"The Englishman said, 'because it was there.' It's the same with the book I am going to research, and maybe write. One of the three that has been published is not very good. Another is very partisan, but the third is an excellent scholarly work by a professor of history at the University of California. So, for a long time I've been thinking that maybe more can be said about the legal part of the Tijerina story than has been written. So, to answer your question about why I am in Espanola today, it is because the closest library to Tierra Amarilla is here. I want to see if there is anything in the Espanola library."

"Do you know the Spanish words for the English 'be careful'?" Pablo asked.

"No," Jon answered.

"They are *'ten cuidado'*," Pablo said. "Take it from me, Mr. lawyer-from-New-York, even after twenty years Reies Lopez Tijerina is a touchy subject for a lot of people up here in north central New Mexico, especially his raid on the Tierra Amarilla courthouse."

"Thanks for the advice," Jon said, sincerely. "I know a little about that already."

As he reached for his wallet, Jon asked *"Cuanto?"*

"La casa invita," the proprietor replied.

"Free?" asked Jon, smiling. "Including the Spanish lessons and advice?"

"Si, todo. Everything."

"Gracias," Jon said, as they shook hands and he left hearing Pablo saying *"Hasta luego."*

As he walked back to the gas station to retrieve his truck, he thought, *thank you Señor Marin for the muchas palabras you made me memorize in high school.*

And then Jon remembered that Pablo had not said, *"adiós"*—goodbye—but instead *"hasta luego,"* meaning "see you later." *Was that deliberate?* Jon wondered.

CHAPTER 9

FOLLOWING DIRECTIONS PROVIDED BY THE gas station guy's English-speaking teenage daughter who had just arrived, Jon headed for the Espanola Public Library in the Richard Lucero Center.

It was an undistinguished-looking two-story building of territorial design, which had seen better days. A helpful clerk at the main counter told Willard the chief librarian's office was at the far end of the general reading room and pointed it out. When he got there, a doorplate read "Emmanuel Salazar, Chief Librarian."

Willard knocked, a voice on the other side said *"Si,"* and Willard entered one of the most cluttered offices he had ever seen, including his own. Behind the book-laden desk sat a Hispanic man probably in his mid-fifties with a dark complexion, steel-gray hair, broad chest, and welcoming smile.

"Good afternoon, sir, what can I do for you?" Salazar said, in a deep, accented, baritone voice.

Jon introduced himself, and said, "Well, for openers, you may be able to save me a lot of time. May I sit?"

"Please," Salazar said, amicably.

Jon then told the Chief Librarian why he was there, and added, "I'll check the card catalogue, of course, but I wondered whether there is anything about Tijerina, the raid and aftermath that was not in one of the three published books. Such as letters, microfilmed local newspaper reportage, and the like. Such as in natural history museums which have countless artifacts in the basement that haven't been examined in decades. That sort of thing, but documents."

"Interesting question. I have been in this library for over a decade, but rarely in the basement and not recently. I do remember piles of random books, magazines, and newspapers, and cartons galore, but I doubt whether any of it has been catalogued."

"Would it be OK if I roamed around down there sometime, for Tijerina material?" Willard asked.

"Sure," Salazar said, glancing at Willard's left leg, "but you should be exceedingly careful."

Misinterpreting, and glancing at his leg, Jon said, "I've had this for over fifteen years, so my balance is well under control. No problem there."

"Glad to hear that, Mr. Willard, but that's not what I was alluding to. I meant you should not make it known in this library or, for that matter anywhere in Espanola, that you are researching the Tijerina affair. What Reies did still earns a lot of respect in north central New Mexico. Please be careful. Some people may misconstrue what you're doing."

"You're the second person in the last hour who told me that."

"May I ask who the other person was?"

"Of course, Pablo Gallegos."

"Pablo . . . from the taberna . . . and elsewhere?"

"Yes, do you know him?"

Salazar laughed. "Everyone in Espanola knows him. Pablo Gallegos wears several hats, and can be found in more than one place," the librarian said cryptically.

Curious, but not wanting to overstay his welcome, Willard asked if he could contact the librarian about investigating the basement, and where else he might look for records.

Handing Willard a card, the librarian said, "Try the county clerk's office at the Espanola Municipal Court, but better not use my name or Reies's. Try to disguise what you're looking for."

There he goes again, using Tijerina's first name. Like he knew him. Was that inadvertent, or was Salazar trying to tell me something?

CHAPTER 10

ALTHOUGH THE COUNTY CLERK'S OFFICE was only a few blocks away, Jon took too many turns and became lost. After about twenty minutes, a polite policeman told him to follow his Crown Victoria cruiser and in ten minutes they were there.

There, on the first floor, Willard encountered a large, elderly woman whose weathered face reminded him of a Native American. She stood behind the counter talking on the phone.

When she finished her conversation, Jon caught himself before asking whether she spoke English. He said, "I'm trying to find the records of a contested divorce case back in the late 1960s, probably around 1968. I have one party's name and would recognize the other if I saw it. I'm hoping that you still have the docket books somewhere."

"That depends, sir," she said, "because like all those World War II and Korean War records in St. Louis that were lost in a fire some years back, we had our own on the Fourth of July in 1981. Some kids shot Roman candles through the courtroom windows across the hall, started a fire. Spread to the basement floor where all the old docket books were kept. Between the fire and water to put it out, not much survived from World War II to 1981. We don't encourage people to go down there."

"Think I'd find what I'm looking for, if I did?" Willard asked.

"No," the clerk answered sympathetically. "Besides, the

company that cleaned up the mess never did get the smell out of there. It's a dead end, sir, you're out of luck, I guess."

"Thanks," Willard said as he left.

From the hallway, he heard shouting from the municipal judge's courtroom opposite the clerk's office and could tell it came from a trial in progress. As a litigator, Willard was drawn to the closed double doors as a moth to an illuminated light bulb. He opened the right-hand door a crack, heard louder shouting, and confirmed it was indeed a trial in progress. Irresistibly, Jon Willard, Esq. was drawn inside, where he found an aisle seat toward the rear, among the scattered audience.

Surveying the courtroom, Jon felt as if he was in a time warp and wished that Andrea were here to see the classic Spanish courtroom. From the ceiling's dark brown vigas, corbels and latillas, to the floor's reddish clay Saltillo tiles, to the hand-carved wood benches, to the counsel tables, chairs, and judge's bench, the courtroom in Rio Arriba County, New Mexico, looked like a Hollywood movie taking place in fifteenth-century Madrid, Spain. But this one was authentic.

The only concessions were that it was a twentieth-century trial, with the participants — prosecutor, defendant, and audience — dressed like Americans and speaking English. While Willard was examining the courtroom's beautiful details, he looked at the judge's bench and was stunned. There sat Pablo Gallegos, bartender, cleaned up and wearing a black robe.

It was not clear which of the men saw the other first, but Gallegos — *Judge Gallegos,* Willard now realized — was speaking to the prosecutor, a tall man who looked like he had just walked out of a Corona beer commercial, with tall, dark complexion, pencil-thin black mustache, and slicked-back dark black hair. Immaculately dressed, down to his shined black shoes. He reminded Jon of Zorro in the old TV series, lacking only a cape and sword. Willard would soon learn that he was the Espanola City Attorney.

"Listen to me, Ricardo," Judge Gallegos was saying, "I understand the defendant is charged with public intoxication and resisting arrest. I get all that. But look at him, he's still half-drunk and he has no lawyer."

"He waived a lawyer, Your Honor," the City Attorney said, pompously.

"Are you serious?" the judge said. "Are you blind as well as dumb?" That was not a question. "Look at him. He couldn't knowingly and intelligently waive another beer, let alone a lawyer."

Even though this was not a courtroom in New York, after years as a criminal defense lawyer Jon Willard, Esq.'s brain was so alert to everything happening, and his antenna so fine-tuned, that instantly he realized what might come next, especially with Judge Gallegos's two pointed comments that the defendant had no lawyer.

As Judge Gallegos scanned the small audience, he smiled and said, "Will any other lawyer present in this courtroom please approach the bench." Dutifully, Ricardo Cardona, Espanola City Attorney, left his seat as ordered and approached the judge's bench.

Willard did not move. *Two can play this game.*

Noticing that Jon had not moved and looking straight at him, the judge said, "Perhaps I should rephrase. Any lawyer in this courtroom, *licensed in any state or territory of the United States*, please approach the bench."

Willard complied, while Cardona and a few audience members looked around at each other, puzzled.

With Cardona and Willard standing before him, the judge said formally, "Mr. Cardona, I would like to introduce Mr. Jon Willard of New York City and Santa Fe." Each lawyer muttered something, and they shook hands.

Gallegos continued, "Ricardo, Mr. Willard is a prominent criminal defense lawyer and part-time professor of law who, among other accomplishments, was recently Special Counsel to the United States Senate Judiciary Committee when it exposed the criminality of a New Orleans federal district judge who was pulled down from the bench and sent to prison. He is not here to practice law, so you don't have to worry about competition, but to do research for a book."

Cardona was thunderstruck into silence. Willard was amazed that the judge knew about the Senate Judiciary Committee hearing.

"Are you suitably impressed, Ricardo?" Judge Gallegos asked, sarcastically. "Is Attorney Willard a worthy opponent, do you think?"

"Yes, Your Honor," the District Attorney said dutifully, but reluctantly.

"Well, here's what's going to happen, gentlemen. Right now, I am going to appoint Mr. Willard to represent the defendant, *pro bono publico.* You know what that means, Mr. Cardona?"

"Yes, Your Honor, for the 'public benefit,' and 'free of charge'. But I do not suppose Mr. Willard is a member of the New Mexico bar."

"Correct, Mr. Cardona. But that is no problem, because I deem him to have made a motion for admission *pro hac vice*, which I have just granted. Do you know what that means, Ricardo?"

"Yes, sir, it means for 'just this one case'."

"Then," Gallegos said, "we will have our trial. Mr. Willard will show that public intoxication and resisting arrest are 'intent' crimes, and that as a matter of law the defendant was too drunk to form the requisite intent. Our friend from New York and Washington, D.C. will then move to dismiss the charges, which I will grant, and then I will order you to help his girlfriend get him home and put to bed."

Throughout this colloquy between the judge and the City Attorney, Willard fought to keep a straight face. He had never heard anything like it in any courtroom, anywhere.

"Unless, Mr. City Attorney," the judge said, "as an act of Christian charity, and because you now know how embarrassed you're going to be if we go to trial, you decide on your own, with no pressure from the court, to drop the charges in the name of the public interest."

Whatever the City Attorney's shortcomings, and there were many, he knew where his self-interest lay. "The city respectfully moves to dismiss the charges."

"Granted," the Honorable Pablo Gallegos said, as he banged his gavel twice, and then said, "Mr. Willard, the court thanks you for your professional willingness to perform a public service. Please see me in my chambers. We stand adjourned." For good measure, Gallegos banged his gavel two more times.

CHAPTER 11

ASKING FOR DIRECTIONS TO THE judge's chambers and drawing a laugh, a uniformed city cop pointed at an ajar door down the hall which said, "Break Room, Police Only." Inside, Jon saw Judge Gallegos struggling to get his robe off.

"If you help me get this shroud off, we can get out of here," Gallegos said, frustrated.

Jon did, and they did.

As they were leaving the courthouse, the now-defrocked judge told Jon to get his truck and follow Gallegos's van.

Back to the saloon, probably. OK, I'm thirsty, and worn out after that intense legal proceeding, he thought to himself, sarcastically.

A different bartender greeted them with "Hey, judge, who's your friend?"

"Ramon Lucero, meet Jon Willard," Pablo said. "The lawyer?" Lucero asked.

Word sure travels fast around here, Jon thought.

"One and the same. Just had a big case over at the courthouse."

"I heard," Roman said, as he uncapped two Coronas.

Pablo grabbed them, and headed for a table, saying, "I guess I have a lot to explain."

"I guess you do, especially why I so easily won my second case in New Mexico."

"Your third, if you count helping that Army reservist from Mora who was sexually assaulted by her commanding officer in Saudi Arabia. That makes three. Rather good, without having a license to practice law here."

I wonder if he knows my shoe size.

As they sat, Jon said, "Okay, Pablo, first explain the revolving bartender."

"Not to worry, Jon. It is not that in Espanola all bartenders are judges, or all judges are bartenders."

My god, thought Willard, *that sounds like it is from an Aristotelian syllogism. All "A" is "B", all "B" is "C", and therefore all "A" is "C." Who is this guy?*

Pablo continued, "My grandfather and then my father owned and operated this place for years. Even though I own it now, I don't operate it. Occasionally, I stand in for a few hours if a bartender has to vote, or gets sick . . . you know what I mean. It's not necessary, plenty of short-term replacements are available. I do it because I enjoy it. Gives me the pulse of the place. I meet interesting people, such as those who live in two places and do interesting things."

"Okay, I understand. Next. The plaque outside that magnificent authentic Spanish courtroom says, 'Municipal Judge.' I assume the judicial hierarchy in New Mexico is, from the bottom up, Municipal Court, Magistrate Court, District Court, Court of Appeals, and Supreme Court. Maybe probate and Family Court, off to the side."

"Correct."

"I assume also," Willard said, "that the jurisdiction of the Municipal Court, your court, is limited to all violations of municipal law occurring within the boundaries of the municipality. Such as that DWI and resisting arrest case I was shanghaied into today."

"Correct, again."

"Last, I assume that a municipal judge is elected, and need not be a lawyer."

"I was, several times," Pablo said, "and, I am not."

As Gallegos signaled Ramon for two more Coronas, Jon asked, "Why?"

"Are you asking why I bother?"

"More or less. I suppose you have a day job, which we will get to, but why do you spend time with municipal law? Note, I am not criticizing, nor would I. As a matter of fact, there are good reasons. I just wonder what yours are."

"Good question. You are correct, there are excellent reasons, but they all come down to the same one. The Municipal Court is the closest most of the People of this city will ever get to 'the law'. The Magistrate Court jurisdiction, one level higher than mine, involves real legal issues, substantial dollar amounts, and serious crimes that most of my friends and neighbors are never touched by. The next rung up, the District Courts, have statewide general jurisdiction for trial of felonies and expensive civil actions. Even most litigants there do not reach the next rung, the Court of Appeals, let alone understand what Appellate courts do. Forget about the Supreme Court of the State of New Mexico, which can decide which cases it wants to take, and where the big-shot lawyers practice."

"So," Jon said, "your court is 'grass roots'."

"Yes, that's where, for better or worse, they feel the impact of 'the law,' and because of that they have the right to fair, honest, and reasonable justice. Like today."

"Well, I saw that," Willard said. "You taught a few lessons."

"I'd like know why you saw that, Jon, from your perspective, which we don't often get out here."

"Happy to oblige," Jon said, enthusiastically. "First, you taught the DA and audience about the importance of intent in criminal law, and how its presence or absence can instantly turn a case around. You conveyed to Cardona, whether he realized it or not, that pomposity is objectionable in your courtroom, and that waiver of counsel can only be acceptable if it is knowing and intelligent. Then you showed him, the audience, and the defendant that if the DA lacked the intelligence or fairness to do what was right, the judge would. All this in respectful, albeit lightly sarcastic, language anyone could understand. The *coup de grâce* was when you appointed not only a lawyer to represent the defendant, but one who was unlicensed and from out-of-state. I can imagine what the community grapevine will say about all this. Kudos!"

"Thank you, I really appreciate your understanding all that."

"Where do you get the legal knowledge?"

"Well, I read a lot, and the State of New Mexico gives classes for the Municipal Judges and has a handbook for the Magistrate Court. Plus, experience. Even though an appeal lies to the District Court from Municipal Court decisions, few of those who lose in my court bother to appeal. And I can always ask Manny."

"Manny?"

"Emanuel, the Chief Librarian."

"He's a lawyer?" Jon asked in wonderment, but quickly realized there was no reason for him to be surprised. It was stereotyping. A Hispanic librarian in Espanola, New Mexico, a lawyer?

"Yes. If you are going to wander around Espanola asking questions you need to know something about some of us. And some of us about you. These are not tales out of school because while you were on your way here, I asked Manny if I could tell you some things about him."

"I understand."

"He told me you were on your way to the county clerk's office. I assumed that when you heard a trial in progress, you couldn't resist seeing what was happening beyond those beautiful antique doors."

"Smart, but what about Manny?"

"Well," Pablo said, "Manny was born in 1931during the depression and grew up in Espanola. Usual upbringing in a family struggling to survive. Always reading, when not doing menial jobs. Salutatorian of his high school graduating class. Drifting. Marine Corps enlistment 1949. June 1950. . . ."

Jon interrupted, having instantly recognized the date, and said, "North Korea invades South Korea."

"Correct. Manny and his unit from the First Marine Division are flown from Okinawa to Pusan, to help 8th Army hold the ever-shrinking perimeter. Soon after, the Marines hit the beach at Inchon as part of MacArthur's surprise invasion."

Again, Jon interrupted. "The Marines make it almost to the Yalu River border with China in northeast Korea. At the Chosin Reservoir, they become encircled, and fight their way to a southern evacuation port."

"You know your Korean War history," Pablo said, somewhat surprised.

"My father was MIA there, and my surrogate father made it back."

"Very sorry, Jon, very sorry indeed," Pablo said. "That's the end of the Korean War part of Manny's story, except that he was wounded at the Chosin Reservoir, got an honorable discharge and a verified disability, but I don't know for what. I don't think anyone does."

"What, then?" Jon asked.

"Not much, except for the last part, which will probably interest you, but I'm saving that for later. College and law school in Albuquerque on the G.I. Bill. Admitted to the bar. Back to Espanola, small town practice. Wills, real estate, Municipal Court appearances and even a little Magistrate Court work. Some court appointments to represent indigent defendants. That kind of stuff. Only enough to live on, let alone marry and have kids. He picked up some hourly part-time work at the library."

"Is he still practicing law, or just Chief Librarian?"

Ignoring Jon's question, Pablo continued, "It's now June 1967. . . ."

Jon interrupted again, and said, "Tijerina's courthouse raid." It was not a question.

"Correct. Manny's a lawyer but has no important

credentials or experience. He has a practice but isn't making more than subsistence money; he's thirty-six years old but has no meaningful prospects. That said, Emmanuel Salazar is a staunch supporter of the land grant movement and its leader, Reies Lopez Tijerina. So, what does Manny do?"

Before Pablo could answer his own rhetorical question, Jon said, "I know what's coming."

"I'll bet you do. Birds of a feather. Another idealist. Tell me," Pablo said, "what Manny does."

Jon answered. "Manny signs on *pro bono* with Tijerina's defense lawyers in the federal prosecution, despite not-so-subtle hints from the United States Attorney that anyone connected with the rabble-rouser Tijerina might have his own problems later."

"Correct, again," Pablo said. "Manny did not heed the advice, and instead stayed involved in Tijerina's case through Reies's conviction and affirmance on appeal. Somehow, the rumor got around that lawyer Emanuel Salazar was toxic, that the 'government' considered him dangerous in some unexplained way. Well, as a practical matter, that was the end of what little law practice Manny had."

"Pity," Jon said, with evident sympathy. "That was years ago. He stayed with the library, climbed the ladder, and became Chief Librarian?"

"Yup, that's about it. He's now in his mid-fifties, with a useless law license and a Korean War disability of some kind. It has been a decent living, though he never married," Pablo said, sadly.

Because Jon wanted to dispel the depressing mood, and satisfy his insatiable curiosity, he insisted that Judge Pablo Gallegos admit if he had a day job and, if so, what it was.

"Okay," Pablo said, smiling. "I'm chairman of the board and president of the Zapata Credit Union here in Espanola. My father organized it back in the Fifties. I went to work there after college and took control when he died. College was Anderson School of Management, UNM's business school. Majored in management and finance."

"So," Jon said, "you juggle full-time at the credit union, your Municipal Court duties, and tending bar in your spare time?"

"That's pretty much it."

"Married?"

"Widower."

"Sorry."

"Thank you," Pablo said, sadness crossing his face. "Now, back to business. You must wonder why I'm telling you all this?"

"It crossed my mind."

"Well, by population, at the last census Espanola was the twenty-third 'largest' city in New Mexico. That is not saying much, because the population was only about nine thousand. If you subtract the three thousand schoolkids, you get about six thousand adults in twenty square miles."

"You're telling me that Espanola is a small town."

"Correct. If you picture a rectangle of five miles by four miles, that's twenty square miles. It's a small town, where for starters most people on any given level of society tend to know others of the same social level. With crossovers, for example, I know cooks, financial folks, and a handful of physicians. A physician knows an auto mechanic, a teacher has an auto loan from my credit union."

"I get it. So, in the end," Jon said, "most people in Espanola know most people in Espanola."

"And talk to most people," Pablo quickly added.

"Especially about outsiders," Willard said.

"Yes. So, here's this Anglo New York lawyer John Willard, dressed like a fake cowboy, roaming around their small town asking questions about what a local hero did twenty years ago."

"Fake?" Jon smiled. "I buy my New Mexico wardrobe at Walmart, probably like you."

Ignoring Jon's remark, Pablo said, "I'm telling you all this for two reasons. Because I'm going to let it be known around town that you're a legitimate guy who is researching a potential book on a man who was, to put it mildly, controversial. That you have no pre-formed opinions. Also, I want people to know that you are not a carpetbagger, having had a second home in Santa Fe for many years, and knowing a good many folks there and in Albuquerque. Also, that you have done some legal work in New Mexico, including representing a Mora County female reservist, *pro bono*, when she was sexually assaulted by her commanding officer in Saudi Arabia. And that you did important legal work for a former governor when he was a congressman representing this district."

"I understand, and I'm grateful," Jon said. "I hope that will open some doors for me."

"Well, you have opened an important one yourself. Manny Salazar. He and I can start you with Rachel Castellano. She's the daughter of a Tijerina cousin. Rachel was born in Mexico and some of her family is probably still there, in Guadalajara, I think. When he raided the courthouse, the family repudiated him, and when Rachel supported Tijerina, they repudiated her."

"Is she still in Mexico?" Jon asked.

"No, no. When Rachel was disowned by her family, she moved to New Mexico to help Tijerina. Now, she lives in Abiquiu, about twenty miles north of here. That's Rio Arriba County. But she is often in Espanola. Rachel has an account in my credit union."

"How far is Abiquiu from Tierra Amarilla?" Jon asked.

"About forty miles."

"After the debacle of Tijerina's raid, does Ms. Castellano have any contact with Tierra Amarilla?" Jon probed.

"Plenty, she runs a very large ranch up there."

"Cattle?"

"Some, but a large sheep herd. She rents thousands of acres, between Tierra Amarilla and Abiquiu."

"How old is she?"

"Probably early sixties. During the Tijerina raid, she was in her early forties. I'm going to ask Manny to arrange a meeting, either in Espanola or Abiquiu. It's important that you talk to her."

"Manny can arrange it?" Jon asked, surprised.

"They have some kind of relationship, maybe Platonic friends. Probably, a bond because they both supported Tijerina. Maybe more. *Quin sabe?*" *Who knows?*

CHAPTER 12

Back in Santa Fe waiting for a call from Pablo, Jon spent the rest of the day making notes about everything he had learned in Espanola.

When Jon told Emiliano about his trip, Romero seconded what Pablo had said about Espanola being a suspicious place which did not easily countenance outsiders.

The following morning was catch-up time.

On a call with Andrea, most of which was about Jon's trip to Espanola, she told him that winding up her outstanding Innocence Project cases was proving more difficult than she had anticipated. It would probably be at least another week or so before she could get to Santa Fe. She passed on regards from Miles Stewart, who missed Jon, and a message from her father who, after seeing photos of Jon's Juniper Drive house, said his daughter and future son-in-law needed a larger one.

A lengthy call with Jon's secretary took care of old and new business.

Regarding the old, the media was still chasing him for comments about the disbarment cases he had recently won, the imprisonment of New York's Chief Judge, the Senate Judiciary Committee Hearings, and the removal from the federal bench and prison sentence of Amos J. Deveroux. She referred them all to Willard's spokesperson, Karen Newman, who told the bothersome media to get lost. There was a message from Senator James Thomason that he and Ava might be in Scottsdale in a few months and could drive to Santa Fe. A few calls about Willard representing just-indicted defendants were referred to criminal defense lawyer Henry Rothberg. Willard's secretary was under strict orders not to reveal to outsiders where he was, with two exceptions. If Judge Julia Bart or New York Attorney General David Feldstein was looking for him, it was OK to give them Jon's contact information in Santa Fe.

It's great, Jon thought, *to be away from New York City. New Mexico continues to grow on me. I wonder if Andrea and I would be happy living here permanently.*

He took a few days off to reconnect with old friends and acquaintances, among them physician Scott Shirley, lawyer Madison Williams, and top realtor Virginia Serella.

Jon then spent some time with the Santa Fe and Albuquerque librarians looking for Tijerina material but came up dry.

He had lunch with Stan Horden, telling him about his day in Espanola and asking about any connection of that city with the Converso phenomenon. By unstated agreement, they stayed away from any mention of land grants.

Then, the call came from Manny Salazar.

"Good to hear from you," Jon said warmly. "Pablo Gallegos told me a few things about you. I'm interested in meeting."

"That's why I'm calling. Your visit last week sparked my interest because of my association with the Tijerina episode, and what followed. So, yesterday I spent some time roaming around the library basement. There are nine cartons labeled 'RLT' which I take to stand for 'Reies Lopez Tijerina.' I have had them moved upstairs and thought you would want to go through them. I can help."

Although Jon wanted to ask some questions, he quickly decided not to press the Chief Librarian. Instead, he said, "I'd certainly like to come up and see what you have, when would be convenient?"

"Sunday," Manny said, "the library will be closed, so I

won't have any duties and there'll be no one else around. If 10:00 a.m. is okay, I'll meet you out front."

"Done."

"By the way," Manny said, "after your talk with Pablo, he called and filled me in about Rachel Castellano. You and I can talk about her on Sunday."

CHAPTER 13

MANNY SALAZAR GREETED JON WILLARD warmly outside the Espanola library, and they walked through the main reading room where Jon saw nine cartons piled on a long reading table. In his office, Manny had set up a coffee machine and some breakfast pastry.

After they had helped themselves and were seated, Manny spoke first.

"Pablo told me in some detail about his conversation with you last week, and I want to be sure that you didn't come away with a misimpression on one salient point."

"About your relationship with Tijerina."

"Exactly. So let me give you some historical background before I get into why and to what extent I was involved in his Quixotic cause."

"I'd like to hear about that," Jon said, quelling his reaction to Manny's reference to Don Quixote of La Mancha, with whom Willard was well acquainted.

"Okay," Manny began. "There are two crucial dates to keep in mind, 1848 and 1967. Although you are interested in Tijerina, I have to start way back before him, so bear with me."

"You're in charge," Jon said, smiling.

Manny began. "Spain settled Mexico, and Spaniards and Mexicans moved north into what became New Mexico. Some Mexicans were given grants of land to colonize there, in one case a half-million acres. Whether they owned land or not, many Mexicans farmed or were ranchers. Then came the

Mexican American War. The United States won, and the parties agreed to the 1848 Treaty of Guadalupe Hidalgo. Significantly, the Treaty originally contained a provision that expressly recognized land grant titles from Spain and Mexico, but it was rejected by the United States Senate during the ratification proceedings."

"Article X?" Jon asked.

"Yes."

"President Polk's 'Manifest Destiny,' for America to march west," Jon said.

"Exactly, that was a crucial turning point in Mexican and American history. While many people believed the Treaty unambiguously recognized the validity of the land grants, especially the Mexicans, others did not. Some grantees and their descendants began selling land. Titles and ownership became cloudy, and the battle which began lasts to this day."

"Didn't Congress get involved in the mid-1800s?" Willard asked.

"It did," Manny said, "but let me relate this my way."

"Okay."

"As long ago as the 1930s, well before Tijerina arrived in New Mexico from Texas, there had been considerable land grant litigation in New Mexico. Many Americans of Mexican descent, Chicanos, felt they were discriminated against and lacked a voice in their own destiny. The United States was seen as a foreign, occupying power, and New Mexico as a mere colony."

"So," Manny continued, "having first heard of land grants in 1945, in the late 1950s Reies Lopez Tijerina shows up in north central New Mexico, which was then a hotbed of land grant fever. He falls under the tutelage of some descendants of the Tierra Amarilla land grant. He takes up the issue as his principal cause as a Pentecostal minister firmly believing it is God's will and that he is doing God's work. Eventually, he founds the Federal Alliance of Land Grants, but for years neither he nor the cause gets anywhere."

"Do you think his lack of success was because of his Pentecostal, mystically based motivation and, let's say charitably, 'eccentric' beliefs and behavior?"

"Well," Manny said, surprised at how much Jon knew about Tijerina, "that's another subject, but for now let's just say Tijerina's excessive passion could not have helped."

"Understood."

"Now we get to the second crucial date in the Tijerina history, 1967, the year of his courthouse raid, the details of which are well recorded and not worth wasting time on now. For a while, he is headline news, a celebrity. But after a few years in federal prison, he faces the problem of being overshadowed by the civil rights movement, the Vietnam War opposition, the women's liberation bandwagon and other headline-grabbing movements."

"So, what does he do?" Jon asked.

Manny answered, "Chameleon-like, and not for the first time, Tijerina reinvents himself, latching on to the anti-war movement and the so-called 'Jewish conspiracy to rule the world.'"

"When he dies impoverished in El Paso, Texas, years later, his life is a mere footnote to the activism of the Sixties."

"Please do not misunderstand this, Manny," Jon interjected, "but I sense that you're critical of Tijerina, even though you were with him through a federal criminal trial and an appeal to the United States Court of Appeals for the Tenth Circuit. No offense intended."

"None taken. I understand why you say that," Manny replied, "but you won't yet. You will when I'm finished."

"Okay, so please continue."

"Reies Lopez Tijerina was one of the vilest persons I have ever known. One can put aside his hyper-mysticism, which was his own business if it did not hurt anyone else. But there is strong evidence that it did."

"How so?" Jon asked, his curiosity fully engaged.

"There is credible evidence that he was cruel to his wives and may have committed incest. He unabashedly lived off other people, like a leech. His Alliance stood for, among other schemes, land redistribution, reparations, and other socialist principles. As to outright Communism, Tijerina's preaching often revealed political admiration for the USSR, parting company with the Communist slaughterhouse only over the worship of God. He had dubious relationships with Communists, and some of the authorities suspected him of being an actual Communist. One conservative writer compared him to Cuba's Fidel Castro."

When Manny made the Communist references to Tijerina, Willard almost interrupted to reveal that was what his research was really about, but he decided to keep that to himself for the time being.

"The Communism part of Tijerina I could swallow," Manny said, sincerely. "After all, it was a belief, an ideology, that was his own business. What made me abhor the man was his anti-Semitism. Tijerina had a selective morality about discrimination. He rightly cried for enslaved Africans and their descendants, he identified with Native Americans and bled, literally and figuratively, for the Chicanos. But as to the Jews," Manny continued, now speaking very emotionally, "as to the Jews, he insulted and disparaged them, turning a blind eye toward their persecution and suffering from a thousand years before Christ to and including this morning."

Manny's face was red, tears forming.

Jon was stunned because he knew what caused Emanuel Salazar's passionate outburst. *The man sitting before me is a Jew. Emanuel Salazar is a Converso.*

* * *

With that, Jon made an excuse to leave the room, leaving Manny alone. He had locked the library's front door when they arrived, so Willard walked around the main reading room half-looking at the shelved books but staring at the Spanish Mexican architectural design and flavor of the room, much like Pablo Gallegos's courtroom.

Yes, Jon thought again, *New Mexico is growing on me.*

After a few minutes had passed, Jon rejoined Manny in his office.

To break the ice, before Manny could speak Jon said how much he liked the interior design of the main reading room and municipal courtroom. Then, they eased back into where the conversation had left off.

Manny continued. "You are probably not surprised, Jon, that my emotional condemnation of Tijerina revealed that I am a Jew, a Converso, albeit it a crypto one. You and I share a friend in common."

"Stan Horden," Jon said. It was not a question.

"Yes, for years he's been telling me about this New York lawyer who went to UNM and has long been interested in, and knowledgeable about, the Converso phenomenon and Stan's research."

"And here I am," Jon said, warmly. "A small world. We will have to talk about crypto Jews, sometime."

"Of course," Manny replied, adding, "and we have something else in common."

Before Manny could continue, Jon said, grimly, "War. Pablo told me."

"Yes, that too."

"I wonder," Jon asked, "as an American patriot having fought and bled in Korea, how could you have countenanced Tijerina's anti-American flirtation with Communism?"

"Because my Jewish ancestors in north central New Mexico owned a Mexican land grant the Santa Fe Ring stole from them."

"I see," Jon said, understanding the myriad implications.

"I believed not in the man, Jon. I believed in the cause. Reies Lopez Tijerina was the wrong messenger, but he had the right message."

CHAPTER 14

S TILL SEATED IN MANNY'S OFFICE, Jon asked, "Do you mind if I ask you about Korea? Pablo told me something about that, too."

"No, go ahead."

"Pablo told me that you were with the Marines."

"Yes, a gunnery sergeant with a battalion of the First Marine Division."

"Were you at Inchon? I have a reason for asking these questions."

"I was, yes, when 8th Army broke out of the Pusan Perimeter, and MacArthur landed us on Inchon's mud flats and beaches."

"That was not the end of anything, was it?"

Manny stifled a reaction, and said, "Hell no, it was just the beginning. After Inchon, MacArthur sent us by ship around the entire Korean peninsula to the Northeast coast. Regiments of the First Marine Division, part of Army X Corps, were soon at the Chosin Reservoir in Northeast Korea, near the Yalu River."

It was clear to Jon that Manny was on a roll and could not stop himself, even if he wanted. The Marine combat veteran had something to get out of his system that Willard recognized personally, and Jon was going to help him.

"Then, hundreds of thousands of Chinese hit you," Jon said, softly.

Manny seemed mesmerized, staring, transported back to that frozen wasteland so far away.

"They did, yes. So many. Swarms. It was way beyond insufferably cold."

"Were you in Hagaru-ri, Yudam-ni or Koto-ri?"

"All three."

"So, you were part of what General O.W. Smith called a non-retreat, just 'attacking in another direction', fighting your way to the sea for evacuation at Hungnam."

"I was, and I made it out, but so many Marines, GIs, Brits, and South Korean troops did not."

Jon suppressed his emotions, and said, "My father was with X Corp's 7th Infantry Division. A major."

Manny was stunned. "A lot of Army guys got out, did he?" he asked, cautiously.

"Apparently not," Jon said, near tears. "He went MIA and was never heard from again. A captain who became my surrogate father survived your trek south, barely making it."

Solicitously, Manny asked, "Are you OK to look at those documents now?"

"Are you?" Jon asked in reply.

"Damn right," Manny said.

At that moment, Jon realized that he had to tell Manny the truth about what he was really looking for in Tijerina's life, not the cover story he had used about whether he had been treated fairly by the judicial system. "So," he said, "Manny, look for anything that has to do with Communism. I will explain later."

"Let's open all the cartons first and tackle any that contain books. They should tell us something," Manny suggested.

Each of the men stood in front of an unlabeled carton, box cutter in hand, and working in unison they sliced open all nine cartons. Three appeared to contain books.

In Jon's first carton, he found books and several magazines in English and Spanish on such diverse subjects as desert agriculture, long guns of the West, self-repair of automobiles, mail-order clothing, cooking recipes and other non-controversial subjects. His second carton contained children's toys. As he began to replace them, Manny exclaimed, "Jon, you're not going to believe this. Come around here."

Manny had removed only five books so far. One was *Marxism and the Spanish Civil War.* The second book was *Will Mexico, Central America, and South America Accept Marxism?* Another was the Marx and Engels *The Communist Manifesto,* and the fourth, *Communism and the American West.* The last book on the pile was *Homage to Catalonia,* a memoir by George Orwell who had fought for the Left in the Spanish Civil War. Inside the front cover, each contained a bookplate that said, "Property of RLT" and an illegible signature. Manny's carton contained a few similar books, magazine articles, and newspaper clippings about international Communism.

Shocked, before they could react there was a tapping on the library's glass front door. Both men walked over and saw Pablo. On the sidewalk next to him were two Domino's insulated red pizza delivery boxes and a cooler. He was smiling broadly. Manny unlocked the door, and Pablo said cheerfully, "Lunch time."

CHAPTER 15

SEATED AT ANOTHER LARGE MAIN reading room table, the three men dug into the pizza and Corona beer.

Jon began the conversation, saying, "Manny, I owe you and Pablo an explanation for why I told you to look for any books related to Communism. As I told you both, my research is primarily focused on the broad topic of whether Reies Tijerina was treated fairly by the United States government and its judicial system back in the Fifties and Sixties. Because that was the time of rampant anti-Communism and the Cold War, since my college days at UNM I have wondered whether, if Tijerina was maltreated for other reasons, it was because the FBI believed him to be a Communist."

The other two indicated they understood, and then Manny told Pablo about the five books piled on the other table. Pablo had read Orwell's *Animal Farm* and *Nineteen Eighty-Four*, so he retrieved *Homage to Catalonia* from the other table while the others kept eating. Inside the book, Pablo found a newspaper clipping referring to Orwell as a "combat volunteer with the Marxist party unit in Barcelona."

"I'll grant you," Pablo said, "that these books, with bookplates saying they were the property of 'RLT' next to a scrawled signature, are strong circumstantial evidence that they belonged to Tijerina, but they do not prove that he was a Communist."

"As a lawyer, I agree with you," Jon said, "but a determination of whether he was or was not, is premature.

If I ever say publicly that he was, rest assured that there will be plenty of proof. But there is more circumstantial evidence than these five books. Manny told me about it, and some of it I knew already."

"Let's hear it," Pablo said, interested.

Jon continued, "Tijerina's *Alianza Federal de Mercedes,* 'The Federal Alliance of Land Grants,' stood for land redistribution, reparations, and other socialist doctrines. Tijerina's preaching often expressly revealed admiration for many of the USSR's dogmas. Mainly, he disagreed only with the Communist slaughterhouse's antipathy to religion. He had dubious relationships with Communists, and some of the authorities suspected him of being an actual Communist. One conservative writer compared Tijerina to Fidel Castro."

"All true," Manny said, emphatically.

They finished the pizza and beer, and Manny cleaned the table of boxes and empty bottles while Jon brought two cartons over to Pablo and said, "Start digging. Anything that has to do with Communism, revolutions, Stalin, USSR, Soviet Union."

The books had been easy. The documents not, because most were single pages or several stapled together. As they dug into the cartons, they found piles of miscellaneous documents. Unpaid bills, letters from relatives, maps of Tierra Amarilla, out-of-date railroad timetables and yellowed announcements of Tijerina speaking engagements. Detritus of years.

After about a half-hour of digging, sometimes having to examine scores of individual pages, Pablo waved a small Mexican saddle blanket, and exclaimed, "Guys, you are not going to believe what was wrapped in this." He held what was obviously a thick handwritten manuscript, yellowing at the edges. "It is entitled," he said with awe, "*The Communist Revolution Comes to North Central New Mexico.*"

"And the author, of course," Jon said, "is Reies Lopez Tijerina."

CHAPTER 16

PABLO'S DISCOVERY OF TIJERINA'S MANUSCRIPT spurred the three men's examination of the remaining documents. Nothing more of interest was found. They filled the cartons, Manny and Pablo returned them to the basement, and at Jon's request Manny allowed him to make a copy of the manuscript on the library's copying machine. Manny stashed the original in his office safe. They then agreed Jon would take the manuscript copy and books back to Santa Fe, review all the material, and return to Espanola when he finished. Manny said, lightly, that Jon did not need a library card.

Jon started with George Orwell's *Homage to Catalonia*, which he had read in college for a course in Twentieth Century European history. He thought then, and again after perusing the book, that Orwell volunteering to fight for a Spanish Communist Party militia in the 1936 Civil War was naïve in the extreme because a decade later he explained that "Every line of serious work that I have written since 1936 has been written, directly or indirectly, against totalitarianism and for Democratic Socialism, as I understand it."

"In other words, Orwell believed that in fighting for the version of Communism euphemized as Democratic Socialism, he was opposing totalitarianism, which every brand of socialism inevitably led to.

"Next came *Marxism and the Spanish Civil War*, which delivered what its title promised. The book tried to unscramble the mélange of combatants, their European sponsors, the ideology that compelled each of the various sides and whether it was genuine, convenient or both. *Trying to understand and integrate all this*, Jon thought, *must have addled Tijerina's brain even more.*

"So, too, *The Communist Manifesto,* the core of which is an economic and political theory of an uber-collectivist and ultimately totalitarian state, where classes, and thus class struggle, have been eliminated. In college, Jon had read this naïve and puerile, albeit dangerous, screed against individual rights, limited government, capitalism, and free markets.

"The last two books — *Will Mexico, Central America, and South America Accept Marxism?* and *Communism and the American West* — were closer to home and, as Jon would soon discover, provided much of the grist for Tijerina's unpublished manuscript entitled *The Communist Revolution Comes to North America.*

"Both books slavishly followed the Communist Party line in lauding socialism, and denigrating capitalism. They exalted the poor and condemned the economically successful. Using euphemisms such as 'democratic socialism' and 'classless societies' the leftist propaganda studiously avoided the destructive implications of their cherished ideology, and the incontestable fact that eventually Communism by any name had failed miserably, killing, or ruining literally uncountable humans in the Twentieth Century, let alone throughout history. There was not a single reference to the approximately one hundred million men, women, and children who died in the Twentieth Century at the depraved hands of Communist and socialist states."

Then Jon turned to Tijerina's twenty-four-page undated manuscript.

By then, Willard knew what to expect, and the author did not disappoint. In essence, the book was warmed over Communist gospel as applied to the unique factual situation of Spanish and then Mexican occupation of north central

New Mexico, prominently featuring the land grant grievance. Tijerina's manuscript was no more than a political-religious tirade against mostly Anglos, containing in its conclusion his promise that he would work to establish a form of Hispanic Communism in north central New Mexico. The land grants would not be returned to the descendants of the original grantees, but instead owned by collectives. Tijerina's strategy and tactics, were akin to a 'bait and switch' scheme. He would use the land grant issue to regain ownership of the land grants, and then divert them into Communist collectives.

CHAPTER 17

WHEN PABLO, MANNY AND JON had finished searching the Tijerina cartons several days earlier, they talked briefly about the importance of him talking to Rachel Castellano about Tijerina. Having revealed to them that he was focused on the Communist aspects of his research and sought to expose Tijerina, Jon urged Manny to arrange a meeting as soon as possible. Now that he had circumstantial evidence that Tijerina was more than a mere socialist or Communist fellow-traveler, a meeting with Castellano was imperative.

Several days later, Manny called. Rachel would meet them the following Sunday at her home just north of Abiquiu, at 10:00 a.m.

Back in Jon's college days at UNM, he and his mother would take day trips to Abiquiu, charmed by its beauty and authentic New Mexico flavor compared with the big-city largeness of Albuquerque. When Abiquiu was part of the Spanish province of Nuevo Mexico in the 1730s the hamlet was the third largest. World famous artist Georgia O'Keeffe had died there in 1986 at ninety-years of age, after residing there for nearly four decades. Jon was anxious to get back to Abiquiu and meet Rachel Castellano.

The men agreed to meet at an Espanola diner for breakfast at 8:00 a.m., which would give them an hour to talk, and time to arrive at Rachel's by 10:00 a.m.

After ordering, Jon had several questions about the woman he was about to meet.

He began with a broad one. "Can you give me a broad-strokes chronology of her life?" Jon asked.

"Being born in Mexico and educated in Guadalajara to parents fluent in Spanish and English, she is fluent in both."

"A native," Willard said.

" Very much so," Manny said, with a touch of pride in his voice. "Her parents sent Rachel to Yale for a Master of Fine Art degree. After graduation, she moved to Abiquiu because of Georgia O'Keefe, who mentored Rachel. She became involved with Tijerina, he went to prison, she remained in Abiquiu, and awaits us in less than two hours."

"Where do the sheep come in?" Jon asked, now curious.

"She'll probably tell you, without being asked."

"Does she make a living from her art?"

"Some."

"How close was she to Tijerina?"

"That is a highly personal question, Jon. If you really want to know, ask her. Although she might volunteer the information."

"Her first name, Rachel, is biblical in origin, appearing first in the Book of Genesis." Jon's statement was an implicit question.

"Jon," Manny said, "I know what you are asking. The answer is 'yes.' Rachel Castellano, like her parents and their parents and their ancestors, is a Jew. That is one of our bonds."

CHAPTER 18

RACHEL CASTELLANO'S HOME SAT A few miles north of Abiquiu village at an elevation of nearly seven thousand feet. Situated on a hill a half-mile from the nearest neighbor, she had an unobstructed three-hundred-and-sixty-degree view of mile after mile of the beautiful Chama Valley.

As Manny and Jon drove up the gravel driveway, Rachel stood outside to welcome them. Behind her stood the oak front door, faded by years in the New Mexico sun, banded and studded with iron. It looked like it had come from a Spanish castle. The blazing sun, nearly at its apogee, illuminated the single-floor light brown stucco-and-adobe house. She appeared to be nearly six feet tall, wiry with a full body. Years spent outdoors had darkened and weathered her face, her lips revealing a warm smile. Rachel's erect posture and steel-gray hair made the tableau perfect, even though Doña Castellano leaned on a carved walking-stick from a recent injury.

When they were seated comfortably in her Spanish-décor living room with vigas, latillas, corbels, brick floors, wood paneled walls, and large, colorful Mexican rugs, Rachel asked if she could serve Manny and Jon anything to eat or drink. When they declined, she said, "Manny told me some things about your professional and personal background, Mr. Willard, but I'm most curious about your interest in the political side of Señor Reies Lopez Tijerina."

"Broadly, yes, I am interested in his political side,"

Jon replied, "but more narrowly his apparent affinity for Communism. If that is established conclusively, what may be left of his reputation can be further sullied, which would suit me very much. I was hoping you could share with me some knowledge of Tijerina and his Communist sympathies." As an afterthought, he said, "By the way, how shall I address you?"

"'Rachel' will be fine. We are all friends here, or I hope will be soon."

"Fine, then please call me 'Jon'."

"I understand, Jon, that you know something about New Mexico history, but to understand Tijerina, his land grant *Alianza*, and why Manny and I were involved with him, you must understand the context of New Mexico and the land that sustained its people for centuries. It is those seeds that made Tijerina possible hundreds of years later."

"The more contextual history, the better," Jon said, sincerely.

"Okay," Rachel began, "feel free to interrupt. You, too, Manny. The American Southwest had been sparsely populated by Indian tribes long before white Europeans arrived. In the 1600s, Spanish explorers claimed for Spain much of what later became New Mexico and other Southwestern states, but, still, Spanish law recognized Indian rights to real and personal property. Franciscan friars followed, dedicated to converting the Indians to Christianity. The friars were quite successful. In any event, to encourage settlers and recognizing that the people who were tending the land needed a stake in their efforts, the Spanish authorities granted them individual and community land, timber, and water rights, which they exercised."

"Based on what legal system were those rights conveyed?" Jon asked.

"Excellent question," Rachel replied. "There was only one legal system available, the Castilian laws of Spain."

Manny said, "Now we must jump a couple of centuries.

During those years, there was a restiveness incubating of Mexican opposition to distant Spanish rule."

"Yes, that's correct," Rachel continued. "The Mexican war of independence, a rebellion against Spanish colonial rule, erupted during 1820 and 1821. When Mexican-born Spaniards, others of mixed European and Indian blood, and full-blooded Indians defeated the Spanish, the newly formed Mexican government assumed ownership and control over all former government land, purporting to recognize and protect the Spanish land grants' validity. The power and right of the Spanish Crown to make the grants in the first place was simply assumed."

Jon interrupted again, impatiently. "What about the Treaty?"

"That's next," Rachel said, smiling.

"A quarter-century later, in 1846, war broke out between Mexico and the United States. Two years later, the defeated Mexicans signed the Treaty of Guadalupe Hidalgo, transferring to the United States Government ownership of a huge area of land, much of which became the American southwest."

"President Polk's 'Manifest Destiny'," Manny said, coldly.

"To this day," Rachel continued, "the argument rages over whether in the Treaty itself or in Congress's ratification of it, the United States agreed to respect the land grants made by Spain and acknowledged by Mexico, especially because one Article providing exactly that was expressly rejected by the Senate when it approved the Treaty."

"But there is language in the Treaty that does seem to acknowledge the land grants," Jon said.

"Some think so," Rachel replied. "For sixty-four years New Mexico remained an American territory, awash with outlaws, cattle barons, ranchers, and farmers—as well as avaricious businessmen, corrupt politicians, and crooked lawyers. New Mexico's admission to the Union in 1912 did nothing to quell the long-seething land grant dispute between old Mexican families and land-grabbers, aided and abetted by the federal and state governments."

"I have always believed," Manny said, "that when the United States won the Mexican American War and succeeded to Mexico's problem with the land grants, under the Treaty and otherwise, morally and legally it had a duty at least to adjudicate the land grant mess it inherited."

"Well," Rachel said, "to some extent it did. While the original version of the Treaty created a *presumption* of good title which shifted the burden of proving bad title to the claimant, the final version shifted the burden of proving good title back to the grantee. You lawyers know how important the burden of proof is in disputed legal claims."

Jon said, "In civil disputes, how well that burden is carried determines the outcome. In criminal cases, it is crucial because the prosecution has the burden not only of proving all elements of the crime but doing so beyond a reasonable doubt."

"Exactly," Rachel said. "When the burden shifted back, the grantee/claimant not only had the burden of proof but had to jump over the hurdles of finding an honest lawyer, obtaining mostly documentary proof, and satisfying all the usual requirements of civil litigation, tasks beyond most claimants. That said, let me add a few more facts."

Not waiting for approval, she continued.

"Apparently, while Congress may have believed it should do something about the land grant mess, it was in no hurry because the politicians waited until six years after the Mexican American War to create the Office of the Surveyor General of New Mexico, at best a naïve attempt to identify and solve the land grant problem, and at worst a cynical way to bury it until claimants died or lost interest. Although, in fairness, it must be admitted that Congress did confirm a few grants, including nineteen to Indian pueblos."

"Which of the two motives do you believe, Congress' naïveté or its cynicism?" Jon asked.

"Both," Rachel replied, "But mostly the latter. The sad fact is that the Office of the Surveyor of New Mexico was impotent and doomed to fail from Day One."

"I agree," Manny added. "Just look at the facts. The Surveyor General had other duties, but had no money, no staff, and his jurisdiction was limited only to claims already filed, not the many more that could have been filed. Moreover, no claim was surveyed until after it was approved, and the application of whatever criteria was used to confirm claims was inconsistent."

"On that point," Rachel interrupted, "most potential claimants were never notified that their ownership was to be examined, and thus never found out until it was too late that their claim had been considered, extinguished, and awarded to someone else."

Manny, who had become more involved in the conversation, added, "Even the first Surveyor General admitted that thoroughly examining and satisfactorily solving the land grant was not possible. So did Congress."

Rachel said, "All this would have been bad enough if some progress had been made during a few of the Surveyor General's early years, even five years, maybe even ten. But the process went on longer than that."

"How long?" Jon asked, impatiently.

"Si, forty years," Rachel answered.

"Forty years," Willard said, incredulously.

"*Si. ¡Cuarenta años!* If the Surveyor General's process of adjudication was not doomed from Day One, as I believe it was, after forty years it was dead and buried. Apparently waking up, Congress tried again in 1891 by creating a five-judge Court of Private Land Claims. But its processes tilted heavily toward the federal government. Pro-claimant presumptions that earlier had help claimants sustain their burden of proof were eliminated, even honest land grant lawyers were outclassed and outfought by government counsel and their experts, courts including the Supreme

73

Court upheld other hurdles claimants had to overcome, and Spanish and Mexican law was ignored."

"Enter Reies Lopez Tijerina," Manny said.

"Lunch enters," Rachel said.

CHAPTER 19

THEY WERE SERVED BY A middle-aged Hispanic woman to whom Rachel and Manny spoke Spanish, while Jon understood enough of the words to enable him to understand they were discussing how much to reveal about Tijerina. A frequent word Jon heard was *verdad*—truth.

"I must apologize, Jon, for our speaking Spanish, but there are some details about my relationship with Tijerina that are highly personal. I will hold them back," Rachel said, "until I am certain they are relevant to what information you are seeking about him."

"Of course, I understand."

As if by prearrangement, Manny spoke next, saying, "Rachel and I agree that concerning our relationships with Tijerina it is enough for now to say, as she just did about herself, that it is highly personal. But for me, not so personal that I can't say a few things."

"Please do," Jon said, "without prejudice."

Manny laughed at the lawyer-expression, and said, "First, in the years before the courthouse raid, I was in my early and mid-thirties with a minor law practice, a part-time library job, a claim to some of the Tierra Amarilla land grant through my ancestors, and a conviction that the land had been stolen. Thus, Tijerina's crusade — as ill informed, often exaggerated, and sometimes psychotic sounding — still had enough truth in it to ring true. So, for a couple of years before the raid I volunteered to do some research for him into Supreme Court of the United States' land grant cases.

He was grateful, and that task led to other legal research. I knew him well, we spent time together, I furthered his education about the legal aspects of the land grant dispute. Then, on June 5, 1967, Reies. . . ."

Jon interrupted, "The day before the courthouse raid. . . ."

Manny continued, "Yes, the day before the raid he sent a messenger to request I come to the courthouse in Tierra Amarilla the next day because they were going to kidnap someone and 'light the fuse of rebellion'. I was instructed to be armed."

Stunned, Jon was about to speak, but stopped cold.

"I did not go, and that was the end of Reies Lopez Tijerina's and Emmanuel Salazar's personal relationship. But, and I am embarrassed to admit this, still believing in the land grant cause, as I do now, I did some research for his lawyers in the federal criminal case through the unsuccessful appeal, but never saw Tijerina again. As you can see from Rachel's stunned expression, I never told anyone about his request that I join his raid."

That explained why Rachel Castellano sat frozen in her chair.

Silence, all around.

Rachel was the first to speak, and said, "Let's get to something I can tell you that relates to Tijerina and Communism. As Manny knows, because I, too, should own part of the Tierra Amarilla land grant through my ancestors, Tijerina's rhetoric fell on very receptive ears. From time to time, he asked me to solicit contributions for the *Alianza* from some of my wealthy artist friends. I asked a few of them, and some money was raised. On two occasions, well before the raid, Reies and I were intimate. After the second intimacy, apparently he trusted me enough to say that back in the late 1950s he had written for help to the President of the United States, then Dwight Eisenhower. Now, in 1966, he wanted to get his memorandum to President Lyndon Johnson, so he asked me to edit and type it from his scrawled handwriting."

As Rachel had looked amazed at Manny's revelation about the raid, so, too, he and Jon looked similarly at her, Manny appearing crestfallen.

"The memorandum," Rachel said, "though not intended as such, was a confession of how much he hated America and respected Communism. I remember that several times he said with admiration a paraphrase from Karl Marx, who said socialism would guarantee 'from each according to his ability, to each according to his needs.' Tijerina's version was 'from each according to his land ownership, to each according to his needs'."

Hesitantly, Jon asked, "Did you do the editing and typing?"

"Because I was still mesmerized by him and so much believed in the cause, I am ashamed to admit I did. The raid later opened my eyes, and I never had anything more to do with him."

Almost afraid to ask the obvious question, lawyer Jon Willard asked, "Is it possible you have a copy?"

Rachel Castellano answered with a single word. "Maybe."

CHAPTER 20

RACHEL'S REVELATION LEFT LITTLE TO be said. She promised to search among her many files for a carbon copy of Tijerina's Memorandum, or any other record of it. They would return the following week at the same time.

On the drive back to Espanola, Manny and Jon conduced held a postmortem of the day's conversations, concluding that if the memorandum surfaced it would be a game changer in destroying what was left of Tijerina's undeserved reputation. While there would probably not be enough for a book about his having been a crypto Communist, Jon could write a blockbuster article and place it with a political magazine.

The following Friday, Jon received an urgent telephone call from Manny. Rachel had just been taken to Espanola's Presbyterian Hospital. The details were sketchy. All Manny knew was that she had fallen at Walmart, took most of the blow on her right leg, and was to be x-rayed and examined in a couple of hours.

Cutting Manny short, Jon said, "A friend of mine is an orthopedic surgeon at the Christus St. Vincent Regional Medical Center in Santa Fe. Can you get her there?"

"Yes."

"Explain to Rachel that I strongly recommend she go there because it's a regional hospital. I have had personal experience at Christus and the orthopedic surgeon there is a friend of mine. I'll meet you at the hospital."

Jon arrived first. Dr. Robert Roybal was in surgery, so

Jon explained the situation to the ER chief nurse and waited in the room reserved for patients' families.

The hospital smells, the waiting room, the trauma center next door, and physicians, nurses, and staff walking and running through the halls brought back mixed memories for Jon. On an earlier visit to Santa Fe, he had tripped on his house's front steps, badly twisted his leg's prosthesis, and was taken by Emiliano Romero to the hospital. There, Dr. Roybal examined Jon's leg, made some adjustments to the socket which connected the prosthesis to the remaining part of his left leg, and that day each had made a new friend. Invariably, they would meet for dinner each time Jon was in Santa Fe, though not yet on this trip.

About forty minutes later, the huge interior metal ER doors swung open and a short, surgically attired man with a stethoscope around his neck walked directly toward Jon.

They embraced, and Roybal said, "They told me you were waiting out here; I didn't know you were back in town. More trouble with the prosthesis?"

Jon explained about Rachel Castellano.

"Well," Roybal said, "I'm through for the day, so let's wait in my office. We can catch up until she gets here."

Not surprisingly, the first subject was Jon's recent notoriety. Not only was Robert Roybal a first-rate orthopedic surgeon, but he was also a law buff who closely followed prominent criminal cases. As such, Roybal insisted on hearing every detail about Willard's disbarment case and his stint as Special Counsel to the United States Senate Judiciary Committee for the Deveroux hearings. Before they could get to the end of the story, Dr. Roybal was paged to the Emergency Room.

"I'll finish the story at dinner soon," Jon promised.

"Okay, I'll hold you to that," the doctor said, smiling.

In the ER they found Manny and, in a wheelchair with her right leg elevated, sat Rachel Castellano.

Jon took over, making the introductions.

"Rachel," he said, "This is Bob Roybal, a good friend and the chief of orthopedic surgery here who's going examine your leg." The patient and doctor shook hands.

"Manny, you and Bob have something in common," Jon said.

"My legs are okay," Manny said, to ease the tension.

They all laughed.

"Bob," Jon said seriously, "Manny was with the Marines at Chosin." As the men were shaking hands, Dr. Roybal said, "8225th Mobile Army Surgical Hospital, fall and winter '50 and '51. Our MASH unit got a lot of you guys."

Manny nodded but remained silent.

Uncomfortably, Dr. Roybal took over, saying, "Well, let's get down to business. First a quick examination. We'll do the paperwork later."

Taking charge, Bob led them into an adjoining examining room. Then, he moved Rachel from the wheelchair onto a sitting position on the examining table, motioned the two men into a corner, began examining her right leg from the knee to the ankle, and asked, "What happened?"

"I was shopping at Walmart in Espanola, pushing a half-filled cart. Suddenly, from behind, I was shoved, the cart went flying forward, I went down hands first and instantly my knees hit the floor and I could feel my right ankle bounce and twist. There's pain if I put pressure on it by standing."

"You're correct about that, Rachel," Dr. Roybal said, "we have a lot of swelling there." He added, "If you gentlemen will excuse us, I want to conduct a thorough physical examination of Rachel. Please ask the nurse to come in."

Jon Willard, the lawyer, stepped in. "Before we leave, Bob, can I ask Rachel a few questions?"

"Okay but make it fast."

"Rachel, was Walmart crowded?" Willard asked.

"No, it was only a few minutes after the store opened."

"Are you sure you were pushed?"

"Absolutely, in the small of my back. The lumbar area."

"After you were pushed, did you see who did it?"

"Not really, I was on my way to the floor."

"Are you certain?"

"Well, I did catch a split-second glimpse of the back of a jacket."

"What did it look like?"

"Camouflage, like a soldier. Or a hunter."

"Jon . . ." Dr. Roybal started to say.

Manny and Jon took the cue, left, and the nurse entered.

CHAPTER 21

HAVING BEEN A LITIGATOR FOR fifteen years who relied heavily on investigators to ascertain the facts of a case — such as the Pinkerton International Detective Agency in the *Quade-Vardas* cases — Willard had developed a keen instinct for the existence of hidden facts.

When he and Manny were seated in the waiting room, about fifteen minutes later, Jon said, "Rachel leans on a cane, today she was deliberately pushed to the floor, likely to re-injure her bad knee and perhaps even destroy it, let alone what seems to have happened to her ankle. No one except you, Pablo, Rachel, and I know about my interest in Tijerina's Communist leanings, nor about our meeting last Sunday, Yet, five days later she is attacked, perhaps with the intent to cripple her. I cannot make a connection between Tijerina and the attack. What the hell else is going on?"

While Jon was speaking, Manny had become increasingly and visibly uncomfortable.

"It's not up to me to tell you, Jon, I'm deeply sorry."

"Who can?"

"Only Rachel."

"Will she?"

"I don't know. I hope so. In the meantime, without revealing what I learned in confidence, I can tell you today's attack, and the previous one, have nothing to do with Reies Tijerina. Nothing."

"So, there was a previous attack!" Jon exclaimed. It was not a question.

"I can't say."

Manny's terse answer shut down conversation for about forty minutes, each man absorbed in his own thoughts.

Finally, the examination room door opened. The nurse was pushing Rachel in the wheelchair, her right leg still elevated, followed by Dr. Roybal. She waved to Jon and Manny as the nurse wheeled her in another direction, and the doctor approached the two men.

"Okay, guys, all is well. Let me explain what happened in the examining room and in the imaging department. Before we get to the knee, know that I did a thorough physical examination. I checked her extremities, that is the upper arms, elbow, forearm, wrist, hand, fingers, and thumb. Also, her feet, left knee, ribs, spine, and head. All fine, and not affected by her fall."

"Great," Manny and Jon said, almost in unison.

Dr. Roybal continued, "As to her right knee, you saw for yourselves that it was swollen. We call it 'effusion,' better known as 'water on the knee.' It can be caused by many things, but we know in Rachel's case it was caused by the trauma of the knee hitting the floor. I drew some of the fluid, which will not only reduce her pain, but also allow us to test for infection, disease, and the extent of her injury."

"Is infection a possibility?" Manny asked.

"Yes, but unlikely. We're just checking all the boxes."

"What about her ankle?" Jon asked.

"Please, *Dr.* Willard," Dr. Roybal said, smiling. "Be patient."

"A quick x-ray has told us that the knee is okay, just some trauma and a little swelling from the fall. The ankle is not. She has two hairline fractures, one in the first metatarsal, the other in the second. She needs to keep her leg elevated and stay off it as much as possible, using a crutch when it is necessary for her to stand or walk. Ice to take down the swelling, and Tylenol for the pain. I want to see her in about a week. For now, I gave her a mild pain killer. Does Rachel have some help at home?"

Manny said "Yes," and Jon added, "We can provide additional help if needed."

Manny then volunteered to be Dr. Roybal's contact, and the nurse wheeled Rachel back into the waiting room. All three thanked Dr. Roybal, and as Manny pointed Rachel's wheelchair toward the exit door, Jon told Bob that he'd be in touch.

"Better be, I want to hear the end of 'Tales of Willard.'"

CHAPTER 22

As Jon drove home, he realized there were few facts available even to begin thinking outside the box. about Reies Lopez Tijerina, especially because Manny had assured Jon that the firebrand had nothing to do with the Walmart attack on Rachel Castellano. As to that, all Jon knew was that she had been attacked, Manny and Rachel knew why, and she might or might not tell him.

At the hospital, I told Manny to review the Walmart security cameras, they might tell us something about the assailant, Jon thought. *It should be easy because the store was not open too long before Rachel was attacked.*

Introspectively, Jon had begun to think about what occurred during the past several hours, and he was not happy with himself.

I am at home. Manny calls with news of Rachel's fall at Walmart. I go into automatic. Get the cameras, Manny. Right now, come to Santa Fe to my friend Dr. Roybal. I make the introductions, telling the guys they have Korea in common. Interrupt Bob's examination with lawyer questions. Express skepticism to Manny and want to know what is really going on. In automatic mode. Tijerina involvement? No, but then what? Why won't Manny tell? Will Rachel? If not, why not? Whoa! I am too curious. This has nothing to do with me. I have not come to New Mexico for this. It is not my problem. I do not need this. Danger. Peligro.

As Manny drove Rachel to Abiquiu there was a related

conversation, initiated by Manny, about Jon asking whether Tijerina was connected to the Walmart attack.

Manny's denial to Jon that there was a connection, necessarily implied that there was some other reason. Unable to let that implication pass, Jon naturally asked what the other reason was. When Manny refused to answer, saying only Rachel could, but might not, tell him, Jon's interest in an explanation increased.

This dilemma put Rachel in a damned if she did, damned if she didn't position, Jon thought. *If she told me why she was attacked and what was behind it, I might think she was trying to get me involved. If she didn't, with the campaign against her seeming to be growing exponentially she would have to face unknown enemies with only Manny's help. But he was not capable of providing much, in or out of court.*

CHAPTER 23

A FTER RACHEL RESTED AT HOME over the weekend, she was up to meeting with Manny and Jon on Monday. Her neighbor's teenage daughter had been hired to help Rachel around the house and on this day made her comfortable in the living room, even though she was still in a wheelchair. There was a lot to discuss.

Jon seized the moment, and said, firmly, "Rachel, what happened Friday, and what I suspect is behind it, dwarfs our conversation last week about Reies Tijerina. If you want to build on our growing friendship, I insist we sideline him for now, while you tell me what is going on. I'm afraid it's 'take it or leave me'."

"I agree," Rachel said, sincerely.

"I, too," Manny added, with evident relief.

"It's a complicated story with different parts, but all are connected. As with many stories in New Mexico, it begins with the land."

Manny said, "Jon, when we met at the library for the first time, I said two dates were important, 1848, the Treaty of Guadalupe Hidalgo, and 1967, the raid on the Tierra Amarilla courthouse. Because we were discussing them in the context of Reies Tijerina, I said little about the land grant issue itself. When we were here last week, Rachel explained more about them."

"I remember," Jon said. "Basically, you said that Tijerina had taken it up as his primary cause."

"Right. But now you need to know more, with an emphasis

on the Tierra Amarilla grant, which was justification for Tijerina's raid. Rachel and I have land grant claims through our ancestors. So, Rachel, you have the floor."

"Okay," she said, with alacrity. "What became the original Tierra Amarilla land grant in north central New Mexico consisted of about 600,000 acres. Spain had claimed the land by virtue of conquest, and whatever the Spanish Crown's legal entitlement was, it passed to Mexico in the early 1800s. In 1832, the Mexican government made a *community grant* – and I am emphasizing *community grant* – to settlers from Abiquiu. But for an unknown reason, the grant application and other documents contained only the *individual* petitioner's name, not the community's. His name was Manuel Martinez, in Spanish the designated *poblador principal*, which in English means 'principal settler, inhabitant or colonist.'"

"A community grant," Jon said, "but naming the grant's recipient principal as a single individual. I can guess what that led to."

Rachel continued, "Manuel Martinez died in 1844, his property, including land grant rights, passing to his son Francisco."

"So," Manny interjected, "without notice to any other of the Abiquiu settlers, Francisco Martinez petitioned to confirm individual— *not community* ownership in the Tierra Amarilla land grant in the names of the heirs of the original grantee, Manuel Martinez. In 1860 Congress confirmed the land grant as a *private* grant, rather than a *community* grant, due to mistranslated, concealed, and other questionable documents. Later, attorney Francisco Catron even obtained a judicial degree acknowledging that owned the original Manuel Martinez grant.

"If that kind of fraud was exposed in any American court, the entire process beginning with the ownership confirmation petition should have been thrown out and community ownership recognized," Jon said, angrily.

"There's more," Rachel said. "Although a pre-condition of confirmation was that a survey be conducted, some Manuel Martinez heirs began to sell their interests to land speculators such as Catron. He resold, and by 1883 owned virtually the entire grant except for the original community ones that had survived the original 'mistake,' the massive fraud, and sales and resales."

"On top of all this," Manny added, "there was another way Catron and the Santa Fe Ring stole land grants. Together with what Rachel has just explained, it is among the worst abuse of American land law in our history."

"That's hard to believe, given what I've just heard," Jon said, disgustedly.

"Well, let's see," Manny challenged.

"I know and understand what Manny is about to tell you, Jon," Rachel said. "Don't worry about the legal jargon."

"So," Manny began, "let's say a claimant community, or for that matter an individual or non-community group of settlers, want to confirm a land grant claim. They need a lawyer, so they go to one such as Catron. If he obtains confirmation, his fee will be one-third to one-half of the value of the land, which will make him a co-owner. So far, he's doing well."

"I'll say. Even today, in the United States, a contingent fee of one-half is almost unheard of, and closely monitored by the court," Jon interjected.

Manny continued, "Enter the New Mexico partition law of 1896. In an issue involving land, a co-owner such as Catron had two choices. One was to ask the court that the land be physically divided among all owners, or, *if the in-kind division would diminish the land's value, the land must be sold.* Guess what? Back in the day, the courts would invariably find diminution existed and that the land had to be sold. Thus, would the lawyers such as Catron be able to cash out."

"Wait a second, Manny," Jon said quickly. "You told me

that that under Spanish and Mexican law, community land could *not* be sold."

"Correct, and lawyers have an ethical duty to act in the best interests not of themselves, but of their clients. Pardon my cynicism."

"I take your point," Jon responded. "The original Tierra Amarilla grantees, the 'community', and descendants of Miguel Martinez, including eventually you and Rachel, were cheated by various factors. There were inequities, incompetence, and corruption in the Surveyor General and Court of Private Land Claims systems, and the Congress that enacted them. Judicial decisions that interpreted them were mostly erroneous. Crooks and land speculators like Catron and his Santa Fe Ring exploited all of it. Spanish law was not determinative of the claims that somehow managed to be made despite the practical and legal hurdles."

"You grasped it well, Jon," Rachel said, impressed. "So, now I will get you to my sheep, and today's problem. But first, lunch."

When seated, though, the conversation's momentum could not be stopped.

Rachel began.

"It is authoritatively accepted that when in 1598 Don Juan de Oñate and his followers explored and settled northern New Mexico, they brought with them from Mexico several thousand sheep, among other livestock. And so it was in 1832, when the Abiquiu settlers in the name of Miguel Martinez received the Tierra Amarilla land grant. So, it was nearly a century later, when my grandfather and his community of settler descendants was doing what his father, and his father's father, and their fathers, had done since the time of Don Juan de Oñate.

"And so, for nearly four hundred years sheep have provided meat, milk, and wool to local New Mexico ranchers and others."

Jon had been listening intensely to Rachel and interrupted.

"Hang on, you said your 'grandfather and his community'. I thought you said that the original community grant had been confirmed as an individual grant to Miguel Martinez, and then sold and resold to other individuals."

"True, Jon," Rachel replied, "but the grantees' descendants were absentee owners, developers who never developed, the state and federal governments. All ignored the sheep grazing, until 1912."

"Someone woke up?" Jon asked.

Rachel replied, "Yes, a lumber company that had owned much of the land on which today I graze my sheep decided that the party was over. While they had no need to use the land just then, the company wanted that option against unforeseen future events. With New Mexico having achieved statehood on January 6, 1912, and Arizona, the forty-eighth on February 12, 1912, the lumber company anticipated great national prosperity, especially in the American Southwest."

"It was correct about that," Jon said.

Rachel picked up her thread.

"Instead of again litigating the land grant legal issues, the owner offered my grandfather and others like him a ninety-nine-year grazing, water, timber, and mineral rights lease. He had no choice but to accept. All others similarly situated did the same."

"I've seen that kind of lease," Jon said. "Not just for land, but also other kinds of indebtedness, like railroad bonds. They contain a so-called 'gold clause,' meaning that payment must be calculated at the current value of gold. It is to protect against devaluation of paper money during the period of indebtedness. FDR illegalized the use of gold clauses in 1933, but Congress relegalized them in 1977. A friend of mine, Professor H. Marcus Holder wrote a book about them, *The Gold Clause.*"

"Correct," Rachel said, "And family records show that my grandfather made payments that way until the 1934 illegalization. As a matter of fact, once gold clauses were relegalized, the lumber company went to court, arguing that relegalization operated retroactively and that my family owed recalculated rent based on the increase in the value of gold between 1933 and 1977. However, the relegalization statute, drafted by Professor Holder and championed by Representative Phil Crane and Senator Jesse Helms, was quite clear about 'no retroactivity,' so the lumber company lost. But the payments, in inflated dollars, continue to this day."

Jon said, "If it is a 1912 ninety-nine-year lease, it expires in 2011."

"Correct," Manny said, "which finally brings us to what is happening right now, and explains what Rachel is facing today."

"Jon," she said, "in the last half-century alone, the number of sheep in New Mexico has declined from some 2.5 million to maybe 100,000 statewide. I have one of the few sheep ranches left in this state. I employ people, my Churu sheep are an heirloom breed just now coming back from near extinction. My herds number about seven thousand. There is more to be said, but there is one reason above all the others that explains why I keep at it, rather than living on income from my art and investments."

"I think I know," Jon said, softly.

Just as softly, Rachel said, "I am keeping alive a tradition started some four hundred years ago by New Mexico's founder, Don Juan de Oñate. Sheep herding was in the blood of our Hispanos, as it is now in mine. It is something I must have as part of my life."

Puzzled, Jon said, "But the lease does not expire soon. Surely you can make other arrangements. What's the hurry?"

Rachel and Manny looked at each other knowingly, and she said, "Your question brings us to you wanting to know what is going on."

CHAPTER 24

AFTER LUNCH, BACK IN THE living room, Rachel restarted the conversation.

"The last piece of 'what is going on' takes us to a man named Antonio Carranza, who showed up in Espanola a couple of years ago, rented an apartment and spent a lot of time in and around Tierra Amarilla in the company of mineralogists and surveyors. For a while, it was unclear what he was doing there, but about a year ago he approached me directly with an offer to buy my lease."

"Was he acting on his own behalf, or representing someone?" Jon asked.

"Good question," Manny said. "I have been helping Rachel with Carranza's offer since the beginning, but without success. Carranza would refer to 'me and my people,' or 'potential investors.' Sometimes, 'our group,' or just 'me.' I never did pin him down. Let's just refer to him as 'Carranza,'" Manny said, "if this goes anywhere, we'll have to find out who the real party in interest is."

"Bad sign, him being so evasive," Jon said. "What was the offer?"

"In essence," Rachel said, "Carranza would buy the lease. Period."

"Is it expressly assignable?" Jon asked.

"Yes, unequivocally."

"What transfers with it?"

"Everything," Rachel replied. "The land and mineral rights, sheep, buildings, equipment. *Todo*." Everything.

"Did Carranza say why he wanted to buy the lease?" Jon asked, his curiosity growing.

Manny laughed. "At the beginning of our conversations, he claimed it was because he wanted to raise sheep. When Rachel and I laughed in his face, he claimed that was a joke and finally admitted that he wanted to reopen a turquoise mine in northern Rio Arriba County, near Tierra Amarilla. That made more sense, but not a lot. Those mines have been closed for years and are not easy to find."

"I had no intention of selling the lease, for reasons I just explained," Rachel said, "but Manny and I prolonged the discussions so we could learn as much as possible about what he was really up to. He came here to my house, we had drinks, went out to dinner, telephone calls, that sort of thing. He drank heavily. Carranza would be in Espanola for a while, then disappear, and resurface. It was all very odd."

"Did you ever find out who he was, and what he wanted?" Jon asked.

"No, we tried, but never could find out anything about him," Manny said.

"Are the discussions still ongoing?"

"No," Manny said, "about two months ago, on Rachel's behalf, I told Carranza that under no conditions would she sell the lease. Period."

"Within a week, someone 'accidentally' slammed a shopping cart into my back at COSTCO, and since then we have found some sheep with their throats cut. Two of my shepherds have been roughed up, an equipment shed has been burned to the ground and the equipment stolen."

"Obviously, Carranza is sending a crude message," Jon said.

"Of course, he is," Rachel said, "but I will not be intimidated."

"Well," Manny said to Rachel, "tell Jon what else happened before you were knocked down at Walmart the other day."

With apparent reluctance, Rachel said, "I mentioned that

Carranza was a heavy drinker. On several occasions here and in restaurants, he would 'come on' to me with obnoxious comments, innuendo and once a flat-out proposition."

"Jon," Manny said contemptuously, "Carranza was out-and-out lusting after Rachel, even though he is at least twenty years younger than she is, and always made it clear that she had zero personal interest in him."

"Twice," Rachel continued, "Carranza has shown up banging on this front door, drunk, screaming barely understandable obscenities and demanding that I sell him the lease. Most recently, about ten days ago, he came here about 2:00 a.m. less drunk than usual, and threatened to kill me so, in his words, he 'could deal with my estate,' and 'not have to suffer my stupid female unwillingness to sell'."

"Did you report the two intrusions?" Jon asked, now concerned.

"Well," Manny interjected, "there are no cops in Abiquiu, but there are police in Espanola and a sheriff for Santa Fe County. But the Espanola chief of police said that because Rachel lives outside the city limits, he had no jurisdiction."

"What about the Santa Fe County sheriff?" Jon asked, impatiently.

"I went to the Espanola substation," Manny said, "saw the deputy in charge, and told him the whole story. He asked a lot of questions, promised to investigate, but then reported back ten days later and said he couldn't find Carranza."

"I noticed cameras outside and inside the house," Jon said, "and panic buttons strategically placed here and there. And I've noticed you wear one around your neck. That's good as far as they go, but who monitors them from a central station and calls the sheriff if there's an alarm?"

"I have that service, but the sheriff is responsible for all of Santa Fe County, and if he got an alarm call it would probably take him a week to get here."

"What about weapons?" Jon asked, hopefully.

"I have Mossberg pump guns inside at all three doors,

and Smith and Wesson .38 caliber revolvers stashed here and there. When I am outside, I open-carry a Colt .45. All are always loaded. If you are about to ask if I know how to use the guns, the answer is yes. I go to the range in Santa Fe frequently and in the woods behind the house. And I'm a lifetime member of the NRA."

Coming from New York City, Willard was impressed.

"On the two occasions Carranza tried to break in, I fired one shot way over his head through the top of the front door and ran him off."

Curious, Jon walked over to the door to see for himself. Sure enough.

The two shots appalled Jon even more at how Rachel had to live, all because of some mystery man who was making her feel like a defender of the Alamo. Against his better judgment, knowing he was getting too involved with Rachel Castellano's affairs, he said, "Stand fast, and I'll see if I can find out who Antonio Carranza is, and what he really wants."

Truth and justice, he thought. *The Paladin Curse* awakens, *Don Quixote* rides again. *Be careful.*

After effusive thanks from Rachel, Jon and Manny left, on their way to the Espanola Walmart and its surveillance cameras.

CHAPTER 25

THE ESPANOLA WALMART STORE MANAGER was Manny's second cousin and had checked several surveillance cameras when the event occurred. One, inside above the front doors facing the rear, had caught Rachel's assailant pushing her, dodging around the woman's falling body, and fast walking out of the store. He wore camouflage, and his face was obscured by a boonie hat, sunglasses, mustache and a thick but obviously fake beard. The parking lot cameras were more helpful. They had captured the assailant as he exited the store, providing a full body picture, and another photo of the pickup truck whose passenger seat he jumped into as the driver gunned the accelerator.

Unasked, the manager had already had his photo department print the pictures. He gave three sets to Manny, who asked whether his cousin could identify the assailant or the truck.

"Not the guy, too much disguise," the cousin said, "but the truck, yes. It belongs to Nestor Garcia."

"Nestor Garcia?" Manny exclaimed. "As in the Garcia brothers?"

"You guys know them?" Willard asked.

"Everyone knows them," Manny said derisively. "Broken home, Bad Conduct discharges from the Army, petty thieves, smalltime pot dealers, strong-arm guys. Troublemakers."

"How old are they?" Jon asked, feeling himself being drawn further into the Rachel Castellano affair, despite his increasing misgivings.

"Nestor is the oldest, probably in his mid-thirties now. Felipe must be late twenties," the manager replied. "Bad hombres, always in trouble."

The next stop for Jon and Manny was Pablo Gallegos's bank. He greeted them warmly, and they got comfortable in his office. Pablo ordered lunch and while they waited for it to be delivered his two visitors brought him up to date, beginning with their work in the library examining the Tijerina cartons, to, and including, showing Pablo the Walmart surveillance photos.

"The reason we're here, Pablo," Willard said, "is to ask for your help." That said, Jon realized that beginning last Friday when Rachel was attacked, and during all the time since, he had automatically taken over from Manny, Dr. Bob Roybal, Rachel, the Walmart manager, and now Pablo Gallegos. As if by default, everyone seemed to understand that Jon Willard, Esq. was in charge.

I do not want this. It has nothing to do with me. I had enough in New Orleans and New York. I returned to New Mexico for R & R, and to research a potential book about Reies Lopez Tijerina. Now, like the pull on a magnet as it gets closer to steel, hour after hour I am allowing myself to become more and more involved in Rachel Castellano's woes. I must extricate myself. ASAP.

While they were eating, Pablo asked, "How can I help you?" visibly upset about what Jon and Manny were telling him about what was happening to Rachel.

"In at least two ways," Willard answered. "One, is if you have a close relationship with anyone in the Santa Fe County sheriff's office, particularly in the Espanola substation. Second, if you know anyone in town with information about a man named Antonio Carranza who has been in and out of Espanola in the last year or so."

"Yes, as to the first. The Chief Deputy in charge of the substation is Walt Duran. I often work with him as a judge. Tell him I sent you."

Jon had a flash from his subconscious, but it was gone as fast as it had arisen.

"That's the guy I talked to," Manny said.

"As to the second, I'll ask around."

"Thanks," Jon said, "If you find out anything, tell Manny and he'll pass it along to me. We're going to head out to the substation when we finish this great pizza."

CHAPTER 26

THE SHERIFF'S SUBSTATION WAS A block behind the main street, on the first floor of the courthouse. The middle-aged receptionist asked if she could help them, Manny replied that Judge Pablo Gallegos sent them over to see Chief Deputy Sheriff Duran, she took their names, pointed to a group of chairs, and said, "Wait one."

Ex-military, Jon and Manny thought at the same time.

A few minutes later, a heavy wood door opened behind the receptionist. Through it walked a tall, thin man in his fifties who reminded Jon of the cowboy featured in the Marlboro cigarette ads, complete with lizard boots and a ten-gallon hat.

Instantly, Jon's subconscious told him why he recognized the man.

Before either Jon or Manny could speak, the Chief Deputy crossed the room and shook Jon and Manny's hands.

"Mr. Salazar, you and I have met before. And you, Mr. Willard, have a reputation that precedes you. And, from the expression on your face, you know who I am."

"Indeed, I do," Jon said, warmly. "You're John Duran's brother, Walt. The resemblance is uncanny, he mentioned you a few times recently."

Not wanting to leave Manny out of the conversation, Jon said, "Chief Deputy Duran's brother is a Special Agent of the FBI. He and his partner and I recently worked on sending a corrupt federal judge to prison."

"Indeed, they did. My brother told me all about it," Walt

said. "Thanks to Mr. Willard, my brother and his partner were promoted, commended, and allowed to choose their next assignments. They split up. I don't know where his partner is going, but after John's leave, vacation days and reassignment processing are over, he's coming home."

"Coming home?" Manny asked.

"That's another story," Walt said, "but yes, our family is originally from Las Cruces, down south. Enough about that for now. Let's get inside and see what I can do for you."

Walt Duran's office looked like a movie set director's idea of a western sheriff's office. Rifles and shotguns in a wall rack, Mexican rug on the floor, battered desk covered with files and loose documents and souvenirs from Las Vegas and Wyoming rodeos.

The Chief Deputy sheriff sat behind his desk, while Jon and Manny sat opposite.

"Mr. Salazar," Walt said, "I suppose you're here about that Carranza guy we talked about. Believe me, we did check, but turns out he is like a ghost. Only connection to Espanola is a monthly-rental studio apartment over on Mountain Street. Landlord told us," Walt paused, grabbed a file, and removed a single sheet of paper before continuing. "landlord told us he pays his rent on time, in cash, never any trouble, comes and goes."

"Walt," Jon said, "you're wondering what I'm doing here, right?"

"I sure am," the Chief Deputy said.

Jon and Manny spent the next half-hour explaining in detail how a New York criminal defense lawyer — recently Special Counsel to the United States Senate Judiciary Committee — was sitting in the Espanola movie-set-like office of the Chief Deputy Sheriff of Santa Fe County.

"So, I have a question for you, Walt," Willard said, respectfully.

"Okay, ask away."

"Based on what we've told you — Antonio Carranza is

a mystery man who likely ordered two attacks on Rachel Castellano, threatened her shepherds, destroyed and stole her property and twice tried to break down her residence door in the middle of the night and threatened to kill her — is it enough to get a search warrant for his apartment?"

"Will Rachel Castellano sign an affidavit incorporating everything you've just said?"

"Yes," Manny said. "Will you sign a warrant application saying you looked for Carranza, but could not find him?"

"Yes," Walt answered.

Willard asked Walt, "Does the Espanola Municipal judge have the authority to issue a search warrant?"

The Chief Deputy thought for a moment, and then said, "Well, the threats to her life and some of the other things happened outside the city, so no, but the assaults at COSTCO were inside city limits, so, yes. Judge Gallegos has the power to issue a search warrant."

All three smiled and shook hands. Already, a team.

* * *

Immediately after their meeting, Walt Duran ordered surveillance on Antonio Carranza's apartment. The next day, accompanied by Jon, Manny, an assistant deputy sheriff, and the local crime scene investigator, Walt rousted the landlord, served him with the search warrant, and ordered him to unlock Carranza's door.

While the civilians watched, for two hours the sheriffs and investigator looked in every nook and cranny of the studio apartment, patiently searching for latent fingerprints. In finding only four – on the refrigerator door handle, an open bottle of Corona beer, the inside doorknob, and a can of Gillette shaving cream – it was evident that Carranza had tried his best to scrub the place free of fingerprints.

Back in Walt's office, he explained how the state crime lab would process the fingerprints, something Willard was well acquainted with, but that it would take a couple of weeks. Walt had obtained a copy of Carranza's lease from the landlord, but declined Manny's request for a copy, explaining that the chain of custody had to be preserved.

Saying that he had two questions, Jon asked if while being watched by Walt, he could copy some information from the apartment lease. Walt nodded yes, and Jon did.

Choosing his words carefully, while Manny observed the lawyer-to-lawman pretense, Willard, who knew the answer, asked the Chief Deputy sheriff, "Is New Mexico plugged in to other states' databases for criminal records, driver licenses, fingerprints, and such?"

"Yes," Walt said, "we have excellent state working relationships. You said you had two questions."

"What about *federal relationships*?" Willard asked pointedly.

"Sometimes," was the Chief Deputy's smiling, but deliberately ambiguous, answer.

CHAPTER 27

WHEN JON PULLED INTO HIS driveway on Juniper Drive, Emiliano was washing his truck. "What's going on, you are spending so much time in Espanola?" he asked.

"It's about that research I'm doing for the book I might write about Reies Tijerina."

"Mercedes mentioned that the other day she saw you at the hospital emergency room."

Emiliano was fishing for information.

Surprised, Jon stalled for a couple of seconds, saying, "Mercedes, your daughter-in-law, the nurse?"

"Right."

"The woman I went to interview in Abiquiu had an accident, and my friend and I took her to the orthopedic department at St. Vincent's. I didn't see Mercedes."

"She had an emergency page from intensive care. Said she ran right past you and some other guy. By the way, Lorraine has a surprise for you, asked you to stop in when you got back."

Jon walked to the Romeros' front door and rang the brass bell. Lorraine opened the door, they exchanged hugs in the foyer, and she said, "Come into the kitchen, there's a surprise for you."

Puzzled, but obliging, Jon turned the corner. Standing behind the kitchen counter wearing a half-smile accompanied by the beginning of tears, was his fiancé, Andrea Vardas.

"My god," Jon said, as he rushed to embrace her, "what

are you doing here? No, I don't mean that. What I mean is, why are you here? No, not that either. Of course, I know why you're here," he stammered, the surprise wearing off. "I didn't expect you for at least a week."

Separating herself from their embrace and taking Jon's hand, she thanked Lorraine for helping with her surprise and led Jon out the door to their house across the dirt road.

After two hours in bed expressing how much they had missed each other, they sat outside on the patio ready to begin the catchups.

"Last time we talked," Jon said, "you said there was still much case work for you to finish at the Innocence Project."

"There was, but it was the kind of stuff others could do, so I spent a few days organizing the material and turning it over to two of the guys."

"You were doing the work of two guys?"

"Well, there are a lot of innocent convicts in prison, and not much in donations and grants available to help them. But I was overworked, needed a rest, and wanted to be here with you. Those were some of the reasons I left."

"What were the other reasons?" Jon asked.

"We'll discuss that some other time; I don't want to spoil this wonderful homecoming."

To help change the subject, Jon asked how her father was.

"Well," Andrea said, now upbeat, "he's good. Retired. Investor, philanthropist, discreet financial advisor. He still talks about our engagement party, where he and Attorney General Feldstein became buddies."

"I wonder why," Jon said, amused.

"Well sure, campaign donations, and Feldstein's aspiration for the governorship and then United States Senate. But partly because of what you did to Bobby Jackson and the other conspirators, especially Mike Quade. Oh, yeah, there's also golf and fishing. And Nick's villa in St. Thomas. He told me Feldstein wants to name him to some commission that's studying reformation of the New York securities laws. Ironic, no?"

Jon laughed. "As long as they're happy together."

"*Estas feliz aqui?*" Andrea asked, seriously. *Are you happy here?*

Jon, too, did not want to ruin their homecoming, so he dodged her question and asked, "Are you hungry? From New York to Phoenix to Albuquerque, and then a cab to Santa Fe. You must be."

"I'm famished. I want some Southwestern food, and décor. Let's go to Maria's."

"I thought the mariachis played too loudly."

"Sometimes," Andrea said, "but tonight it's exactly what I want."

They ate at Maria's, "the home of one hundred margaritas." The mariachis' sound level was perfect.

CHAPTER 28

A FTER DINNER, THEY RETURNED TO the patio and Jon started to answer Andrea's question about whether he was happy in Santa Fe. He began by reminding Andrea how during the disbarment case, and especially when it was over and the loose ends resolved, he had experienced what he characterized as the "glass full" epiphany.

"I remember," Andrea said, "at our engagement party your toast that your 'cup runneth over, that it was full.' When we got home you explained that the defamation case had caused an epiphany, that the pessimism was gone, that you believed you could win, that the world in general and judicial system in particular was not arrayed against you."

"I meant it," Jon said. "Then."

Andrea noted his word, "then," but kept silent.

Jon continued. "But afterwards, when we parted in New York and I began my drive out here, doubt began to creep in."

"Doubt?" she asked, cautiously.

"Doubt whether I could sustain the epiphany. Whether it was real or illusory? I closely examined everything that had happened. The *Vardas-Quade* and *Chow* cases, my Farber radio appearances, the defamation case. I asked myself why I took those cases, why I attacked Deveroux, and I knew there were good reasons. Truth and justice."

"Are you saying there has been slippage?"

"Good word," Jon said. "Yes, slippage. In a few minutes, I'll explain why I think so, but first I want to give you a general update, the context of what has been going on here in Santa Fe."

He told her that early research for the Tijerina book strongly suggested he was a crypto Communist, that Judge Pablo Gallegos had appointed Jon to represent a drunk defendant, that Korean War veteran chief librarian Manny Salazar who was a lawyer was once close to Tijerina, that artist and land grant descendant Rachel Castellano was under a death threat, that Antonio Carranza was likely trying to kill her, and that Deputy Sheriff Walt Duran would try to protect her.

Jon continued, shifting gears to Rachel's assaults at COSTCO and Walmart, and more important his reaction to them. And what it might mean for him. He paraphrased for Andrea the essence of the introspective conversation he'd had with himself on his long drive to Santa Fe.

"I was here, in this house. Urgent call from Manny Salazar. All he knows is Rachel fell in the Espanola Walmart. I go into automatic. This is important, Andrea, and will sound familiar. 'Get the store's surveillance cameras, Manny. Right now,' I ordered. 'Bring Rachel to Santa Fe, to my friend Dr. Robert Roybal in the emergency room.' Manny asks no questions. He does it. Do you get this, Andrea? I took over."

"Please slow down, Jon."

"They get to St. Vincent's hospital. I do the same thing. I took over, again."

Andrea, attentive to Jon's every word, said, "You know what facts are missing, what questions need answers and what others are not doing, or doing correctly. You thrive on conflict, on knowing what's broken and how to fix it, and if it is about lies and injustices, then the Paladin Curse seizes you, and Don Quixote rides again. So then, when you engage, the cynicism takes over, and you see the glass as empty, anticipating defeat in this rotten world. 'Can't win. Won't win.' Is that's what you're afraid of happening again?"

"Although," he answered, "I know better, but I feel with

Rachel's problem I'm allowing myself to be pulled into something serious that I can't handle."

He paused for a moment, thinking, and then said, "No. It's more than that. I'm running headlong into it. Worse, I feel that I'm gazing once again into an empty glass. That whatever I undertake is doomed because the universe is a malevolent place. I fear my epiphany could be left dead on the roadside."

CHAPTER 29

FOR THE REST OF THE week, while awaiting Duran's call about Carranza, Jon made copious notes about what he had learned from Rachel, Manny, and Walt; changed the Ranger's oil and fluids; bought new tires; replaced cracked roof tiles; reinforced the patio supports; talked to his New York secretary as little as possible; and read books on New Mexico and its crypto-Jews that he had borrowed from the Santa Fe library. Andrea, anticipating that the two of them were headed full bore into the Rachel affair, caught up with her museum and gallery deficiency by spending considerable time on Canyon Road.

When the call came, they agreed to meet the next day in Espanola at Duran's office.

After Jon introduced Andrea to Manny, Walt, and Rachel, her beauty and western dress too obvious to hide, the five made themselves comfortable in the small conference room. Rachel was still in her wheelchair because Dr. Roybal thought her ankle had not yet healed.

Walt opened the conversation by passing along his brother's well-wishes to Jon.

"He thinks very highly of you and is grateful for what you did for him and his partner."

Immediately, Walt said cryptically, "I've learned a lot about Mr. Carranza since our last meeting, but then I've had a lot of help if you take my meaning."

Jon did.

"For openers, folks," Walt said, opening a thick file and

passing around photographs, "although Manny and Rachel know what Mr. Antonio Carranza looks like in his current, mid-forties' incarnation, here are some photos when he was younger that may surprise you."

Instantly, Jon said, "Mug shots, looks like when he was in his twenties."

"Correct," Walt said, looking like a dealer handing out cards as he passed out more papers, "rap sheet. Everything from petty theft to arson."

Looking closely at the pages, Jon asked, "Who's Adam Campbell?"

"Good question," Walt said. "An alias. 'Adam Campbell' did prison time in New Mexico for rape."

Manny, who had been looking closely at the Campbell-Carranza rap sheet said, "Looks like there's nothing for several years, from about his mid-thirties until he showed up here in his mid-forties. What is the story with that?"

"That is an excellent question, Manny. It's probably the most important one because it underscores that we are dealing with an extremely dangerous man."

Willard cut into the conversation, asking, "Military, or CIA, or Defense Department contractor, Walt? Covert? Afghanistan, or maybe Africa?"

Without answering Jon's question directly, Walt passed out more papers, which he re-read while the others were reading them for the first time.

Jon, used to reading legal documents quickly, finished first, but waited for Rachel, Manny, and Andrea while casting a woeful glance at Walt.

Taking the lead, Willard said, "If I read this report correctly, Carranza was cashiered by the 'government' because of 'instabilities', meaning alcohol and/or drugs."

"That's how I read it," Walt said.

"He did time in New Mexico, which is probably how he got this job of trying to frighten Rachel into selling her lease," Manny observed.

"But let's hold the analysis for a few minutes more," Walt said. "Here are the last documents, which we obtained from his lease. You will notice that he signed it 'as agent for New Mexico Land Investors, LLC.' Of course," Walt continued, "there is no such entity in this State or any other. But someone did us a colossal favor and found one elsewhere."

"Who?" Jon asked, to cover his tracks.

"I really can't say. It is not that I don't want to, it's just that literally I don't know. These documents came to me yesterday via an international courier service from the Grand Cayman Islands. There is more. Our benefactor was apparently able to learn something about that LLC, which is owned by a Mexican corporation, which is owned by a Gibraltar trust, which is where the trail ends. Except for one more thing. *The Mexican corporation is indeed in the mining business. Gold, copper, lead, zinc, and . . .*" before Walt could utter the last word, Manny finished the sentence. "Silver, not turquoise. Silver. Carranza is fronting for a silver mining company."

When that registered on the others, Manny continued. Looking at Jon and Andrea, he said, "While this information is new to you and probably to Walt, it isn't to Rachel and me. About five years ago, a mining company tried to locate several abandoned silver mines in the former Tierra Amarilla land grant."

"In New Mexico," Rachel clarified.

"Right," Manny said. "But the opposition was fierce. There were two main groups, the environmentalists, and individuals such as Rachel and me."

"Did the groups work together?" Andrea asked.

"No," Manny said. "The environmentalists were against the project because of silver's toxicity, and its 'capitalist' presence everywhere in this country and around the world as both an industrial metal and investment vehicle."

"The second group, individual descendants of land grant owners like Manny and me," Rachel said, "objected on principle. What I mean by that is that even today we claim land grant rights and selling our leases would be a concession that the stealing was okay, and our property was gone forever. I would not sell out my heritage then, and I will not sell it out now."

"Which," Jon said, "takes us back to Mr. Antonio Carranza. If you find him, can you make an arrest because of his threats to Rachel?"

"For banging on the door, and making verbal threats? We could arrest him, warn him, but it's unlikely the glory-hound DA would charge him. We would need more."

"Unless there's an outstanding warrant out on him, somewhere," Willard said.

"We're looking," Walt said.

"Then, you'll pick him up, and turn him over to whomever wants him?" Jon asked.

"In a heartbeat," Walt said, cheerfully.

CHAPTER 30

THAT EVENING DOÑA RACHEL CASTELLANO sat dozing in her wheelchair, bits and pieces of her life bobbing into and out of her conscious mind. *Juan de Oñate. Silver mine. Walmart. Willard. Fracture. Carranza. Grandpapa. Painting. Georgia. Love. Death. Reies.* Dozens, maybe hundreds of fragments in the two hours she had been sitting there.

The wheelchair, with Rachel's right leg still elevated, was in the living room facing the inside of the front door about ten feet away. She had been on and off it for the eight days and nights since the meeting with Walt Duran, sometimes dozing. Every light in the house and the outdoor floodlights were blazing.

On Rachel's lap lay a loaded 12-gauge Mossberg pump gun, a round in the chamber. Instinctively she knew Carranza would come sooner or later, probably after sundown. If he got into the house, he would die. Not Rachel.

The banging, drunken obscenities and murder threats began at 3:21 a.m. just as before, except this time the chopping and pounding was not random. It was focused on the door's metal lock and bolt. As Rachel sat calmly, almost like a disinterested observer, she realized that Carranza was trying to separate the metal from the door's wood, so that it would then swing open on its hinges and he could simply walk in.

Well, she thought, *the sooner the better.*

For the next ten minutes, Carranza chopped, pounded,

and shouted. In between, Rachel shouted back, "Get the hell out of here, you drunken, impotent son-of-a-bitch. I'm calling the sheriff."

But she wouldn't. Not until the deed was done.

Finally, about 3:42 a.m., the door's hardware and splintered pieces of wood to which it was attached fell to the floor.

Carranza pushed the shattered door open and stepped over the threshold holding an axe with one hand and a sledgehammer in the other. Rachel was squarely in front of him, sitting in her wheelchair, the shotgun now at her hip.

His break-in was the last thing Antonio Carranza would hear on God's green earth.

As Rachel pumped the riot gun and pulled its trigger, more and more of Carranza's body was shredded by the shotgun's rounds.

Calmly and purposefully, Rachel put the shotgun on the floor beside her. Next, she pushed the button on the alarm hanging around her neck, causing the house's exterior alarm to sound and telephone messages to be sent to the sheriff in Santa Fe and in Espanola to Walt Duran's office and Manny Salazar's home. That done, Rachel pushed the button again, turning off the alarm.

Then, Rachel Castellano looked down at the threshold to what was left of the man who had threatened to kill her. She smiled. And waited.

CHAPTER 31

IN ABOUT TWELVE MINUTES, THE first to arrive were her neighbors, the husband, a former military policeman in Vietnam—now a contractor—and his wife, a medical assistant to an Espanola gynecologist. Both were armed, he with a semi-automatic rifle, she with a handgun. The front door was open, the threshold partially blocked by the former Antonio Carranza. The neighbors stood outside.

"Jesus," the husband said, "looks like 'Nam. I won't bother with taking his pulse."

"Are you okay, Rach?" the couple asked almost in unison.

"Never better."

"What happened?" the former military cop asked, automatically.

"Pretty obvious, no?" Rachel replied. "Listen, I hear a siren, so that's the cops. Get out of here, so you don't get involved. If you can help, I'll call."

They left.

A few minutes later, siren blaring, an Espanola Crown Victoria sheriff's cruiser pulled up. Out jumped a uniformed officer so young as to look like a Boy Scout, except for the shotgun he carried. As he walked to the front door and took in the bizarre tableaux laid out before him — a shredded human form across the threshold; open door; beyond, an elderly woman in a wheelchair, a shotgun on the floor — he pointed his weapon at the floor just as Rachel yelled, "All secure, officer, bad guy at your feet, my shotgun on the floor next to me, only ones alive are you and me. Careful, this is a crime scene."

"No shit," the officer said. "What happened?"

Why, Rachel wondered, *do people ask what "happened" when what happened is so demonstrably obvious?*

"Pretty obvious, no?" she said. "Please don't take it personally, officer, but I will have nothing to say until I have spoken to my lawyer, Manny Salazar."

"Understood. I know Manny. I used to work in the library after school."

Rachel asked the boy to pour her a stiff bourbon from the sideboard, which he did, saying "I'd like to join you, but I'm on duty."

"That's why I didn't ask you to join me. While we're waiting for the others, look around closely and set this scene in your mind."

The young man did so.

While Rachel drank her I.W. Harper and the officer reconnoitered, her adrenaline level and heartbeat began to come down. The bourbon was working.

Chief Deputy Walt Duran, with the crime scene technician aboard and seeing another cruiser in the driveway, rolled up with his siren off. One look, and he did not need to ask what happened.

The Chief Deputy's first words were to the young on-scene officer. "All secure, no tampering?"

"No, sir. Everything as I found it a few minutes ago, all secure, no tampering."

"Where did Ms. Castellano get that drink?"

"At her request, I got it."

"Okay, from the look of this mess, she must have needed it."

The two sheriffs had been talking as if Rachel were not there, so Walt turned to her and asked, "You okay? Can I get you anything?"

Before she could answer, he continued, saying, "I'd like

to keep you in that wheelchair until the forensics guy gets some pictures."

"Fine," Rachel said, "but only if I get a refill."

Walt laughed, told the crime scene guy to get the pictures, and poured another bourbon for her.

Once the photos were finished, Walt wheeled Rachel to the couch and gently moved her onto it, putting an ottoman under her right foot.

"I assume, Rachel, that if we're going to do this by the book, you want to wait for Manny before you talk to me, and we record the conversation?"

"Yes, Manny, Willard and Vardas, his two 'investigators'," she said.

Walt laughed.

While waiting, Walt, the crime scene guy, and the young deputy puttered around without disturbing the area.

In about forty minutes Manny arrived, followed by Jon and Andrea. None of them had to ask, "What happened?"

When the five were seated in the living room, Walt said, looking at Jon not Manny, "You four can talk privately, I'll clear out."

Jon, having quickly assessed what had happened and that the scene was a classic self-defense situation, said, "That's not necessary, Chief Deputy, I'm sure that Rachel has nothing to hide in explaining what happened and why, and no hesitation in fully and honestly answering your questions, so why don't you interview her right now?"

Andrea, who had seen Jon operate before, knew that he was building a record of cooperation and transparency for later. Manny and Rachel quickly caught on. Walt, too.

There were "sures," "okays," and affirmative head nods all around.

"Then let's begin," Walt said, authoritatively.

Jon, taking over again, asked Walt if he could suggest how to proceed, and the Chief Deputy turned on a cassette recorder. After dictating the day, date, hour, and the names of those present, he said, "Ms. Castellano, for openers, please begin and continue chronologically from when Antonio Carranza first contacted you, to when he showed up a little while ago and Officer Scott here arrived."

Answering occasionally interposed questions from Walt, Jon, Manny, and Andrea, and making some clarifications, Rachel did so for nearly two hours.

When the deputy sheriff departed, Manny said, "I'm not much of a lawyer, but this is an open-and-shut case of self-defense, no doubt about it being a justified 'defense of habitation' shooting."

When Andrea realized Jon had remained silent, she followed his lead by not commenting.

"Well, that's good to hear," Rachel said with a sigh, "because I hope the DA indicts me."

Instantly, Manny blurted out, "What? Are you serious? Indict you?"

Trained to listen, Willard said nothing. Obviously, Rachel had an ulterior motive and was damn serious. Again, Andrea followed his lead.

Manny, naively unaware of the dynamics, looked at Jon and said, "When the DA hears the facts, all the evidence, what happened, about Carranza's threats, the smashed door, all of it, the self-defense, she would be crazy to indict Rachel. Right?"

"Wrong," Jon said, sympathetically. "The DA may be in this for her own reasons, even if she loses at trial. An ulterior motive. Just as Rachel has an ulterior motive, and I hope right now she'll tell us what it is."

Rachel smiled and said, "Well done, Jon, indeed I do. It is rooted in my conviction, no pun intended, that if I am indicted for murder I would likely be acquitted or there would be a hung jury, though one never knows. Correct?"

"Correct," Jon said emphatically, "Never."

"Why are you smiling?" she asked him.

"Because I know where you're going."

"Well," Rachel said, returning Jon's smile, "the others don't, so I'll tell them by asking you some questions. If you were to defend me – and I realize you have not signed on officially– would the case get much national attention?"

"Depends on *what* is on trial," Jon said, still smiling. "Not whom."

"What attention-getting national issue could that be?" she asked.

"You tell them," Jon said, "it's your idea."

Rachel turned to Manny, and said, "*My murder case will put on trial the stolen land grants.*"

CHAPTER 32

THE SANTA FE COUNTY DISTRICT Attorney, Maria Quintana, was in her first term. She was a third-generation New Mexican, and graduate of UNM and its law school. The choice of hometown education, dictated by her lawyer-father, had been required by his ambition that eventually his daughter would sit on the New Mexico Supreme Court. To that end, he bought his daughter the senior class presidency by throwing a huge party a week before the student election, made substantial contributions to the University of New Mexico during Maria's undergraduate years and again when she was in law school, and contributed heavily to the state Democratic Party.

The contributions bought his daughter her first patronage-induced job, Assistant District Attorney for the County of Santa Fe. It was well known around the courthouse that Maria Quintana was inexperienced, and thus unreliable. Accordingly, she was assigned low-level misdemeanor cases, and to handle scripted guilty pleas in felony cases negotiated by senior assistant DAs.

Two years later, Maria's manager-father's next accomplishment was to finagle and buy for her the Democratic Party nomination for District Attorney, in the heavily Democrat County of Santa Fe. Even with a well-financed campaign against a nondescript Republican lawyer, Maria won by only a half-percent margin.

During her three years as an ADA, and now two years as DA, Quintana was a publicity hound of the worst kind, inserting herself in matters over which she had a tenuous or nonexistent connection. Being only in her early thirties and attractive, she was often in the newspapers and giving local radio and television interviews. A climber.

Walt Duran had immediately informed Santa Fe County sheriff Dave Foster of the Carranza killing, and he in turn briefed DA Quintana. She immediately took the case under her personal supervision. While subordinates would do the grunt work, she would reap the glory. Others in the office wondered, would it be the whirlwind?

Quintana immediately assigned her Chief Deputy, Fred Zimmerman, to collect all the information that the sheriff's office had, conduct a thorough investigation, assemble the facts, compare them with the law, and report back to her in three days.

The Chief Deputy District Attorney did a credible job and met with his boss five days later. He related the facts, displayed photos, summarized sheriffs' statements and twice he and Quintana listened to Rachel Castellano's recorded nearly two-hour interview.

"By the way, Fred, at the interview who were these other two, that guy Willard and the woman, Vardas?"

"No idea, probably friends or neighbors."

"Okay, now what about the law?" the DA asked her subordinate.

"A classic 'Castle Doctrine' self-defense, defense of habitation case. The perp threatened twice to kill Castellano, twice tried to bang into her home. The third time he got in, she killed him. Case closed."

This guy, he works for me. Why the hell is he telling me something he should know I don't want to hear? Quintana thought.

"Not so fast, Fred. The defendant was locked and loaded, waiting for him. Doesn't that count for something?"

ADA Fred Zimmerman was a career prosecutor, and with Quintana's reference to the not yet indicted "defendant" he knew exactly where this conversation and the case was going. He had seen Santa Fe District Attorneys come and go, had never kowtowed to any of them, and he was not going to start now. So, he answered Quintana's question by saying, "It doesn't mean a damn thing, Maria. The Castle Doctrine case law says that you can defend your home with lethal force, and a statute says you can defend your home in self-defense. The late Mr. Carranza was the aggressor, Ms. Castellano was the threatened person. There is no legitimate, conviction-beyond-a-reasonable-doubt prosecution here. Frankly, if Rachel Castellano had not been locked and loaded, she'd be dead, and we'd be talking about indicting the perp instead of burying what's left of him."

As if Quintana had heard nothing her Chief Deputy said, she instructed him to "find something we can hang a prosecution on."

Zimmerman noted that his boss did not use the word "legitimate."

CHAPTER 33

ACHEL SPENT THAT NIGHT AND the next at her sister's home in Santa Fe. The following day, she and Rose returned to Abiquiu to collect clothes and other necessities she would need while staying in Santa Fe. Not only was Rachel's home a locked-down crime scene, but even when it was eventually released the cleanup was not going to be quick or easy.

Jon understood with every step he took to help Rachel Castellano he was being pulled toward the ultimate showdown with himself. His realization was underscored when two days later Manny called asking for help.

He had received a telephone call from the DA herself. She said legal ethics prohibited her from contacting Rachel directly if she was represented by a lawyer, and because Walt Duran had mentioned Manny's name she wanted to know if Salazar was representing Castellano. When Manny said he was, Quintana invited him to come to Santa Fe for a discussion about "the case."

"I didn't know what to say, or ask," Manny told Jon, "so, I agreed. No one knows better than me that I'm way over my head with this, so will you come with me? I'll say you're my 'investigator.'"

Willard could almost palpably feel that he was being drawn into the quicksand of what was beginning to look like *State* v. *Rachel Castellano*, but since he had not formally decided whether to get involved, he agreed.

The next day, the two lawyers sat in carved Mexican chairs

across from Quintana's matching desk. After she introduced herself and Fred Zimmerman, Manny introduced himself and Mr. Willard, his "investigator." When the requisite lawyer-talk wound down, she said to Manny, "As we see it in this office, Mr. Salazar, your client has a serious problem."

Willard instantly noticed two reactions. Manny was physically uncomfortable, his butt shifting on the chair's soft cushion. Zimmerman was physically comfortable, but his eyes were downcast, ostensibly looking at notes on his lap. *Something is bothering this guy. Probably realizes there's no case here.*

Composing himself and trying to act professionally, Manny responded to Quintana by safely saying, "What serious problem is that?"

"Well," the thirty-some District Attorney pompously said, "from all we've seen it looks like we have a case of Murder 1."

While she spoke, Willard looked not at the posturing young DA, but at her ill-at-ease Chief Deputy. He was even more uncomfortable than Manny. Jon had been around prosecutors long enough to know he was seeing serious disagreement between the Chief Deputy and his boss.

Manny, of course, did not know how to reply.

Willard did, wondering if any of the others would realize what he was about to do.

"If I remember," Willard said, "and I am partly paraphrasing here, Miss Quintana, Murder 1 in New Mexico has three facets. Correct me if I am mistaken, Miss Quintana, I may have the order wrong. One is the 'depraved mind,' 'greatly dangerous act' crime. Another is the 'felony murder' crime, and the last is the 'willful, deliberate *and premeditated'* crime."

Quintana had frowned at Jon's use of "Miss," twice, in back-to-back sentences.

While he spoke, Willard looked not at the DA, but at the uncomfortable Chief Deputy who now knew for sure that

Willard was neither Rachel Castellano's friend, neighbor, nor investigator.

"You don't have any of that. Not any of it," Willard said with authority. "Nada *depravity,* nada Ms. Castellano committing a *felony,* and nada her *premeditating the late Mr. Carranza's demise.*"

Quintana countered with, "Murder 2 is a lesser included offense of Murder 1."

"Agreed, it's sort of a half-assed manslaughter count. So what?"

Willard was certain Fred had suppressed a smile. *Old Fred knows better than this crap she's selling. He is not on board with it.*

With that, Quintana finally woke up, and asked, "Mr. Willard, are you a lawyer?"

"Sort of."

"Sort of?" she asked.

"I am, yes, a member of our legal fraternity." It was a Willard-laid trap. *Does she let "fraternity" slide, or, standing up for the militant sisterhood, correct me?*

Quintana chose the latter, saying, "And don't forget sorority."

"I stand corrected, Madam District Attorney."

"Are you trying to get under my skin, Mr. Willard?" she asked, Manny and Fred now mere bystanders to the colloquy. "Are you a New Mexico lawyer? I've never heard your name," she managed to ask.

"No, I am a New York lawyer. Speaking of which, I have a closing statement to this unproductive meeting, if you would like to hear it."

"Of course," Quintana said, feigning indifference.

"Among other things, we have bullet-proof cases of self-defense and habitation defense, no pun intended. You have SOS."

Manny, a veteran, and probably Fred, suppressed laughs.

"SOS, what the hell is that?" the DA asked.

"An old military food description, Madam, creamed chipped beef on toast. 'SOS' stands for 'shit on a shingle'."

With that, Jon and Manny rose. Ignoring the DA, Manny headed for the door. Jon shook hands with Fred and thought the Chief Deputy had squeezed too hard. Sending a message?

CHAPTER 34

A s Jon and Manny left the building, he pointed to a small park exhibiting a bronze statue of St. Francis, patron saint of animals, and pointing to a bench, said, "Let's sit down over there for a few minutes."

Jon said, "Let's cross the street first. I have to do something in that delicatessen."

"Delicatessen?" Manny said. "You're a vegan, and I don't eat stuff like cow tongues."

"Trust me."

They went in, and Manny was shocked when Jon ordered a ham sandwich. He was more shocked when Jon wrote a note and told the counterman that he wanted it and the sandwich delivered across the street to District Attorney Maria Quintana.

When they were seated on the bench, Manny said, "I don't know where to start, so let's work backwards. What did the ham sandwich note say?"

Jon smiled broadly, and said, "Happy indictment. See you in court!"

"What," Manny almost shouted. "You sent the Santa Fe DA a ham sandwich, with that note?"

"I guess you never got the memo out there in Espanola. Most every criminal lawyer — prosecution and defense alike — knows the saying that a prosecutor has so much power that he could 'indict a ham sandwich'. The saying is attributed to a former New York State judge."

"What was your point?"

"I was sending the message that we expected her to indict Rachel, and that she should get to it. Between the lines, I was daring the DA to do it. If she didn't get the message, her deputy did."

"Indict Rachel?" Manny repeated. "For what?"

"Murder 1."

"That's crazy," Manny said, indignantly.

"Why," Jon asked, "from Quintana's perspective?"

"Because we have an iron-clad self-defense and defense of habitation case, which she can't overcome," Manny said naïvely.

"Check your premise," Jon replied, "Does she care about winning? No, Manny, what that no-nothing kid DA wants is the notoriety. I checked on her family. Word is her lawyer daddy bought her everything she ever wanted with his wife's money, including the DA job. She wants to prove that she's no longer daddy's little girl, so he can keep pushing her up the ladder to the New Mexico Supreme Court. *State* v. *Castellano* will not be about law, Manny, it will be about professional advancement through politics and publicity."

"You mean," Manny said, angrily, "that the DA would indict Rachel for Murder 1 just for publicity?"

"Throw of the dice. Never know what a jury will do."

"Can Quintana get away with this?"

"If you mean, convict, almost certainly not."

"Well," Manny said, "you certainly 'got under her skin' with that business of you being a lawyer, calling her 'Miss,' forcing her to use the word 'sorority' to describe female lawyers, calling her 'madam' twice and characterizing her case as 'shit on a shingle'. What was all that about?"

"Psychological warfare, Manny. You use insults to establish dominance and fear. I want her to be afraid of us. She needs to be knocked down a few notches. We are the strong, confident. She the weak, unsure. Look, we'll almost certainly get a 'not guilty' verdict. At least a hung jury. But that's not what this is all about, Manny," Jon said forcefully.

"What then?"

"What I did to Mike Quade who tried to frame Nick Vardas for a double homicide, and what I did to him and his conspirators when they tried to have me disbarred. If I get into the case, I will attempt to destroy any reputation Maria Quintana might have, or ever get, as a serious lawyer in New Mexico or anywhere else. At best, she will wind up in her father's one-man fender-bender law practice. You heard Rachel explain why she is willing to risk an unlikely Murder 1 conviction to expose the stolen land grants. Mine will be that, too, plus using the trial as a tool to drive Quintana out of the legal profession. That's what you and I, and the others, will try to accomplish."

Manny looked embarrassed, and said, "I guess I have a lot to learn."

You do, my new friend. But what scares me is that you might not, because of inexperience and lack of grit.

"If you read the DA correctly, and I'm sure you do, what happens next, Jon?"

"Next, we must do at least four indispensable things while we wait for the indictment. So that when it comes down, we don't have to start from scratch."

"Four?" Manny asked, now along for the ride.

"Very quietly, we will have someone reliable set up a defense fund."

"We prepare to post bail, which will be provided by a bonding company or in cash immediately after the amount is set. That way, Rachel will not be stuck in the Santa Fe jail until this case is over.

"We get an investigator, expert witnesses, and a first-class criminal defense lawyer." *God help me.*

"We put the investigator to work providing information about a Gibraltar trust that owns a Mexican corporation that owns New Mexico Land Investors LLC, that owns Rachel's leases. Also, about Antonio Carranza, Maria Quintana, Fred

Zimmerman, and anyone else who can tell us something of importance we do not know already."

As Jon reeled off the steps necessary to organize a well-financed, structured, and professional criminal defense, he felt like he was banging nails into his own coffin, seemingly unable to stop himself.

He was acting as he did in all his criminal cases. Willard would organize and conduct the equivalent of a large symphony orchestra, each instrument responding to the direction of Maestro Jon Willard, Esq. Sometimes — as in the Vargas-Quade and defamation cases — he would make beautiful music. Other times – as in the *Chow* case – he would fall flat.

What the hell am I doing? he asked himself silently. *I am like an addict who needs a fix, and mine is the endless pursuit of truth and justice. I have been kidding myself, because there is no doubt whose case this is already, who will organize it, and who will try it. But what if my Malevolent Universe premise takes over, making me doubt, undercutting my efficacy and God forbid there is a conviction?*

Manny was aware that Jon's thoughts were elsewhere, so although he was bursting with comments and questions, he remained silent. When Jon came up for air, Manny said, "Jon, my head is swimming, and I don't know where to start."

"Slowly."

"Okay, you talk of a defense fund. I understand. But between the bail and all the people who will need to be hired, it's going to cost a lot of money."

"Maybe," Jon replied.

"Where will it come from?"

"Don't worry about that. It will be provided. 'Build it, and they will come.' Apart from the insurance premium or cash for the bail bond and the trial lawyer's fee, the costs for the investigator and expert witnesses should run no more than about forty thousand dollars. If we obtain a cash bail, the money will be returned after the acquittal or hung jury."

Unused to numbers like that, Manny almost gasped. "Can you make a guess about the bail bond premium?" he asked.

"Well, we can get all we want for a ten-percent premium, but we can't speculate because we don't know how much the bail will be. If it's one hundred thousand, the premium will be ten thousand dollars. But likely we will put up a cash bail."

"And the trial lawyer?" Manny asked, carefully and reluctantly.

"Let's leave that aside for now," Jon said. "Maybe someone will come forward *pro bono*." *Who am I kidding*? he thought. *That's what I'm worried about. Guess who*? He knew the Paladin curse and Quixotic urge were inevitably pulling him toward a dangerous place, one where the glass was always empty.

Jon Willard, Esq., now stood gazing into the abyss.

"Still," Manny said. "That's a lot of money."

"To most people, but not to others," Jon replied equivocally.

CHAPTER 35

A S THEY WERE ABOUT TO part, Jon asked Manny how he had been able to spend so much time helping Rachel, having a full-time job as chief librarian.

Manny replied that he was beginning to get complaints from the staff, and that sooner than later the library board would get wind of it.

"What are you going to do, Manny?" Jon asked, concerned. "You know from our meeting with the DA that this mess is going to get much worse before it gets better."

"I know. And there's another complicating 'worse' right now that you don't know."

"Try me."

"I'm not breaching a confidence, because I asked Rachel if I could tell you."

"What did she say?"

"She laughed and said you probably already had figured out that we were in an intimate relationship."

"She was correct, I had. But put that complication aside for now because you have two immediate tasks. First, you must accurately and thoroughly report to Rachel everything you learned at the DA's office, and what we discussed just now. Second, you must solve your job problem while I attend to other matters."

"How fast do we have to move?" Manny asked nervously.

"Not urgently, but fast. I checked on the grand jury. Its work for this month is finished, and the jurors have been discharged. The DA will convene a new one in sixteen days, so there will be no indictment until then."

"But there will be one," Manny said, reluctantly. It was not a question.

"Yes, Rachel Castellano will be indicted for first-degree murder."

CHAPTER 36

EVER SINCE THE MANY HOURS of introspecting Jon had done on the drive to Santa Fe and even more since he had been there, despite the distraction of Rachel's legal problem he had been conscientiously trying to dig deeper and still deeper into the *why* of his hopefully now-gone Malevolent Universe premise.

While Ayn Rand's explanations and prodding and his own psychological honesty had identified *that* he suffered from that problem, until recently he was stymied as to *why*.

Okay, when I told our guests at the recent engagement party in New York that finally my glass was neither half-full or half-empty, but instead completely full, that liberating epiphany was so welcome I did not then dig deeper and try to expose the reason I had for having so long allowed that premise to dominate my life. I might have deliberately suppressed or repressed the "why" of my Malevolent Universe premise—why I believed the universe was malevolent, and the good, the righteous, doomed.

Indeed, during Jon's introspective cross-country drive from New York to Santa Fe, and despite the distraction of his Tijerina research and increasing involvement in Rachel Castellano's forthcoming Murder 1 indictment, he had been obsessed by *why* the Malevolent Universe premise had pervaded his adult life. Not *that* it had, because in New York he had been able to recognize the toll it had taken. But, *why*? What was the cause, the triggering mechanism that replaced normal optimism with ceaseless pessimism? Before

Andrea's arrival Jon felt he was getting closer to the answer, and with the benefit of their recent conversations he believed he was almost there.

As Jon walked home on Paseo de Peralta to Juniper Drive after his meeting with the DA and his follow-up with Manny, Willard began once again to put the disparate pieces together in the hope that by fitting they would reveal the picture that for so long he had fought to bring into focus.

From the moment I became involved in Rachel's legal problem, I began to lose slivers of the New York epiphany, seeing that she was suffering and would need help. Indeed, already needed it. But at the same time, I felt my help would be doomed. Back where I started, it seems. Before my New York epiphany.

But as disheartening as that identification was — that his epiphany fell short of understanding the *why* of what caused his Malevolent Universe premise — at least Jon hoped he now knew that the answer to *why* held the key to the door which had locked him into cynicism and fear his entire adult life.

The depth and intensity of Jon's thoughts were apparently revealed on his face because the moment Andrea greeted him, she saw he was struggling.

Sitting on the rear patio, Jon told her everything he had been thinking on the walk home, adding, "While I was alone here, and even after you arrived, I have been agonizing about this dichotomy, this 'damned if I do, damned if I don't' almost schizophrenic way I see life."

"Has the dichotomy been made real to you by the looming first-degree murder charge against Rachel?" Andrea asked.

"Yes, this *fake* charge. I *can* help her, but more and more I feel emotionally that because the system, especially here in New Mexico, is so corrupt, in the end I won't succeed. And it is going to be an indictment for Murder 1. And today at the DA's office made it worse."

"Tell me about that."

He did.

When Jon was finished, she said, "The last time we discussed this, you told me all the thinking you've done recently may have enabled you to understand the *why* for your Malevolent Universe premise. Tell me about that."

"Okay," Jon said, "here goes. Interrupt if necessary."

Looking at her fiancé intensely, Andrea said softly, "We have to resolve this once and for all, here and now, and only we can do it. Only the two of us can get to the bottom of this."

He began.

"I started my analysis literally at the beginning. As you know, I was born in Tokyo in 1948. My World War II veteran father, Major Max Willard, was doing occupation duty in Tokyo, with the Army's 24th Infantry Division. Two years later, after North Korea's June 1950 attack on South Korea and MacArthur's invasion at Inchon, his unit was close to the northeast border of Korea and China, at a godforsaken place called the Chosin Reservoir."

"Miles was there, too," Andrea said.

"Yes, Miles was also in the infantry, in a company of my father's battalion. They were together when my father was wounded in his right shoulder and arm by a Chinese grenade. Miles helped Max to a rear aid station and went back to his unit. Two days later, the Chinese overran the aid station, killed the wounded who could not walk, and marched the survivors north. My mother was notified that her husband was MIA, 'missing in action.'"

"How long was Miles in Korea?"

"Until he was seriously wounded on the retreat from the reservoir, some weeks later. That's late 1950. He was sent to Okinawa for recuperation. Then back to the States, and later to Tokyo again."

"That's when he visited you and your mother there. Do you have any memory of that?"

"No, later I found out his visit was in 1953, I was about

five years old, but I remember a couple of years later my mother telling me of Miles's visit, and that my father had been a prisoner of war since 1951. This is the most important part, Andrea, and may provide the *why* of what happened to me. I now remember it clearly."

"What happened?"

"There was a negotiated cease fire, an armistice, in July 1953, one condition being the repatriation of POWs from both sides. It was called 'Operation Big Switch' and took place at a place called Panmunjom near the 38th parallel. By then, I remember my mother's joy that 'Daddy is coming home.' Exultations like that, over and over, louder and louder. Mom surrounded by other Army wives, a few of whom had MIA/POW husbands."

"They had good reason to be happy."

"Indeed, they did. The Big Switch repatriations began on August 6, 1953. On that day, and every day of repatriations of American POWs until the last day in December 1953, over 120 days, my mother and I were glued to the radio, newspapers, and telephone, and in contact with other MIA/POW wives. And the army in Seoul, Tokyo and at the Pentagon."

"Was there any news of your father during that time?"

"No, not one word."

"Still, there was a relentless drumbeat in our home, from my mother, Army social workers, other wives, friends, relatives back in the States, even strangers at Camp Drake in Tokyo who knew Mom was waiting for her husband. 'Daddy is coming home.' Newsreels. I cried myself sick, Andrea. My mother and I prayed at bedside. I had dreams, and nightmares. I didn't sleep, to get to the radio and other news early in the morning. Anything to tell us when 'Daddy is coming home'."

"Jesus," was all Andrea could say, tears now running down both their faces.

With Jon in her arms crying uncontrollably, he managed

to say, "Andrea, Daddy *never* came home. I now recall that my anger and disappointment was unbearable. I grew up simultaneously hating and fearing the world."

That moment, Jon Willard's emotional dam broke, his repression of decades flooding his conscious mind.

CHAPTER 37

L ATER, AS THE BLAZING WESTERN sun surrounded by purple-tinted clouds began its nightly red-orange journey to the other side of the world, they sat in the patio silently trying to absorb and understand what Jon had experienced: A child's understandable, relentlessly drummed anticipation that his long-lost father was being restored to him had been crushed by reality.

"You never connected your childhood mega disappointment with what Rand diagnosed as a Malevolent Universe premise?"

"Never, until now. But I was a child. As I recall now, once my mother unsuccessfully beat the bushes in Seoul, Tokyo, and Washington for more information about her missing husband, she got on with her life as best she could. She was a normal adult, who could cope with adversity. Her husband was a professional soldier. His job was to fight, and maybe die. He survived World War II, but not Korea. 'Okay,' she must have said. 'I'm a young woman with a six-year-old child. My husband is gone, and he is not coming back. So, pick yourself up and get on with life.'"

"You were a child, Jon. You were not equipped psychologically to cope with what happened. Think about it. Your father was lost to you *twice*. Once when you were told that he was MIA and maybe POW. Then, in August 1953 he was not MIA or POW. He was coming home. Except he never did. Way back in Tokyo, as soon as you lost him for the second time, young Jon Willard needed serious psychotherapy."

"Instead," Jon lamented, "the surviving two-thirds of the Willard family moved to Albuquerque, and I brought with me my emerging conviction — not belief, Andrea, but *conviction* — that the world is a rotten place, and nothing good can succeed. Happiness cannot be attained."

Silence.

"But that's over," he said. "I am not going to ruin *our* lives, now that I know why I *have* crippled mine and probably others'."

Silence.

A few minutes later, Jon stood abruptly. Looking at his fiancé, he said, "There is too much evil in the world, and too many rotten people, but many more decent ones. Among them is Rachel Castellano. I am going to defend her, and I am going to win. For her, and for me!"

CHAPTER 38

THE NEXT FEW DAYS WERE a flurry of activity.

Jon and Andrea called her father to update him about what was happening in otherwise quiet Santa Fe. When they reached the part about Jon representing Rachel Castellano in her first-degree murder trial and setting up a defense fund, Nick jumped in, as he had when Jon was fighting the conspiracy that was trying to disbar him.

"How much do you need?"

Andrea responded with a hearty laugh.

"That's not why we called," Jon and Andrea said almost in unison.

"I know that, but you know this sort of thing, helping innocent people getting screwed by politicians, lawyers, judges, legislators and such has become kind of a hobby for me. Like that Innocence Project Andrea has been doing *pro bono* work for. I told Mrs. Cooper to send them a check every few months."

Surprised, Andrea said, "I didn't know that. Why didn't you tell me?"

"Well . . . Anyhow, it's right there on their contributor list," Nick said.

Not wanting to ask her father how much he regularly donated, Andrea said, "Under your name, right?"

"Right, just look for 'Mr. Anonymous.'"

By the time their conversation had ended, Nick had volunteered to have a "trusted friend" open and manage a defense fund, line up a bondsman in Albuquerque, and have the Rachel Castellano Defense Fund put up cash for bail or pay for the bail bond fee. Also, Nick would take care of an office, expert witnesses, the Pinkerton International Detective Agency, and anything else they needed. The "trusted friend's" services were *pro bono*.

So, too, Jon thought, *would be the trial lawyer's services.*

As a parting shot to Andrea, Nick said, "Maybe I'll come to the trial. I enjoy seeing my future son-in-law destroy his opponents. That's become another hobby."

"Typical," Jon said when the call ended. "I'm not surprised doing good has become a hobby; your father is a decent man. He probably will show up for the trial."

Lightheartedly, Andrea said, "On a related subject, regarding this case I want a title, since I can't practice in New Mexico."

"I thought you knew. You are the chief-of-staff, my liaison to everyone else. Substantively, as in the disbarment case, you will handle the expert witnesses, investigators, the Friedmans, and whatever discovery we may get. Okay?"

"Great," she said. "The whole eight yards."

"Nine yards."

"I know. Just wanted to be sure you were listening."

Jon laughed.

"Most important," Jon said, "I want your mind thinking like a lawyer at every step in this case. But viewing it from the outside. Yours truly and Manny Salazar, who doesn't know he's going to be second seat at the trial, will be under fire inside the courtroom, and your outside perspective will be indispensable."

"All you want is my mind?"

"Very funny. Don't rub it in."

CHAPTER 39

J
ON, ANDREA, MANNY, AND RACHEL met two evenings later at her sister Rose's home in Santa Fe because Rachel's in Abiquiu was still considered a crime scene.

The purpose was to put Manny and Rachel in the picture. To preserve the attorney-client privilege, Rose had to be excluded.

The first order of business was the problem of Manny's job. He had approached the president of the library, explained what was happening, and, in confidence, revealed his personal relationship with Rachel. The conversation's upshot was that Manny could use his lunch hour and steal a few hours here and there until the trial. Then, he could use accumulated vacation and sick days, and a brief unpaid leave of absence.

After informing the others about this arrangement, he asked Jon how long the trial might take.

"Maybe five to seven trial days if the judge works all day. How much do you make per year in salary?"

"Forty-two thousand."

"That's not a problem. Whatever income you lose, the Rachel Castellano Defense Fund will reimburse you."

Jon could see that Manny and Rachel's heads were swimming, so he jumped in before either could speak.

"I wanted to resolve Manny's job situation, for two reasons. First, I am going to defend this case."

As Manny and Rachel began to speak at the same time,

Jon said, "But we'll get to that later. Second, Manny is going to help me defend it, in what is called the 'second seat'. We will get to that later, too. Third, if it has not been created by now, the Rachel Castellano Defense Fund will soon be formed and preliminarily funded in the next day or two. Its location, complete with a secretary and everything else necessary, will be in Santa Fe along with the defense office."

Overwhelmed, and grasping only the essence of what Jon had said, Rachel was in tears, Manny, well on the way.

"I know you both have questions, so let's address them in the order of what I just said, starting with my trying the case."

"Why you?" Manny asked.

"Who else? Don't you want to win? Seriously, folks, as you will soon know, there is no one in New Mexico with the combined experience and material resources Andrea and I can bring to a first-degree murder case."

"Yes, I understand that Jon, of course, and I'm grateful for the mere possibility. But" Rachel said, "and please do misunderstand my question, what is in it for you, Jon?"

"Two things, as we have previously discussed. Exposing to today's public the immorality and illegality of the stolen land grants, and perhaps motivating the government to redress that grievous wrongdoing. Second, to drive DA Maria Quintana out of the legal profession. Truth and justice, with concrete results."

"Thank you," Rachel said somberly. "But you're not licensed to practice law in New Mexico."

Manny, who now saw where the case was headed, said, "The trial judge will admit Jon to the New Mexico bar as a professional courtesy and because you have a constitutional right to a lawyer of your choice. But only for this case."

"Correct," Jon said. "Manny knows what he will do in the second seat during the trial, so to save time I'll let him explain it to you later.

"The case will need money for the bail bond, expert

witnesses, investigators, office. That's the purpose of the Defense Fund. All that and more is the only way to defend a serious criminal case correctly and successfully. There's nothing more serious than Murder 1. Trial counsel comes *pro bono*."

Having regained more of his composure, Manny said, "This sounds like a Hollywood movie."

Laughter, and Jon said, "In a sense it is a drama. The pretrial jockeying is the beginning, then the trial itself, which is the middle, and finally the post-trial aftermath for the participants, which is the end. A story, play, book, movie, in three acts."

Rachel asked, "Where will the Defense Fund come from?"

Andrea answered, "For now, that's classified. But I can assure you one hundred percent that the funds are from a legitimate source that hates lies and injustice as much as Jon and me. You both must take me on faith about that. Without adequate funding, this case cannot be defended properly. Eventually, you will meet the source. If there are no more questions for now, there's one more piece of business."

There were not.

"Manny," Andrea said, "if you don't have a professional letterhead, make one up on the computer. Your name, Attorney at Law, address, phone number. Professional looking. I want you to send this letter to the District Attorney."

Andrea handed Manny and Rachel a single sheet of paper.

After the formal obligatory "Maria Quintana, District Attorney, County of Santa Fe," address, and "Dear Madam District Attorney," it said:

> This letter is sent on behalf of Rachel Castellano of Santa Fe County, whom, as you know, I represent.
>
> It is my understanding that the current grand jury has finished its caseload and has been discharged.

It is my further understanding that a new grand jury will be empaneled in approximately two weeks.

Accordingly, on behalf of my client I hereby demand that *before* the new grand jury votes whether or not to indict my client, she be afforded an opportunity to appear as a witness in her own behalf.

I also demand that at the same time Santa Fe Deputy Chief sheriff Walter Duran be called as a witness for my client.

I make the same demands if you choose to proceed against Ms. Castellano by means of a prosecutor's information instead of by an indictment.

It is my opinion that Rachel Castellano has a federal and New Mexico constitutional right to have these demands honored.

Because I do not know whom the next grand jury chairman will be, as a professional courtesy and because of your ethical and legal duties, I expect you to forward the enclosed copy of this letter to such person as soon as you know his or her identity.

Cordially,

Manny's signature.

cc. Jon Willard, Esq.
Walter Duran, Chief Deputy sheriff, Santa Fe County.

Rachel understood what the letter said and had a general idea of what it meant.

Manny, however, was skeptical, and said to Jon, "I don't

know much New Mexico criminal procedure law anymore, but I don't think there's any such statute."

"There isn't, that's why I didn't cite one," Jon said, smiling.

Andrea laughed.

"What about the New Mexico and federal constitutions?"

"Well, there are no cases in either jurisdiction that expressly hold that there is *no* such right, so we're writing on a clean slate regarding any precedent *against* us. On the other hand, there are express provisions for procedural due process — notice, and an opportunity to be heard — in the New Mexico and federal constitutions. So, again, we're writing on a clean slate as to what procedural due process means in the context of grand jury testimony."

"So," Manny the lawyer-librarian asked naïvely, "what's the purpose of my letter?"

"You are going to see, Manny, that I answer a lot of questions with more questions. Starting now."

Andrea, a veteran of Jon's Socratic technique, laughed.

"But" Jon said smiling, "you'll be a better lawyer for it. So, here's my question in answer to your question. If you were Madam District Attorney, what would you do with the letter?"

Now in the spirit of the Socratic dialogue, Manny said with no embarrassment, "Honestly, I feel like I'm back in law school."

Andrea laughed again, looking at Jon. "I know that feeling. So do a lot of lawyers who ask Jon questions."

"Ok," Jon said, "let's get to it."

Thinking out loud, Manny said, "She has two choices. She could grant our demands, which she won't."

"Right," Jon said.

"Or she can ignore it, do nothing. If she does nothing, I'm sure you'll make something out of it when we get before the judge."

"Right."

"Okay. Then the judge has two choices. He can sanction her, which would make her look bad for whatever that's worth, or even dismiss the indictment as invalid so the DA would have to start over, and I suppose let Rachel and Walt testify, which is obviously beneficial to us. Or, more likely, the judge would rule against you because there is no New Mexico or federal law allowing such testimony. Then, we would have a brand-new, undecided appellate issue."

"Right, all from one brief letter."

Manny, now obviously enjoying himself, said, "We will have sent a message to the DA and judge that they're in for a 'creative' trial."

"Exactly. So, we stand adjourned. Send the letter. No typos."

CHAPTER 40

Manny sent his letter the next day. Because Walt had to remain neutral, there was no response from him.

When the DA received the letter two days later, she summoned Chief Deputy DA Fred Zimmerman and showed it to him. He read it twice.

"So?" he asked the DA.

"So, what do you mean, 'so'?" she barked. "Have you ever seen anything like this before?"

"I have. Back in the day, I stumbled on a law review article about revision of New York's Criminal Procedure Law. There was a grand jury section that mentioned this kind of provision. Several other states have a comparable law."

Fred Zimmerman was a scholar of New Mexico criminal law, which explained his decades in the DA's office, calling things as he saw them, not as his bosses wanted to see them. Often, they ignored him. Especially newbie Maria Quintana.

"I don't care about any other states, only about New Mexico," she spat, the harshness in her voice not surprising her subordinate.

Used to his boss' frequent outbursts, Fred simply said, "New Mexico has no such law, either in our constitution or a statute that can be construed as providing the right that Salazar is trying to invoke."

"Okay," Quintana sighed, "thanks, Fred, I'll just chuck this."

As she turned to the waste basket at the side of her desk, Fred said, "Stop, please don't do that."

"Why not? You just told me that New Mexico has no law forcing me to comply with what this guy Salazar wants."

"Maria, damn it, have you asked yourself a few important questions?"

"Like what?" she said irritably.

"First, like who really wrote it."

Fred's question got the DA's attention.

She thought for a moment, and replied, "Willard?"

"Willard!"

Now engaged, but puzzled, the DA asked, "Why would he do that, if there's no law to support him?"

This stupid kid, Fred said to himself, *doesn't know her ass from third base.*

Smiling, he said, "Maria, there are three questions here. First is, why Willard? The answer is that Emmanuel Salazar, though a lawyer, isn't clever enough to have thought up the letter gambit. Second, why did Willard write the letter when there is no legal support for Salazar's demand? The answer to that is, he wrote it precisely *because there is no law,* and thus he writes on a clean slate. Which brings us to the third question: What is his game?"

Ducking Fred's questions because she was unable to answer them, the Santa Fe County District Attorney said evasively, "I have my own idea, but I'd like to hear yours first."

This neophyte must think I was born yesterday. I was trying felony cases in Baltimore when she was screwing high school jocks under the stadium seats.

Tired yet again of nursing this slow kid, Fred took a deep breath and said, "If you do not comply and we indict, the first time Jon Willard gets in front of the trial judge he will make some kind of a cockamamie motion complaining that his client has been deprived of her New Mexico and federal constitutional rights, and demanding the indictment be dismissed."

"But she has no such rights."

"What court has ruled that?" he answered, managing to suppress his growing frustration. "No court, anywhere."

"You said so, you Fred Zimmerman, Chief Deputy District Attorney for the County of Santa Fe. You said so."

Near the end of his patience, Fred managed to ignore his frustration and say, "That's the damn point. There is no decisional law, no precedent, no answers to this question from a New Mexico court. Fred Zimmerman, Esq. does not count."

By now, the DA was beyond trying to hide her ignorance. "Okay, what does the judge do?"

"He has two choices. One, he can grant Willard's motion, and dismiss the indictment, which is the last thing you seem to want. Anyhow, the judge will not do that. Or he can deny the motion, which is what he will do."

Relieved, the DA said, "Great, that's that."

That did it for Fred.

"Goddamn, Maria," he shouted, "it is not 'that's that'. It is only the *beginning*. Willard will have created for himself what we lawyers call a 'naked appellate' question."

"What the hell is *that*?"

"An *undecided* core constitutional-criminal law question that he can ride to the New Mexico Court of Appeals, Supreme Court of New Mexico, or even the Supreme Court of the United States." Needling her, Fred added, "That's what *that* is."

Maria Quintana may have been slow, but now realized she was in trouble.

"What if we proceed by a prosecutor's information, instead of an indictment?"

"No can do. Read the letter again. Willard covered that."

"Look, Fred," she said pompously, "I am determined to try Rachel Castellano for Murder 1. I need to do that, to show this town I am a tough prosecutor. Win, lose or draw, we are going to indict her for Murder 1, and that's final, 'naked appellate question' or not. I, Maria Quintana, District Attorney of Santa Fe County, am going to try the case on behalf of the people in the State of New Mexico who want justice."

That grandstanding, delusional bitch.

As Fred got up, the DA held up her hand as if she were stopping traffic. "I'm not finished. Who the hell is this guy Willard, and why have you been referring to him and not Castellano's lawyer, Emanuel Salazar?"

Fred sat down, took twenty-five minutes to recite Jon Willard's pedigree, and saved the frosting for last. "Jon Willard will try the case. It is not Manny Salazar you will face in court."

Hearing that, quickly changing gears, Quintana said, "No Fred, not me, *we.*"

CHAPTER 41

RUE TO HER COMPULSIVE, IRRATIONAL need to indict Rachel Castellano for first-degree murder, DA Quintana convened her grand jury, ignoring Manny's demands. In due course, the foreman reported a 'true bill' charging Rachel with murder in the first degree.

Under Section 30-2-1 of the New Mexico Statutes Annotated, that charge was defined as "the killing of one human being by another without lawful justification or excuse, by any of the following means with which death may be caused: (1) by any kind of willful, deliberate and premeditated killing; (2) in the commission of or attempt to commit any felony; or (3) by any act greatly dangerous to the lives of others, indicating a depraved mind regardless of human life."

At Jon's direction, Manny had been in contact with Fred Zimmerman and negotiated Rachel's surrender and processing after court hours. The deputy DA assured Manny that she would be segregated in the county jail, and a carefully chosen female officer assigned to watch her until she was released on bail, if she was. After all, it was a Murder One case.

All the details were explained to Rachel. She understood and seemed fearless. Even impatient.

It was obvious to Jon that Fred knew there was no case, but whatever his other agenda he had to be a team player in the prosecutor's office. That explained the white-glove processing treatment Rachel would receive. As a further accommodation, Fred had arranged the arraignment for the next morning in front of the judge who had already been assigned to the case.

Santa Fe County District Court Judge Horace Baldwin was different from most trial court judges in New Mexico. Although descended from a family that had lived in the Territory and served the territorial government before statehood in 1912, Baldwin had graduated with honors from Harvard undergrad and its law school, returned to Santa Fe to practice law, and was eventually tapped by the then governor to serve as a District Court judge. His reputation included descriptions such as "self-protective" and "no nonsense." Some thought him devious. Horace Baldwin did not dally, nor easily suffer fools.

CHAPTER 42

A T 8:45 A.M. ON THE morning after Rachel's surrender, she and Manny were seated at the defense table in a semi-modern courtroom, lacking the Spanish décor and flavor Jon had seen in the Espanola courtroom. She was dressed in her own clothes and not shackled, another accommodation of Fred Zimmerman. Manny looked like a Hispanic lawyer in a New Mexico small town.

Behind the railing, in the spectator section, sat Jon Willard, Andrea Vardas, Walt Duran, Pablo Gallegos, Rachel's sister, Emiliano and Lorraine Romero, Stan Horden, Dr. Robert Roybal, and Santa Fe's version of court buffs who had nothing better to do with their time. Maria Quintana's parents sat off to the side in the middle of the courtroom. Standing room only, for the Murder 1 trial.

While waiting for the indictment to come down from the grand jury, the Willard team in Santa Fe and elsewhere had not been idle, as the DA would soon learn. A few weeks before, Jon had hired Pavel and Natasha Friedman, young New York contract lawyers whom he had used before for research and drafting. Their current task was to prepare two motions, one admitting Jon as *pro hac vice* defense counsel and the other pertaining to Rachel's bail.

At 8:45 a.m. Fred Zimmerman entered the courtroom, followed by the DA. Fred shook hands with Jon and Manny, who thanked him for his professional courtesies. Maria Quintana ignored both as the prosecutors sat down at their table.

Promptly at 9:00 a.m., the bailiff called the court to order with the universal "All rise," and Judge Baldwin took the bench.

He was tall and thin, with dark brown hair, a face that had seen much of the outdoors, and eyes that had seen too much.

The judge said a *pro forma* "Good morning, ladies and gentlemen," followed by "Let's get down to business. We are here for the case of *State of New Mexico* versus *Rachel Castellano*, on a charge of murder in the first degree. But first, we have three other issues to deal with."

Both teams expected two other issues, but not three, and were puzzled.

"My wife told me this morning that four years ago she bought one of Ms. Castellano paintings at an SPCA auction. Accordingly, I am prepared to recuse myself if counsel wish. Please take a few minutes to decide."

Willard had prepared for everything except something like this. Manny knew the judge's pedigree, and Jon was hopeful his inexperienced second seat would act accordingly.

Without consulting Willard, Manny stood and said, "The defense does not move to recuse Your Honor." Fred Zimmerman, who had his own agenda, echoed Manny's statement.

The judge said, "Thanks to the parties and their counsel for their confidence in me."

He then looked at Manny and said, "I understand, Mr. Salazar, that you have a motion seeking to admit Jon Willard of the New York and other bars *pro hac vice* for the duration of this trial."

Manny stood and said, "Yes, Your Honor, that is correct."

"Has the State received a copy of Mr. Salazar's motion papers?"

"We have, Judge," Fred replied.

"You have the floor," Judge Baldwin said, "Mr. Salazar."

The well-rehearsed second seat stood with notes in his

hand, and said, "May it please the court, since you and the State have seen my motion, I will only summarize."

"That is welcome news, Mr. Salazar. I note for the record that your motion is about seventy-five pages long, including exhibits. Perhaps a tad excessive, do you think?"

"Point taken, Your Honor. If I may continue?"

"Please."

"Mr. Willard was admitted to the New York Bar about fifteen years ago. His specialty area of practice is criminal defense, federal and state. Since that initial admission, he has been admitted to several state and federal trial and appellate courts and appeared in others *pro hac vice*. He is a member of the bar of the Supreme Court of the United States, where he has filed briefs and petitions for *certiorari*. Mr. Willard has always been, and is now, in good standing in all those courts. He has taught law at two ABA/ASLS accredited law schools, has lectured widely, and conducted close to fifty criminal trials to verdict. There have never been client complaints. There has never been a blemish on his personal or professional reputation, except for the recent proceedings in New York which we have fully documented, nor has he been involved in any personal litigation."

"What he said on the radio about former Judge Deveroux being biased and unfit for the federal bench was a tad over the top, don't you think?" the judge asked.

"I agree," Manny replied quickly, "as does Mr. Willard, whom I might add has apologized to former Judge Deveroux and former District Attorney Quade."

"I understand," the judge said with a barely visible smile, "that former Judge Deveroux is in prison, and former District Attorney Quade may be hiding in the federal witness protection program."

"That is Mr. Willard's understanding, as well. To continue briefly, Your Honor, I want to add that Mr. Willard has appeared in the federal district court here in Santa Fe and the Tenth Circuit on behalf of the then governor in a First Amendment campaign finance case.

"You are too modest about your client, Mr. Salazar. Mr. Willard won that case in the Tenth Circuit on a 2-1 vote and on remand to the district court the trial judge in Albuquerque held the statute unconstitutional."

"Correct, Your Honor. May I continue?"

"Perhaps, Mr. Salazar," the judge said, still wearing that barely visible smile, "a summary of your summary of your motion papers would be better. Are you finished?"

Manny got the message.

"I am now, Your Honor."

Laughter through the courtroom. Judge Baldwin managed a slightly more visible smile.

From Manny's colloquy with the judge, Willard had drawn two conclusions. His second seat had done well and had promise, and there was more to this judge than was apparent, though Jon did not yet know what.

When the laughter subsided, the judge turned to the defense table and asked if the State had any objection to the defense's motion seeking Willard's admission *pro hac vice.*

While Fred closed his eyes, District Attorney Maria Quintana rose, and said, "May it please the court, the State is leery about consenting to the defense motion because of what Mr. Willard said on the radio about a federal judge."

It was evident to Willard that the judge was not happy with her non-response to his simple, yes or know, question.

"Madam District Attorney," he said, "I did not ask you if the State was leery. You can be leery all you like on your own time, and anywhere else except in my courtroom. I asked if you have an objection. If you do, please state it now. If not, sit down."

When the DA looked at Fred Zimmerman, he not only had his eyes closed, but was staring, head bowed, at his blank yellow legal pad.

Quintana's reply to the judge was, "I guess not, Your Honor."

Willard joined the judge in being startled at her non-answer, but both hid it well enough.

"That's that," the judge said. "Mr. Willard, please take the witness chair."

While he was coming forward, the judge asked Rachel if she wanted Mr. Willard to represent her. She instantly answered in the affirmative.

By then, Willard was in the witness box, and the judge addressed him.

"Your reputation proceeds you, Mr. Willard, but for good or ill that has no place here where your client is going to get the best trial the jury and I can provide."

Christ, Willard realized, *Baldwin's comment about my reputation preceding me was what Judge Bart said in the disbarment case.*

"Perhaps you have heard this comment elsewhere," the judge said pointedly, with a faint smile.

That cinched it. Judge Baldwin, Willard thought, *must have spoken to Judge Bart in New York.*

"Thank you, Your Honor, that is reassuring, though neither my client nor myself had any doubt about her receiving a fair trial in your courtroom."

"Okay, Mr. Willard, if I grant Mr. Salazar's motion, will you abide by New York and New Mexico Rules of Professional Conduct?"

"Yes."

"No shenanigans."

"No, Your Honor. But to be clear, I respectfully reserve the right within those rules to do everything possible to represent my client. Not any of what I say or do will be intended, or should be construed, as disparaging you or this court."

Well, the judge thought, slightly taken aback, *that's a new one on me. Willard just told me that on behalf of his client he's going to fight like hell, maybe even get close to going too far, but I shouldn't take it personally. This is a tough guy.*

"I would have expected no less, Mr. Willard. Let the record show that Mr. Salazar's motion is granted, a formal order to follow. That's enough business for now. In forty-five minutes, Jon Willard, Esq., appearing *pro hac vice* can tell us why his client is entitled to reasonable bail in a first-degree murder case."

On cue, the court officer called out the "all rise," everyone did, and the judge left the bench.

CHAPTER 43

D URING THE BREAK, JON AND Manny were besieged by Rachel's supporters and strangers but had to brush them off because the forty-five-minute hiatus was too precious to waste.

Fred Zimmerman understood that, so he grabbed the lawyers and Rachel and half-pulled, half-pushed them into an adjoining room reserved for waiting attorneys.

Once inside, Jon commended Manny effusively, and said he would elaborate in the postmortem they would conduct after court.

He asked Rachel how his client was holding up, and she enthusiastically reassured him she was fine, especially because she was not shackled and was wearing her own clothing. She, too, commended Manny.

Jon asked Andrea for her thoughts. She knew the drill, and that there would be a thorough postmortem later, so she was brief. Judge Baldwin reminded her of Judge Birnbaum who conducted the arraignment of her father in *State* v. *Vardas*, and even more of Judge Lang who had handled the *Vardas-Quade* cases. Smart, acerbic, engaged. She added that Judge Baldwin likely had talked off the record to federal Judge Julia Bart in New York, because she recognized Baldwin's remarks as those of Judge Bart.

Manny said that he had been overwhelmed at the thoroughness and persuasiveness of the *pro hac vice* and bail motions the Friedmans had prepared in New York.

Returning to Andrea, Willard asked what she thought

about DA Quintana and Chief Deputy DA Fred Zimmerman. As to the DA, Andrea said, "She's an inexperienced kid without a clue about what she's doing, way over her head. Zimmerman is their whole team, but I believe he knows there is no case and is trying to figure out how he can navigate to its end while keeping his reputation intact. I will watch very closely what he does, and what he doesn't do. He has a tough row to hoe."

"I know we're running out of time, Jon," Rachel said, "but I think there's a reporter out there, someone I recognize from seeing her on local TV news shows."

"Thanks for the tip-off. Pretty soon they'll be coming out of the woodwork. For now, let's get back into the courtroom."

CHAPTER 44

WHEN THE LAWYERS AND THE defendant were at their tables, the courtroom quiet, and the judge on the bench, he nodded to Willard, and asked, "Are you and your client ready for her arraignment?"

"We are, Your Honor, but with the court's indulgence there is one matter I must raise first."

The judge seemed surprised, but said, "Proceed."

"May it please the court, when we first learned that Ms. Castellano might be charged with a serious felony, Mr. Salazar, then her only attorney and now my co-counsel, sent a letter to District Attorney Quintana, copies of which I hold in my hand. May I have the court officer give them to Your Honor and the prosecution?"

"Yes," the judge said, obviously curious.

Willard watched the judge read, and when he put the letter down Jon continued.

"Madam District Attorney ignored it, proceeded to empanel the grand jury, present her case against Ms. Castellano, and obtain the first-degree murder indictment we will deal with later. After considerable research through the Westlaw data base, the defense has come to two conclusions. One, is that while some states, such as New York, have *statutorily* recognized the defendants' right we sought in Mr. Salazar's letter, there is no case law in any American jurisdiction, state or federal, ruling whether there is a *constitutional* right. Our other conclusion is that there is or should be."

From Judge Baldwin's expression, Willard saw

engagement, even enjoyment. He asked Jon, "Are you asking me to be a pioneer, and go where no other judge in the United States has gone? Are you asking me to rule that there is a *constitutional* right for a would-be defendant, and anyone he or she proposes, to testify before an indictment is filed?"

"Not exactly, Your Honor."

"Not exactly? Then what?" the judge asked, obviously intrigued.

"If you would allow me to make an oral motion right now that the indictment should be dismissed because the defendant's procedural due process rights — notice, and an opportunity to be heard — have been violated, I would do so in good faith because I reasonably believe that's what the law should be. However, in making that motion, because of the current state of the law I would expect you to deny it. I would take an exception, and thus preserve the issue for judicial review."

"That's pretty clever, Mr. Willard, so clever, cute even, that it is nowhere near the frivolousness that would require me to sanction you."

"Thank you, Your Honor. I have thought through my proposed motion very carefully."

"You better keep doing that, throughout this trial."

"Yes, Your Honor, I shall."

"Well, let's hear what the State has to say about that," the judge said, looking over to the defense table where the DA and Fred Zimmerman were in a huddle.

The Chief Deputy DA knew a sandbag when he was hit with one, and when he needed to keep his options open. He stood and said equivocally, "May it please the court, the State does not have any control over what ill-founded motions the defense wishes to make, *or how Your Honor chooses to rule on them.*"

Judge Baldwin and lawyer Willard had the same thought, at the same time. *Zimmerman's equivocation shows he is no dummy. This is going to be an interesting trial.*

The judge turned to Willard, and said, "Mr. Zimmerman is correct. The defense can make any *non-frivolous* motion it wants, and I can make any ruling I choose. Hence, consider your motion made. It is denied."

"Thank you, Your Honor. Exception."

"Exception noted. Let's move on to the arraignment."

CHAPTER 45

"M R. WILLARD, ARE YOU AND your client familiar with New Mexico's arraignment procedures."

"Yes, Your Honor. New Mexico Rule 6-501."

"Specifically," the judge asked, "the offense charged, the possible sentence, the right to bail or possibility of pre-trial detention, the right to remain silent, the right to a jury trial, and the right to a preliminary hearing."

"Yes."

"Ms. Castellano, do you concur with what Mr. Willard has just acknowledged?"

"I do, Your Honor."

"Mr. Willard, do you intend to enter the plea on behalf of your client?"

"No, Rachel Castellano will enter it on her own behalf."

"Ms. Castellano, please," the judge said.

Rachel stood resolutely erect, looked at Judge Baldwin, then at Quintana and Zimmerman, and said emphatically, "I am not guilty. Killing Antonio Carranza were lawful acts of self-defense and justifiable homicide!"

Well, thought Judge Horace Baldwin, *that's damn clear.*

"Okay, Mr. Willard, the floor is all yours."

"First, Your Honor, I trust you and the prosecution have received the defense memorandum in support of Ms. Castellano's motion for bail."

Both had.

"I'll begin with what the defense believes is the law of bail in New Mexico. Like the Eighth Amendment to the

Constitution of the United States of America, Article II, New Mexico's Bill of Rights, Section 13, assures a criminal defendant of bail if certain conditions are met and specific disqualifications are not present."

"Correct," said the judge.

Willard continued. "New Mexico statutory text and case law decisions have established certain core principles. (1) There is a presumption of bail, (2) the State has the burden (3) by clear and convincing evidence, (4) to prove that one of two criteria for denial — dangerousness or flight risk — exist."

"Correct."

"There is a corollary to these core principles: (5) neither constitutional law nor rules of criminal procedure permit a court to base a bail decision or the amount of bail *solely* on the severity of the charged offense. In support of this principle, I cite *State ex rel Torres* v. *Whitaker*, 262 P.2d, 16, 23 (1967), and cases cited therein."

"Correct again, Mr. Willard," the judge said. "you've done your homework."

"Finally," Willard said, ignoring the compliment and plowing ahead, "because bail is presumed, and thus the burden is on the State to prove, *by clear and convincing evidence*, that Ms. Castellano is dangerous or a flight risk, the defendant stands down until the State makes its case against bail, at which time we will respond if necessary."

Sandbag!

The judge got it. Fred Zimmerman got it. The DA did not have a clue about what just happened. Willard had just shifted the burden of proof from the defense having to prove why the defendant *was* entitled to bail, to *the State having to prove by clear and convincing evidence why she was not.* And that was limited to dangerousness and flight risk.

"Madam District Attorney," Judge Baldwin said, "Mr. Willard's recitation of New Mexico bail law is correct. Your office has the burden of dissuading me from granting Ms. Castellano reasonable bail."

The moment Willard had started his recitation of New Mexico bail law, Fred Zimmerman knew their anti-bail objection was dead in the water. Also, he knew to a certainty that he, himself, was not going into the ranks of deputies throughout the country who were routinely sacrificed by their bosses. So, when the judge called on the DA, and she tugged at Fred's arm, he sat still.

When the judge repeated, "Madam District Attorney," Maria Quintana rose on unstable legs, knowing she was done for, and said, "May it please the court, the State objects to any bail."

Seasoned trial lawyer Willard knew when to keep his mouth shut. Either she would bury herself, or the judge would. Or, more likely, both.

"Does the State have clear and convincing evidence that Ms. Castellano would be a danger if out on bail? If so, to whom? And why, and how do you know that?" Judge Baldwin asked politely, but pointedly.

"Well," the DA said haltingly, "she did murder Mr. Carranza."

Deeper and deeper.

"Aren't we here to decide if it was self-defense and justifiable, and isn't Ms. Castellano presumed innocent, and doesn't the State have the burden of proof?" the judge asked.

"Well, I guess that's true," the novice District Attorney answered, her falsetto voice sounding like a little girl.

Close to having had enough, but needing to protect the record, the judge asked Quintana, "Does the State have clear and convincing evidence that if Ms. Castellano was out on bail, she would be a flight risk, and if so, why, and how do you know that?"

Silence.

"Madam District Attorney?" the judge asked.

Finally. "Well, Your Honor," Quintana said, barely

audibly, "the defendant is charged with first-degree murder, and lots of defendants jump bail."

That was it for the judge, and he asked Quintana to sit down.

Although Fred Zimmerman was there in body, his mind had shut down the moment Quintana started speaking. He had just witnessed the worst performance of any lawyer in any courtroom in any state in all of America. *And she's my boss*, he thought.

Judge Baldwin turned to Willard, saying, "Do you have anything, Mr. Willard?"

Willard was certain Rachel would get bail, but he knew also that because it was a first-degree murder case the judge needed protection on the record, which Willard was prepared to provide.

"I do, Your Honor. To provide the court with some options for bail conditions, Ms. Castellano is prepared to do the following. We will obtain a surety bond from the Albuquerque office of National Surety Underwriters, whose local general manager is in this courtroom and ready to write the bond as soon as necessary. Or, to save the premium cost, the defendant can post fifty thousand dollars in cash by the close of business today."

Andrea had already arranged that. The $50,000 in cash, and more if needed, was already in the Defense Fund's account at Tom Ramirez's First National Bank of Santa Fe.

The judge made a note on his legal pad.

"Second, Ms. Castellano, who has no passport, will agree not to travel outside New Mexico before the trial is over without your written approval."

"Last, she is amenable, but not anxious, to wear a monitoring device. Of course, she will comply with any other conditions you impose. That is all I have, thank you, Your Honor."

Horace Baldwin was grateful for how Willard had helped him protect the record for any bail the judge might set.

Immediately after Willard sat down, the judge said, "Bail is set at fifty thousand dollars, cash. Ms. Castellano's travel restrictions as stated by her counsel are imposed. There will be no monitoring devices, nor any other conditions. A formal order will follow."

Pointedly but expressionless, Judge Baldwin looked at Willard and said, "Thank you for your assistance, Mr. Willard. It was most helpful."

With that, Judge Baldwin banged his gavel twice and said, "This court is adjourned."

CHAPTER 46

A S SOON AS JUDGE BALDWIN left the courtroom several things happened.

In filling her briefcase, the DA dropped some papers on the floor. As a bystander rushed to retrieve them, she said, "Get the hell out of my way, I can pick them up myself." She promptly left the courtroom, fear written all over her face. Her lawyer father and mother trailed behind her. Daddy Quintana did not look happy.

Fred Zimmerman walked over to the defense table, and the three lawyers shook hands. Fred complimented Jon and Manny. They thanked the Chief Deputy DA for accommodating Rachel in her surrender. Jon quipped that Fred should have brought a shovel, a trial lawyer's way of saying someone had dug a hole for himself. Fred bested Jon by saying, "two shovels." It was clear to Jon that Fred Zimmerman had his own agenda, and it was more than simply having no confidence in the State's case and in his boss.

Utilizing a pre-arranged signal from Jon, Andrea began arranging for the cash bail delivery with Tomas Ramirez at First National Bank of Santa Fe.

Chief Deputy Sheriff Walt Duran, preserving his neutrality, quickly and quietly left the courtroom. With a beaming smile.

Some of the defense's supporters – Pablo, Rose, Emiliano, Lorraine, Stan, and Robert – crowded around Jon, Manny, and Rachel, all talking at once, shaking their hands, asking questions, making comments, offering congratulations. Slowly the crowd drifted away.

Andrea, Manny, and Rachel, who was not in custody thanks to another accommodation of Fred's, were talking to the court's administrator about the bail. Andrea told them that in ten minutes Tom Ramirez would deliver a blank check for $50,000. The administrator told them processing Rachel out of custody would take no more than a half-hour, and they were welcome to wait in his office.

As Jon was about to join them, a tall middle-aged woman dressed in classic western attire approached him.

"Mr. Willard, my name is Joan Davis. I'm a stringer for Associated Press covering New Mexico from the southern to the northern borders. Can we talk?"

"Briefly, you can see I have my hands full."

"Indeed."

They sat at the defense table.

"Let me begin by saying that until about a month ago, I was with the *Yonkers Journal*, until my Air Force daughter was assigned to Kirtland AFB in ABQ. I'm a widow, we're close, she's single, so here I am."

"Shoot," Willard said, "no pun intended."

"To put it bluntly," Davis said, "what the hell is going on here? I have a source who says the late unlamented Mr. Carranza twice tried to break into your client's house threatening to kill her, that the third time he did bust in making the same threat, but instead she killed him as soon as he crossed the threshold. In entering her plea, she said it was self-defense and justifiable. Seems to me it was, so what's this kid DA up to?"

Willard immediately liked this brash woman, not only because of what she said, but also how she said it.

Before Willard could speak, the reporter added, "Being a New Yorker, I know all about your exploits, not just recently, but back in the day. Karen Newman, that physician who was accused of writing too many opiate prescriptions. Nick

Vardas. Quade. These are my calling cards. Will you talk to me about this case?"

"Yes, when I can, but not now and not here."

She handed him a card, and said, "I hope you understand that if we speak on the record, this odd murder case in Santa Fe, New Mexico, and you at the center of it, will go national."

Willard smiled, and said, "Oh, really?"

CHAPTER 47

T HE WILLARD TEAM MET AT Rose's home on Saturday
morning at 10:00 a.m.

Jon began by thanking the others individually for
their contribution to the successful arraignment. Manny,
for handling the *pro hac vice* motion so well, Andrea for
expediting the posting of bail, and Rachel for her dramatic
and effective "not guilty" plea that emphasized their self-
defense and justification defenses.

Each of the three modestly acknowledged Jon's
compliments.

He added, "There are some people in New York whose
efforts we need to acknowledge. Pavel and Natasha Friedman,
who put together the *pro hac vice* and bail motions, and who
may do more legal work before this case is over."

Andrea had already told them of the successful pro bono
motion, and the reasonable bail.

Jon continued, "Thanks to Andrea, the Pinkerton
International Detective Agency is searching for information,
and next week she, Manny, and I will interview two potential
expert witnesses. Then, there is Mr. X, the source of the
defense funds, and Mr. Y, organizer and administrator of
the RCDF, which will pay the bills. And locally, Tom Ramirez
at First National Bank of Santa Fe who is maintaining the
bank account and worked with Andrea on the instantaneous
cash bail."

Rose Castellano asked, rhetorically, "What do poor people
do?"

"Mostly," Jon replied, "they get screwed."

Jon then turned the floor over to Andrea, who said, "As of Monday, the Law Offices of Jon Willard, Esq., lacking a sign or any other identification, and the location of the Rachel Castellano Defense Fund, also anonymous, will be open in a small former residence just off Paseo de Peralta. It will be fully furnished and contain everything necessary to run this case, including a full-time secretary. I will provide all concerned with contact information next Tuesday."

Jon then asked for reactions to the arraignment, already having heard Andrea's at home the evening after the hearing. As to the judge, she thought he knew the DA was over her head, and that Zimmerman understood what was happening and had an agenda of his own. Also, Andrea thought, like judges Birnbaum and Lang in New York's *Quade* and *Vardas-Quade* cases, Judge Baldwin enjoyed seeing Jon's skill and was probably looking forward to jousting with him as the case unfolded. What the grapevine said about the judge was accurate, and Rachel was in good hands.

Manny expressed his gratitude to Jon for giving him a chance to exercise the skills he thought were lost to him.

Rachel said she understood most of what was happening and looked forward to participating in preparation of the defense and the trial itself.

Jon took over.

"I'm now going to give you a chronological look at the order of what happens from now to the end of the trial. Please hold your questions and comments until I'm finished.

"Andrea has already told you about next week's interviews. I will explain about the expert witnesses when they are chosen, because who they are will depend on our trial strategy.

"As to the investigators, we will process their information as we receive it."

"We have a long and fruitful relationship with the Pinkerton detectives." Andrea added.

Jon continued.

"The judge did not set a date for a preliminary hearing and motions, but Andrea will press the judge's law clerk. The purpose of the preliminary hearing is to determine if there is enough evidence to justify holding the defendant to answer the charge. We already know what the evidence is because we know what happened. But my cross examination of their witnesses at a preliminary hearing is a good opportunity to educate the judge."

"I have a question," Rose said. "How much of their evidence do they have to expose at the preliminary hearing?"

"Good question," Jon replied. "It's up to the judge to decide if they have shown 'probable cause' that a crime was committed, and that Rachel committed it. Frankly, I do not think they can distort let alone erase the facts."

"At the preliminary hearing, the judge will set a date for motions to be heard, and a status conference to see how the case is moving along.

"It is unlikely we will receive any 'discovery'. Luckily, we do not need any.

"At the status conference, the judge will set a trial date and ask whether we want to try the case before him alone, a 'bench' trial, or before a jury. We will choose the jury.

"At that point, everything we have been working on comes together for us. Goal, strategy, tactics, investigation product, expert witnesses. Into one seamless package.

"The order of the trial you probably know from books or TV lawyer shows. Jury selection; prosecution and defense opening statements; witnesses; cross examination; maybe motions; jury instructions; counsels' summations; deliberation; verdict."

"The floor is open for questions. Manny?"

"What is your calculation regarding a motion to dismiss after they rest?"

"If granted, the case is over, but we don't get to the jury. I cannot emphasize the significance of that. *To make the land grants a central part of the case, we must get to the jury.* No jury, no exposure of the stolen land grants.

"If there are no more questions, let's call it a day. Next time we meet, there will be a lot more to tell."

CHAPTER 48

O N TUESDAY MORNING JON AND Andrea were getting organized in their new office when, as scheduled, at 9:00 a.m. Allison P. Corrales rang the doorbell.

After Saturday morning's team meeting, Jon had called Tom Ramirez at home and asked if he could recommend someone who could act as a secretary and office manager during the Castellano prosecution.

Tom had a few questions. How long would the job last, what would it pay, what would his or her duties be, and was it a normal forty-hour week?

"I'm asking," Tom said, "because a former assistant of mine at the bank just finished maternity leave and does not want to return to us. She needs a few months' work, while deciding what to do next. She might go back to school. Solid young woman. Her husband is a detective junior grade on the Santa Fe police force and one of us."

"Vietnam?"

"Yes."

Jon and Andrea answered Tom's preliminary questions. The job would probably last about a month; it would pay whatever Tom told them the going hourly rate for that kind of work was in Santa Fe. Her duties would be normal secretarial and office management. It was a thirty-five-hour week, except in emergencies. Tom would send her over to the new office on Tuesday morning at 9:00 a.m.

Jon opened the front door, seeing a tall, dark-skinned,

well-dressed, beautiful young woman in her late twenties. Inviting her to come in, he introduced Corrales to Andrea, who would conduct the interview. He returned to his office, while the two women settled themselves in what had been the former residence's living room.

In about forty-five minutes, after Corrales reiterated the answers she had given to Tom Ramirez the night before, they had covered all the essentials, among them Jon and Andrea's backgrounds and that they were in Santa Fe defending a baseless murder case. Andrea emphasized that everything Allison did and heard was confidential and protected by the attorney-client privilege. Allison's live-in mother would take care of the newborn baby during work hours. Andrea told Allison who Manny, Rachel, Rose, and others close to the case were. The young woman seemed a quick study, and she would begin the next day at 9:00 a.m.

After the team meeting two days earlier, Jon had made two telephone calls. The first was to Joan Davis, the reporter who had introduced herself at the end of the arraignment. She would meet him at the office for an interview.

His second call had been to David Trujillo, a retired Forest Ranger and friend whose family's ties in New Mexico were rooted at least in pre-Territorial days and probably even earlier than that. Their relationship had started when Jon purchased his house, and David was hired to paint it and make some minor repairs. With Jon in New York most of the time, David had, along with the Romero family, become a quasi-caretaker, and, over the years, a friend. During the few weeks Jon had been back this time, David had been out-of-state as a consultant to the Forest Service. He was now back in Santa Fe. Jon and Andrea wanted to see David socially, but also because of special knowledge he had that could help the Castellano defense. This night, David would come to the house for dinner.

Between Allison leaving and Jane Davis arriving, Jon

and Andrea had about two hours available. He used them to tell her part of his defense strategy and tactics.

"Even as stupid as she is," Jon began, "the DA is not going into court with just the facts of this case. On the facts, the prosecution is dead in the water. Fred Zimmerman is a smart guy with his reputation on the line. No matter what, as Chief Deputy DA there is no way he is going to prosecute a first-degree murder case on these facts with the self-defense and habitat justification defenses so obvious and winnable. Someone in that DA's office has something up his or her sleeve."

"He's going to find a plausible out in the *law* and exploit it," Andrea said.

"Exactly, and I think I know what that is. I have been reading New Mexico statutes and cases relating to first- and second-degree murder, and about the defenses of self-defense and justification. I am not going to say more now because I want you to figure this out by yourself. So, first thing tomorrow, have Allison get a copy of a book entitled *Lawyers and Land Grants in Northern New Mexico* by Filipe Ortiz, Ph.D. Read it ASAP, and then we'll talk some more about that part of the defense. Remember, you're in charge of the expert witnesses."

"Okay. David might be able to shed some light on that subject."

"Indeed."

"Indeed, yourself," she said, smiling.

"There's something related to the book I want you to do. Hire the best surveyor between Albuquerque and Tierra Amarilla, that's in Rio Arriba County south of the Colorado border. I want to know if Rachel's Abiquiu home is within the Tierra Amarilla land grant. Complete with written reports and maps. In color."

Andrea, who was a quick study in her own right, was stunned, some of the pieces of the defense strategy having connected automatically. All she could say was "You are one damn clever lawyer."

"Thank you, Ms. Vardas. More to come."

"No doubt."

CHAPTER 49

J ANE DAVIS ARRIVED PROMPTLY AT noon, as did the salads and soft drinks. The three sat in the living room, and the former New York reporter got right to the point, turning on her recorder and repeating what she had asked him at the arraignment.

"What's going on with this case?"

Before Willard answered, he told Davis he wanted an unedited copy of the tape, and that everything was off the record until the interview was over and they agreed what was on the record. Reluctantly, she agreed.

"You've heard of 'show' trials?" he asked her.

Puzzled, she replied, "of course."

"Yes. Well, this is a 'show-off' trial, where our inexperienced neophyte District Attorney shows her lawyer daddy that his investment in making her president of the high school senior class, getting her into UNM and the law school, the job as an ADA, and financing the primary and general District Attorney election, were all worth it in her climb to the top, the Supreme Court of New Mexico. Also worth it for his reflected glory, as the proud papa who barely made it out of law school and never made it as a practicing lawyer."

"Wow," Davis said, "that's a hell of an indictment, no pun intended."

"Jane, those are well-known *facts*. Do you dispute she is an inexperienced neophyte?"

"Well, no."

"The *Santa Fe New Mexican* and *Albuquerque Journal* reported that her father threw a large party for the entire class as part of Maria's campaign for senior class president."

"I get the picture," she said.

Jon continued. "Because her father is an alum of UNM and barely of its law school, and a generous donor to both schools, the *Santa Fe New Mexican* and the *Albuquerque Journal* both ran puff-piece father-daughter articles and photos in her freshman years.

"Daddy also got her the ADA job soon out of law school, and Daddy was virtually the only contributor to her campaign for the top job three years later."

The Pinkertons really did a great job collecting all this information so fast, Willard thought. *They are worth every cent of their fees.*

Taking a deep breath, figuratively and literally, Jane Davis said, "So, you're telling me, or at least strongly implying, that Santa Fe County District Attorney Maria Quintana is an incompetent spoiled brat, who has charged your client with first-degree murder to advance her professional career."

"Please never put words in my mouth, Jane. These are *facts*. What you just said is a paraphrase. You can interpret the *facts* any way you like, just don't attribute your interpretation to me."

"Okay, let's say for the sake of argument I accept, not agree, with the facts, what happens next?"

"Simple, next we prepare for trial, go to trial, acquit and thus vindicate Rachel Castellano, and in the bargain professionally destroy ladder-climbing Maria Quintana. Also, I want to teach Daddy and Mommy Quintana a lesson."

"That's all?" Davis asked sarcastically.

"Except for the land grant motive," he said and then explained in detail.

"Like the destruction you wrought on Chief Judge Robert Jackson, Kristina Liebenthal, Augusta Gonzalez, Amos Deveroux, Mike Quade and, albeit indirectly, Landry

Brussard, Honore Tousant, and two mob guys?" Davis asked rhetorically.

"My compliments, Jane," Willard said sincerely, "you've done your homework."

"Do you think the other side knows what they are up against, with you and the resources you must have organized by now, or soon will?"

"No. Not to sound like royalty, but do you know the expression attributed to Ralph Waldo Emerson, 'If you strike at a king, you better kill him'? We are already way ahead of them on the facts, law, and how to get an acquittal. As you noted a few minutes ago, acquittal will not be the end of the game for the Quintanas."

"Point taken, 'truth and justice'," she said.

Surprised, Willard said, "You know about that saying?"

"I know more than that, Jon," Jane replied, using his Christian name for the first time. "So, let's negotiate about what I can use."

"Here's my nonnegotiable offer. All the facts that are verifiable, you can use as if you did the research. My gift to you. Also, my history that you know, that's in the public domain. By the way, you left out 'Radio Free Willard' on the Barry Farber radio show."

"Thanks for the reminder."

"No references to your paraphrase about 'incompetent spoiled brat,' advancing her career, killing kings, destroying her, what I think about what they think. You are experienced, I'm sure you get the idea. I will not have the other side saying through you that I am misstating, mischaracterizing, distorting, etc. I must appear in the public eye as I am. Tough, but fair. Got it?"

"I do."

"One more friendly reminder," Jon said with a smile, "if you violate this agreement, I will come after you, the judge will enter a gag order, and you will never again get even a nod from me."

"Got it," Davis said firmly, "and good luck. I'll send you a copy of my interview after it goes out on the AP wire."

"Don't forget a copy of the tape."

"I won't. Bye the way, nice office. For a Santa Fe lawyer."

* * *

Jane Davis's story hit the Associated Press wires just after midnight. Because it contained four "hooks" — beautiful Santa Fe, a first-degree murder trial, with a female defendant, being represented by famous criminal defense lawyer Jon Willard — the story went viral in print, radio, and television media.

Davis's story dramatically told of a local artist in picturesque Abiquiu, New Mexico, putting four shotgun rounds into a crazed would-be killer who battered down her door. But there was more. Davis thoroughly explored the land grant aspects of the case, thereby introducing the other prong of Willard's defense. Rachel Castellano was defending her home on land that was stolen from her ancestors.

The national, indeed international, reaction to Davis's story was so substantial, and put Willard so much back in the headlines, that he hired New York publicist, former client, and lover, Karen Newman, to field the press interest. From now to the end of the case, Andrea would refer all press inquiries to Karen. Except those from Jane Davis.

CHAPTER 50

W HEN EARLY THAT EVENING DAVID Trujillo arrived for dinner, it was a grand reunion, he not having seen Jon for nearly a year, and Andrea for longer than that. After the hugs and greetings, consistent with David's near-proprietary interest in the house he spent the next half-hour inspecting it.

"The Romero family is going a good job," David said, "except for the soot on the banco in front of the fireplace." There was a friendly rivalry between Trujillo and Romero family to see who could do more for Jon.

Andrea reminded David there was no damper inside the old kiva fireplace, so every time the wind blew, residual soot came down the chimney and onto the white banco. And every day, she cleaned it up before retiring.

They had drinks and dinner on the patio, catching each other up. Andrea said David, short and naturally dark-skinned, had gained too much weight, which their guest good-naturedly denied. Jon and Andrea told David about the conspiracy to disbar him, what became of it and the perpetrators, and then about her and Jon's engagement. It was then David noticed Andrea's ring and congratulated them effusively.

When asked where he had been, David explained that the special assignment for the Forest Service entailed trying to catch poachers who were illegally cutting government trees. When dinner was over, the dishes washed and put away, they returned outside and Jon said, "I need some advice from you."

"Sure," David said immediately, without asking about what. "I wondered why you're in Santa Fe now."

"Over the years," Jon began, "*apropos* of nothing, you've occasionally mentioned the Tierra Amarilla land grant, and said your mother had a right to some of it, and thus you. Frankly, although I learned something about New Mexico land grants in college at UNM years before, your mother's and your connection with them never registered with me."

"Well, there was no reason they should have."

"Do you remember that book I was thinking of writing about Reies Lopez Tijerina?"

"I sure do. I told you to watch yourself. There are some folks up north who still revere Reies Lopez Tijerina for his preaching and raid on the courthouse. So, what does that have to do with you two being here?"

Jon and Andrea then told David the entire story of how they had come to Santa Fe for peace and quiet to solve some personal problems and work on the Tijerina book. How that led him to Pablo Gallegos, from him to Manny, then to Rachel Castellano, to her land lease, Antonio Carranza, the shooting, the indictment and Jon volunteering to defend her.

"I know a lot about the land grants now, David, probably historically and legally more than you, no slight intended."

"Wow!" David said. "None taken. How can I help?"

"You can be an enormous help," Andrea replied, and said, "at the trial there will be self-defense and justification evidence to counter the first-degree murder charge. So, I need jurors who believe in forcibly defending oneself and home. Veterans, NRA members, former cops, correction officers."

"Okay, got it."

"What complicates our job, and what we want your help for, is that some of those potential jurors need to understand how Hispanos in northern New Mexico lost their land grants. Both issues are intertwined in this case, so, ideally, each juror should possess sensitivity to both issues—self-defense, homicide justification, and stolen land grants."

"That's a challenging assignment, so let me ask you some contextual questions."

"Go ahead."

"Tell me about your defendant."Jon and Andrea did, extensively.

"Does she speak Spanish?"

"Yes. First language. Perfect unaccented English."

"What impression will she make on the jury?"

"She may not testify but sitting at the defense table and comporting herself like a lady with nothing to hide, Rachel will make an excellent impression."

"What impression will the DA make on the jury?"

"Young, inexperienced, bumbler. But the Chief Deputy is smart and capable. As to impression, hard to tell. Short, tubby, bold, East Coast accent."

"What are the judge's three best qualities?"

"Smart, honest, fair."

"What impression will your experts make?"

"Smart, knowledgeable, honest, not trying to sell the defense's case. Factual, giving rise to supportable opinion testimony devoted not to the self-defense of the case, but only the land grants."

"Okay, I'll sleep on this, but here's my horseback opinion. If you are going to load the case, the DA's, and yours, with the history of the land grants, you want elderly jurors or their children or grandchildren whose ancestors were alive in the years following the Treaty of Guadalupe Hidalgo in 1848. As you know, that is when their descendants would have been affected by the government's incompetence and chicanery, and the ability of crooked lawyers, politicians, judges, and government employees, to steal many of the land grants."

"How do I identify them on jury selection?" Jon asked.

"Good question, they won't be wearing a sign. Think not only elderly, but about Hispanos. You want as many of them on your jury as can be fitted into the jury box. Not only Hispanos, but farmers, ranchers, outdoor people, or their descendants. You don't want successful college graduates carrying briefcases who look like they do not live in the non-Hispano world."

Andrea asked, "With a jury of mostly Hispanos, how are the others going to react to a white lawyer from New York defending a murder case in New Mexico, rather than someone local?"

"Excellent question. For openers, Jon knows enough to dress simply, not use big English words. Do not, under any circumstances sprinkle a few Spanish words here and there to show the jury that Jon is 'one of them'. That act would fall flat, and perhaps the defense with it. Jon is just another lawyer doing what he is always doing in his own easy way, but in a different state."

Jon thought for a moment, and Andrea knew he was assembling, or more likely reassembling, several pieces.

"Okay, David, in one sentence give me a generic profile of my ideal juror."

Finishing his after-dinner drink, David Trujillo said, "Me."

Andrea and Jon looked at each other and realized that David had encapsulated what started out seeming like a complicated problem.

"I get it. *You*," Jon said with evident relief. "You've made it simple. You're a combat veteran, whose family had, still has, an interest in the Tierra Amarilla land grant that was stolen. Period!"

Jon's mind was racing. Before David or Andrea could speak, he said, "The 'self-defense, habitat justification, law-and-order' juror can easily be identified with standard jury selection questions about law enforcement. Until later in the trial when I open the door to the land grant part of the case, earlier on in jury selection I can look for the qualities you just gave me. When we look at it this way, it's simple."

"Glad I could help."

"You're not finished," Jon said, excitedly.

Andrea knew why.

Looking at their friend, retired Army Special Forces Sergeant Major David Trujillo, Jon said, "I want you in that courtroom when we select the jury."

CHAPTER 51

THE PRELIMINARY HEARING IN *State of New Mexico* v. *Rachel Castellano* began at 9:00 a.m. on April 1. Counsel was seated as at the arraignment, some of those who attended that proceeding had returned, including District Attorney Maria Quintana's parents.

At precisely that time, the court officer made the usual announcement, and Santa Fe District Court Judge Horace Baldwin took the bench.

Looking around, he said, "Good Morning, Ms. Castellano, counsel, and spectators. We are here today for a preliminary hearing in the case entitled *State of New Mexico* v. *Rachel Castellano.* For the benefit of the spectators, I want to explain what that means. Ms. Castellano has been indicted for the crime of first-degree murder in a one-sided procedure at which the District Attorney presented evidence to the grand jury she considered adequate to sustain that charge. Note that neither Ms. Castellano nor her lawyer were present, and thus none of the grand jury witnesses were cross examined. The formal, written indictment is somewhat sketchy on details, and that is what we are here to remedy."

There were several reactions to the judge's "sketchy" comment.

The DA and her Chief Deputy were not surprised, because vagueness was their intention.

Jon had anticipated the judge would want to know more facts of the homicide, as charged in the "sketchy" indictment. After all, Ms. Castellano was charged with first-degree murder.

Manny took the comment as an indication the judge continued to be unimpressed with the District Attorney.

Most of the audience "sort of" got it.

The judge continued. "We will remedy the indictment's vagueness —" *there he goes again*, Willard thought — "by the District Attorney presenting evidence that an unjustified act was committed by Ms. Castellano, one that constituted a crime under the laws of New Mexico, and that there is *probable cause to believe Ms. Castellano committed it.*"

"By the way, Mr. Willard, for the record," the judge said pleasantly, "I assume that you and Ms. Castellano's presence here today signifies that she has not waived her entitlement to this preliminary hearing."

"That is correct, Your Honor."

"One last word, so as not to confuse the spectators. After the prosecution presents their witnesses, the defense *may* cross examine. Following that, each side *may* make motions. Then, the defense *may* present its evidence, and the prosecution *may* cross examine. After that, I will rule on whether the prosecution has proved probable cause. Or not. Unlike at the trial, there will be no opening or closing statements."

Willard rose, "If Your Honor is finished" — Judge Baldwin nodded affirmatively — "I have a point of clarification."

"Go ahead."

"What level of proof will you apply in determining probable cause?"

The DA wore a blank expression. Fred Zimmerman, a real lawyer, smiled.

"You mean, 'preponderance,' 'clear and convincing,' or 'beyond a reasonable doubt'?"

"Correct."

"Well, of course not the latter. Beyond reasonable doubt is the jury's job."

"Agreed."

"That's an interesting question, Mr. Willard."

No one has ever asked that before, the judge thought. *This is one smart lawyer. It's a trap. He's setting me up for a naked appeal question. If I use the standard of a mere preponderance of the evidence, fifty-one percent, Willard could argue on appeal that it was too easy. Clear and convincing might be too much. Or not.*

"Do you have any statute or case law, Mr. Willard?"

"Well, Your Honor, I'm not arguing for either one. I'm just asking for clarification. But I can tell you I tried the Westlaw database for New Mexico cases by searching 'clear and convincing' and 'preliminary hearing.' As you know, Westlaw searches *both* phrases in *every* opinion in the state of New Mexico, ever, and there is no such case from back in the day to yesterday."

Damn, thought the judge, *I have to get off the horns of this dilemma. I better watch every single move Willard makes before I get set up for a reversal on appeal. He is smart, and dangerous.*

"Mr. Willard, thank you for raising such an interesting law review-like question, but I think your client's interests are best served if I delay my ruling until all the evidence is in, and cross examination has been completed, and any motions have been made."

"That's perfectly agreeable to me, Your Honor."

Partners, Willard thought, *though not in crime.*

"Please call your first witness, Madam District Attorney," the judge said, after thinking *whew.*

"The prosecution calls Andrew Scott."

Scott was the young sheriff's deputy first on the scene. The DA's parents beamed while their daughter led the young man through his direct testimony.

A residential security alarm had come into the sheriff's Espanola substation about 3:30 a.m. Scott answered it. The scene was as bad as he had ever encountered. Busted-open front door, what appeared to be a shredded male corpse lying across the threshold, blood and the smell of gunpowder, and next to the deceased an axe and sledgehammer, Ms. Castellano sitting in a wheelchair about ten feet away, a shotgun next to her on the floor.

"Was there any conversation between you and the defendant?"

"She told me to be careful, not to touch the trigger, there were unspent shells in the shotgun, one of them in the chamber. She said everything was a crime scene."

Although the DA knew the answer from interviewing Officer Scott and thus should not have asked the question, she did. "Officer Scott, did you say anything else?"

Pause. The deputy had just remembered he'd left something out at his interview. *Well, I took an oath to tell the truth, so here goes,* he thought.

"Yes, ma'am. When Ms. Castellano told me the place was a crime scene, I said . . . I said, 'No shit?'."

Laughter throughout the courtroom.

"Then," he continued, "I asked her, 'What happened?' and she said it was pretty obvious."

"Anything more?"

"Two things. One, she said she would say no more until she talked to her lawyer, Mr. Salazar. The other thing was, she asked me to go to the sidebar and pour her a stiff bourbon, which I did."

"Thank you, Officer Scott. Your witness, Mr. Willard."

"This won't take long, Andy. Just a few clarifications, okay?"

"Sure, sir."

"Ever encounter a crime scene with a busted door and a shredded corpse lying next to an axe and sledgehammer? Or an elderly woman in a wheelchair with a loaded shotgun on the floor next to her?"

"Hell no, that was one for the books. Looked like a tank went through that door."

"You said Ms. Castellano was sitting in a wheelchair. How was she sitting?"

"Sitting, like in a regular chair except it was a wheelchair."

"Think back, Andy, was she sitting like in a regular chair with her butt on the seat and her feet on the floor?"

"Now I know what you're asking, sir. No, her right leg was straight out, like elevated, and her right foot was like bandaged or strapped."

"Did you check the shotgun, to see if it was empty?"

"No, sir, I did not touch it because of Ms. Castellano's warning and anyhow it was evidence, but I could see four ejected shells on the floor."

"Did you ask Ms. Castellano why she fired at least four rounds at Mr. Carranza?"

"No, I didn't, and she didn't tell me. Hell, it was obvious she wanted him real dead."

Before either Quintana or Zimmerman could object, or ask that Scott's gratuitous guesswork be stricken, Willard quickly said, "One last question, Andy. Roughly, how tall was the door?"

"The door, the main one in the entry hall where the stiff . . . excuse me, sir, I mean the body, was lying?"

"Yes, that door," Willard said patiently.

"Now I remember something, sir, Mrs. Castellano told me to go look at the top of the door and tell her what I saw."

Almost out of patience, Willard said, "We'll get to that in a minute, Andy, but, for now, how tall was the door?"

"Sorry, sir. That was an eight-foot door because the entry foyer ceiling was ten feet."

"How did you know that?"

"I work construction weekends, and I know eight-foot doors and ten-foot ceilings."

"Did you look at the top of the door inside and outside?"

"Yes. On the inside, I think three holes, exiting on the outside."

"Have you seen those sorts of holes at crime scenes before?"

"Yes. They were bullet holes."

"Thanks, Andy, very helpful." Willard turned his back and walked away.

Judge Baldwin told the prosecution to call their next witness.

It was Santa Fe Chief Deputy Walter Duran. His opening testimony, elicited by Fred Zimmerman, described the physical scene he encountered just as had Andrew Scott. Next, Duran confirmed that he had conducted a nearly two-hour on-scene interview of Rachel and produced a cassette tape. Zimmerman sought to introduce it into evidence, handing what he said were true copies to Willard and to the court officer for the judge.

After Willard satisfied himself about the tape's chain of custody, State's Exhibit was duly marked and accepted into evidence.

However, prosecution-defense cooperation ended when Zimmerman proffered a transcript his office had made, purportedly from the tape.

"The defense has been sandbagged," Willard said adamantly. "There is no way we can ascertain the accuracy of the DA's purported transcript during this hearing. The District Attorney has had weeks to give us the tape and transcript, as a professional courtesy if for no other reason, constitutional and ethical."

When Zimmerman started to respond, the judge stopped him and said, "Madam District Attorney, why did you not do that, and do you think I am going to listen to that tape or read that transcript in the middle of this hearing? Mr. Willard is correct, the defense has been sandbagged, and I'm not going to allow it. He has the tape, now marked as State's Exhibit 1, so give him a copy of the home-brew transcript right now. Then move on. The transcript is not in evidence, nor will it be. We will deal later with whatever impact your non-delivery of the tape may have had on the defense."

Zimmerman tried to pick up where he had left off with Walt's testimony, but the colloquy and the judge's chastisement had thrown him off course. After a few moments, he asked Duran, "Before the shooting, were you aware of a grudge between the defendant and the late Mr. Carranza?"

Willard was on his feet in a millisecond, but, before he could speak, the judge said, "Mr. Zimmerman, you know better than to ask such an obvious, improper leading question. 'Grudge,' indeed. I am not yet at the point where I must admonish you on the record, but I am quickly getting there. I want facts, gentleman and lady, not cute trial tactics. Rephrase, or call another witness."

"When did you first learn that Ms. Castellano was having trouble with Mr. Carranza?"

Before Willard could object, the judge said, "Mr. Zimmerman, you are leading your own witness. Shall I rephrase it for you?"

Some laughter and one or two snickers from the jury.

Zimmerman rephrased, and Duran said, "Several months ago, Mr. Salazar visited me, acting as her lawyer. He reported that Carranza may have ordered two attacks on Ms. Castellano, threats to her shepherds, destruction and theft of her property and twice personally tried to break down her front door in the middle of the night accompanied by his threats to kill her."

"What did you do about Mr. Salazar's complaint?"

"We looked for Mr. Carranza, but were unable to find him, and I reported that to Mr. Salazar."

"When was the next time you heard about Mr. Carranza?" Zimmerman asked.

"Several weeks later, Mr. Salazar returned to my office accompanied by Mr. Willard, wanting an update. I reported that, while we were still looking for Carranza, we could not find him. Mr. Willard asked if the sheriff's office had enough information to obtain a search warrant for his only connection with Espanola, a studio apartment."

"You obtained the warrant."

"Yes."

"Who executed it?"

"Me, two other deputies, and an investigator, with Mr. Willard and Mr. Salazar present as observers."

Zimmerman hesitated, then asked, "Did you find any guns, knives, explosives . . ."

The judge cut in.

"Mr. Zimmerman, apparently you are a slow learner. You are in contempt of court. The fine is one hundred dollars, payable to the clerk of the court by five o'clock today. He will take a check. One more stunt like this, and I will remove you from this case, permanently. Madam District Attorney," Judge Baldwin said, staring at her, "you better rein in Mr. Zimmerman, or I will. Rephrase, or call another witness."

"Deputy, what did your search produce?"

"Only a few latent fingerprints belonging to Mr. Carranza."

"Take the witness, Mr. Willard."

"May it please, Your Honor, may I have a moment with my co-counsel?"

"Five minutes."

Willard pulled his chair closer to Manny's and said, "So far, apparently the DA doesn't know anything about Carranza's criminal record, so we have a choice. Either dismiss Walt and surprise the State at the trial in front of the jury or have him testify now to what a bad guy Carranza was, but in doing so reveal our cards and gild the lily."

Manny said, "The judge already knows Carranza was a bad guy, but to protect himself we know he's going to find probable cause, so we have nothing to gain now and only to lose. Also," Manny added, "we may pick up a few more points from the judge by moving along."

"Good call," Willard said.

When court reconvened, Willard said, "The defense has no further questions, Deputy Duran. Thank you for your testimony."

Next, a technician testified about the crime scene, and that he had taken photographs of it. Zimmerman offered in evidence fifteen, handing a set to Willard and one set to the court officer for the judge. Zimmerman moved that they be marked as State's Exhibits 2 through 16, inclusive.

After defense counsel reviewed the photos, Willard was on his feet. "Before the defense says 'aye' or 'nay' to Mr. Zimmerman's motion, Your Honor, may I ask the witness a few questions?"

"Certainly, proceed."

"When you took your photographs, was the deceased lying in a prone position, face down, or on his back?"

"His back."

"So, that means there are no photos of the deceased's back, because he was lying on it."

"Yes."

"So, the fifteen photos you took were all frontal shots."

"Correct."

"Of the fifteen frontal shots, how many are the best examples? Most inclusive of the body, not merely exact or near exact copies, sharpest, and best angle? Do you understand my questions, and what I'm getting at?"

"Yes, Mr. Willard, I do."

The tech thought for a few minutes, shuffled the photographs, and said, "Three. Three you can take to the bank, that show everything anyone needs to see."

"In other words, and I don't want to put words in your mouth, three photos best depict the deceased's condition at the time of death."

The tech thought about Willard's question, and answered, "True."

Turning to the judge, Willard said, "Your Honor, the defense is willing to consent to use of the three photos, but not for the reasons the witness' testimony has revealed. First, to admit any more if we get to a jury would be inflammatory, and thus prejudicial to my client. Second, we just heard the prosecution's own witness, who works for the county sheriff, tell us which are the best pictures. Thus, if Your Honor finds probable cause and this case is tried to a jury, and the prosecution makes the same fifteen-photo proffer, I will make the same objection and consent to the admission of only these three."

"Understood, Mr. Willard. For now, the three photos will be marked as the State's exhibits 2, 3 and 4."

With no objection from Willard, the four spent shotgun shells were admitted as State's exhibits 5, 6, 7 and 8.

Turning back to the witness, Willard asked about the holes in the top of the front door. The crime scene guy unhesitatingly and unequivocally testified that they were bullet holes, likely from a .45 caliber handgun, either revolver or automatic.

The prosecution had no redirect.

Its next witness was the county coroner, who testified that Carranza died of multiple bullet wounds to the torso, extremities, and head, but it was not possible to attribute his death to any single round or combination of rounds.

Willard's cross examination consisted of only a few questions.

"I know, doctor, that this will be a difficult question to answer with precision, but please try. As Ms. Castellano was pumping rounds into Mr. Carranza, could she know from instant to instant whether he was dead or alive?"

"That's an extremely interesting question, Mr. Willard, and one I have given considerable thought to in attempting to establish the exact time of death. Please don't think my forthcoming answer is evasive because it's not. The fact is that Mr. Carranza could have been dead from the first round through the last. Or not."

Willard paused, for emphasis.

"What do you mean, doctor, by 'or not'?" Willard asked.

"Well," the coroner said, "there were four shotgun shells fired, all nine-ball buckshot. That means thirty-six balls entering a human body at only about ten feet. As I assume you know from your military service, Mr. Willard, that many balls at that short distance are devastating to a human body. Because we do not know which balls struck the deceased in what order and where, we don't know the exact time of his death."

"Can you give us an example, doctor?" Willard asked.

"Of course. Two answers, at each end of the spectrum. Assume the first round hit squarely in the chest cavity or forehead, let alone both, and blew apart the heart or brain or both. Mr. Carranza would have been dead almost instantly."

"Understood," Willard said.

The coroner continued, "But now let's assume that not one of the thirty-six balls hit a vital organ. Some missed, but the others entered his shoulder, foot, stomach, hip, groin, or knee. In that scenario, until the cumulative effect of an unknown number of rounds took their toll, the attacker might have lived for a little while. Please don't ask me how long, because I do not know, and there's no way to tell. In other words, I'm saying that with thirty-six balls of buckshot at that short distance, if the deceased lived at all after even the first round, there is no way to tell when his heart stopped, and he was officially and legally dead."

"Follow-up question, doctor. If after Ms. Castellano fired the last of four rounds Mr. Carranza's body twitched, would that mean he was still 'alive', by any medical definition?"

"Absolutely not," the coroner said, "it could have been entirely neurological. Muscles accommodating themselves to the death of their host. I'm sure some people in this room have seen that happen when they've euthanized a pet. I saw a lot of it in my years as a practicing physician. Especially in my military MASH unit in Korea."

"So, to sum up," Willard said, "When Ms. Castellano

fired the last round, she could have not known whether Mr. Carranza was dead or alive, and a bodily twitch could not have meant whether he was dead or alive."

"Absolutely correct."

"Thank you, sir. Very interesting, informative, and helpful."

"Mr. Zimmerman?" the judge asked.

"No further witnesses."

Judge Baldwin banged his gavel twice. "Forty-five minutes for lunch."

CHAPTER 52

ANDREA HAD ARRANGED WITH THE clerk of the court to use the attorneys' room for the team's pre-ordered lunch, which was delivered a few minutes after the judge gaveled the lunch break.

Jon quickly took charge. "We have a lot to discuss, and some decisions to make, so let's talk and eat in between.

"First, what is Judge Baldwin's attitude? That's Andrea's question, because her assignment was to observe him."

"We've all understood from the beginning that the judge is going to find probable cause, for reasons we don't have to go into now. That said, he is very unhappy with the other side. The 'sketchy' indictment, the tape and transcript problem, acknowledging that we and he were sandbagged, what they tried to do with all the photographs and Zimmerman's antics that resulted in contempt. *Contempt*! In a preliminary hearing. Judge Baldwin is very unhappy."

The others agreed.

"That does not mean that Baldwin will throw the case for us, but in close questions he will at least tilt to us," Andrea concluded by saying.

Jon again. "Another important point is the 'level of proof' problem I created for the judge. Whatever he does about it, we'll know at the end of this hearing, and I'll bring it up again at the trial. We don't have time to get into it now, so Manny please explain it to Rachel later.

"Rachel's assignment was the crime scene."

"Frankly," she said, "between the prosecution's witnesses

and Jon's cross examination, the crime scene recreation was so clear and accurate that I felt like I was experiencing it again. All of it, the door, axe, sledgehammer, shotgun shells. Jon showed through their witnesses what a nightmare that was, that I could not easily run away, and had no way to know when Carranza was dead. So, I kept shooting."

"As you know," Manny said, "my main task was to watch carefully whether they knew Jon and I had a fourth meeting with Walt and learned about Carranza's record and what a bad guy he was. That was the brief conference Jon and I had at the defense table. By our deciding to ignore that in this hearing, the other side will get a big surprise at trial, in front of the jury."

"Now," Jon said, "we come to a crossroads. I remind you that the prosecution has rested without either Quintana, Zimmerman, or any of their witnesses uttering a single word about New Mexico statute Section 30-2-7, 'Justifiable homicide by citizen in defense of habitation,' which, along with standard self-defense, are our defenses."

"They are not that stupid, particularly Zimmerman," Andrea said. "So, let's look at this from their perspective. Certainly, Fred knows this is a classic Castle Doctrine self-defense and justification case. He knows that in the end there will be a jury acquittal, or, at the very best for them a hung jury, or a directed verdict of not guilty by the judge. In other words, they do not expect to win. They expect to lose, the only question is how. So, for whatever twisted reason, the DA wants to get to the jury. Maybe she wants the publicity and will use the loss to get rid of Zimmerman. Or maybe he has trapped her into the trial, for his own purposes. We don't know."

"But we do know," Jon added, "we, too, want to get to the jury, to destroy Quintana and publicly revive the land grant issue. Which means that, like them, we do *not* want a directed verdict of acquittal now or ever, and we *do* want the judge to find probable cause for the case to go to a jury trial. So, how do we accomplish that?"

Answering his own question, Jon said, "We call no witnesses, and do not mention either of our defenses. We go back to court, and the defense rests."

The others understood and agreed.

CHAPTER 53

THE JUDGE WAS BACK ON the bench, counsel and Rachel Castellano were at their respective tables, and the spectators in their seats. The Honorable Horace Baldwin turned to Willard and said, "Call your first witness, Mr. Willard."

Willard stood, saying, "May it please the court, the defense will call no witnesses. The defense rests."

It was like a thunderbolt struck the courtroom. Before he could think, the judge said, "What, no witnesses, you rest?"

Quintana and Zimmerman stared at each other, she stunned, he in automatic trying to analyze what Willard's tactical move had just been on the case's chess board.

Some of the spectators understood what had just happened.

Walt Duran got it immediately, remembering that Zimmerman had not asked him about the last meeting with Jon, Manny, and Rachel, when they examined Carranza's criminal record. Willard would spring it on the prosecution at trial.

Jane Davis understood some of it, especially that now the defense was certain to get the case before a jury.

Rose Castellano trusted Jon Willard, Esq.

District Attorney Maria Quintana's lawyer-father knew instinctively that his daughter had somehow just been screwed but did not know how.

When the judge's head cleared, he started thinking. *That federal judge in New York, Julia Burt, told me Willard was a straight arrow, and I've seen some of that here. But she also warned me that he's smarter than hell. I don't know what he's doing, but I better find out sooner than later.*

"Mr. Willard," Baldwin said, "I understand the defense is not calling any witnesses. Should I assume you are about to move for a directed verdict of acquittal on behalf of Ms. Castellano based solely on the testimony of the prosecution's three witnesses?"

Quintana and Zimmerman held their breaths, as did her father and some spectators.

I better soften this somehow for the judge, not make him look bad. Even if I have to give away something.

"May it please the court," Willard said with utmost sincerity and politeness, "the defense will not make a motion for a directed verdict of acquittal on behalf of Ms. Castellano *at this time.*"

Getting used to, though still not understanding, what was happening, the judge said, "I take it, Mr. Willard, you understand that on the face of the State's *unopposed prima facie* case, I may have no choice but to find probable cause."

You don't get it, judge, we have rebutted their case with their own witnesses through my cross examination. Section 30-2-7 exists, even if no one mentions it. All the evidence the prosecution and I have advanced through direct and cross examination, respectively, add up to classic Castle Doctrine self-defense and Section 30-2-7 habitation justification defenses as a matter of law. There is nothing for the jury. I am just not ready to let the genies out of the bottle by making a motion for a directed verdict of acquittal. I want this case to go to the jury.

"I do understand that sir, and the defense will take its medicine if you do find probable cause," Willard said.

Jesus, Willard wants me to find probable cause and send this case to the jury, the judge realized. *I get it. By God, that's it. My epiphany! That's what he wanted all along. Willard squeezed out the prosecution's entire case and laid out his defense from this probable cause hearing without firing a shot. Why he is so determined to get to a jury, I do not know. But that's what he is going to get.*

"But, Your Honor," Willard added, "there is one loose end. It is what we discussed earlier but left for now, the level of proof you will use in your probable cause determination. I believe we have excluded 'beyond a reasonable doubt.'"

In this posture, the judge wondered, *what level of proof does Willard want, and what am I most protected with? Beyond a reasonable doubt is off the table, that's for the jury. If I apply the 'clear and convincing' standard it looks like I'm holding the prosecution to a tough level of proof. Tough judge, etc. But it won't matter to the prosecution because they're getting my ruling of probable cause and they can gloat that they met the high 'clear and convincing' standard. Willard won't care about the higher standard because he wants to get to the jury. And I will have escaped the horns of the dilemma. Besides, mere 'preponderance of the evidence' looks too faint-hearted. That's it, then, "clear and convincing."*

"Correct, Mr. Willard, we have excluded 'beyond a reasonable doubt. In the absence of statutory or case authority, and because of the importance that criminal defendants like your client receive adequate procedural due process, I am applying the higher standard of 'clear and convincing' evidence.' That is the burden of proving probable cause the prosecution must meet."

"Thank you, Your Honor," Willard said, satisfied.

"Applying that standard," Judge Horace Baldwin said, self-righteously, "my ruling is that the prosecution has proved probable cause."

One judge, four lawyers, and one defendant breathed easier, all for the same reason. Get this case to the jury!

CHAPTER 54

IMMEDIATELY AFTER JUDGE BALDWIN RULED on probable cause, he set April 15 as the date for a status conference.

At that conference, the prosecution represented it had no pre-trial motions, nor would request any discovery *from* the defense. Although discovery *for* the defense in a criminal trial was limited, Willard asked for all reports related to the indictment, including but not limited to those of Andrew Scott, Deputy Chief sheriff Walter Duran, the crime scene tech, and the Santa Fe Coroner. Surprisingly, the DA made no objection, and the judge "so ordered."

Willard then asked how many jurors the judge intended to draw from the pool. Baldwin turned the question around, asking the District Attorney for her thoughts.

Taken unaware, she and Zimmerman came up with the number forty. Willard with fifty.

Looking surprised, the judge asked Jon, "How do you get to fifty?"

"Under New Mexico law, we need to have twelve. It is a first-degree murder case, so I assume Your Honor will seat at least four alternates. That's sixteen. At least four will find a way to escape sitting, using one excuse or another. That's back to twelve. Between the prosecution and defense, eight may be excused for cause. Together, the prosecution and defense have twelve preemptive challenges, I raised the prosecution's forty by ten because something always goes wrong."

Everyone present laughed.

"Okay, that makes sense. Does the state object to drawing fifty prospective jurors from the pool?"

The prosecution did not.

"Settled, then, I will have the clerk of the court draw fifty potential jurors from the pool. Any other business?"

There was none, so the judge said, "Please, get out your calendars so I can set a trial date." As counsel did, Baldwin said, "Today is April 15, the rest of the month is taken, as are the first three weeks in May. Trial begins on Tuesday, May 28. Is that agreeable to all counsel?"

It was.

CHAPTER 55

ALTHOUGH WILLARD'S TEAM HAD DONE considerable work in preparation for the preliminary hearing — most importantly having educated the judge by smoking out the prosecution's entire case, while hiding the defense strategy and tactics — there was still much to do before the trial began in five weeks.

After the Pinkertons came through so fast with useful information about the DA's personal, educational, and professional background, Jon tasked them with another project. Willard had instructed them to analyze Santa Fe County jury patterns, including gender, ages, and numbers and percentages of military veterans.

During pre-trial preparation, Pinkertons' Bill Sherman turned over a large amount of data to Jon, who turned it over to David Trujillo with the request that he analyze and explain what its essence revealed concerning potential jurors.

When David finished ten days later, the two men, Manny, and Andrea sat in the conference room of Jon's office amidst stacks of paper containing reports, graphs, spread sheets and such.

Just as they had at dinner when Jon asked for help, in making his presentation David divided it into the elderly land grant potential juror, and the military/law enforcement potential juror.

At the end of his ninety-minute presentation, David boiled down the data.

"Understand," he began, "this data is solely Santa Fe County. Age-eligible female jurors are 50.75% of the population, males 45.25%. Females and males over age fifty, are 72% of the county population. From these numbers, I calculate that our chance of getting a prospective juror knowledgeable about the land grants is no more than 20%."

David continued.

"The military numbers are interesting. There are a total of just over fourteen thousand male and female veterans in Santa Fe County, comprising just under ten percent of the total population, which is high. Pinkerton reported that they checked twice. Even at fourteen thousand, statistically the chances of getting a veteran are slim."

"That's about what we figured, but it doesn't worry us," Andrea said.

"Why not?" David asked.

"For several reasons. First, the juror pool is pulled from the voter rolls, so there is a decent chance the pool will contain prospective jurors who have at least a high school education. Second, because on its merits, this is a slam-dunk case of self-defense and justified homicide, which means in the end there will be either a 'not guilty' jury verdict, a hung jury, or a directed verdict of acquittal by the judge so he is not reversed on appeal. Third, the land grant issue is known by many New Mexicans whose families have not been directly affected by what happened. Fourth, the DA is a lousy lawyer, and her capable Chief Deputy has already aggravated the judge, as he will the jury. Fifth, the guy sitting to your left is a fair to middling lawyer."

The last thing they discussed with David was his in-court role. Initially, there would be two choices during jury selection. They could accept or reject a juror if Jon and David agreed. If they disagreed, Jon and Manny would thrash out what to do. If they could not agree, Jon would make the call to accept or reject. If the potential juror was to be rejected, the next choice was either to challenge for cause, which would not cost the defense anything, or, if there was no cause, or the judge disagreed, Jon would have to use a precious peremptory challenge.

"Is it okay for me to sit at the counsel table?" David asked.

"Good question," Andrea said. "I researched that. There is no New Mexico statute or case answering it. Nationwide, there are only two cases, one pro, one con. I will not be at the counsel table during jury selection. From left to right facing the judge will be Jon, you, Manny, and Rachel. Jon will introduce you as a member of his team, a word everyone these days uses a lot. If the introduction slides by, so be it. If either the prosecution or the Judge ask if you are a 'jury consultant,' Jon will categorically represent that you are not a *professional* jury consultant, no more than any other member of the defense team. If there is an argument, Jon will deal with it, but in the absence of any New Mexico law, I doubt Baldwin will go out on a limb and prohibit it."

CHAPTER 56

URING TRIAL-PREPARATION, ANDREA HAD BEEN working with the defense witnesses she had hired. As directed by Jon, she had retained the top surveyor in New Mexico, Carlos Santiago, whose father and grandfather had been surveying and charting in the northern part of the state since the late 1800s and were experts on the Tierra Amarilla land grant as far back as the pre-territorial days.

Andrea had tasked Carlos's firm, led by Carlos himself, with a two-fold job. First, to locate exactly where Rachel's Abiquiu property fit physically within the Tierra Amarilla land grant. Second, to create a slide show dramatically demonstrating the relationship.

The defense's second witness would be Felipe Ortiz, Ph.D., the nationally recognized authority on New Mexico land grants, and the Tierra Amarilla grant specifically. Author of four scholarly books and dozens of articles, Professor Ortiz occupied an endowed chair in the history department of the University of New Mexico. For years, he had been chairman.

Andrea spent hours reading Ortiz's books and talking with him about the genesis of the New Mexico land grants from fifteenth-century Spain through New Spain and ultimately to northern New Mexico. Although earlier Andrea had heard an abbreviated version from Rachel Castellano, Professor Ortiz supplied endless detail about the incompetence and chicanery that cost countless Hispanos their lands, livelihoods, and faith in the United States government. As with Carlos Santiago, Andrea asked Professor Ortiz to create a slide show dramatically demonstrating the story of the stolen land grants.

A week before the trial began, Andrea, who had already seen a preview of both slideshows, organized a viewing for the defense team in the conference room—Rachel, Jon, Manny, David, Rose, and Allison.

All were stunned emotionally by the powerfully dramatic impact, which brought two of the New Mexicans present to tears. Allison Penelope Corrales was one of them, although before the viewing she knew nothing about the land grants. As Jon watched the young woman cry and occasionally curse, he thought, *she is a foreshadow of some jurors.*

An invited guest to the preview was Andrea's father, Nick Vardas, whose Gulfstream had landed in Santa Fe earlier that day. Nick was comfortably ensconced in a large suite at the Eldorado Hotel where, after the preview, they all dined in a private room. It was then Andrea told the group that Nick was the mysterious "Mr. X and Mr. Y" who was funding the defense. He was profusely thanked by everyone.

The pretrial preparation included Jon scrutinizing the transcript of the preliminary hearing, prospecting for an overlooked nugget that might be useful at the trial.

Two days before the trial was scheduled to begin, Allison buzzed Jon and said, slightly breathlessly, that the DA and her Chief Deputy were on the phone. Jon told Allison to remain on the line, take notes, and plug in Andrea. When all five were connected, Willard said, "There are three of us on the line, one taking notes. What can I do for you?"

When District Attorney Maria Quintana began beating around the bush, Fred Zimmerman cut in and said, "The DA wants to make a deal."

"What about you, Fred?" Willard asked.

"The DA wants to make a deal," Fred repeated.

"Understood. Why?"

Pause.

Fred said, "The DA says, 'in the interests of justice'."

"If your incompetent, ladder-climbing boss cared about the 'interests of justice', she would never have brought this showboating publicity stunt you people call a lawsuit."

In his office, Zimmerman laughed.

To avoid throwing up even figuratively, Willard hung up. Literally.

CHAPTER 57

THE DISTRICT ATTORNEY AND HER Chief Deputy were seated at the prosecution table which was laden with pads, pencils and paper, documents, folders, and law books.

Also facing the bench, from left to right at the defense table were seated lead counsel Jon Willard, Esq., an unidentified man who had not been there during the preliminary hearing or status conference and at whom the prosecutors were staring intently, co-counsel Emmanuel Salazar, and Rachel Castellano. In front of each was a carafe of water and a glass, a yellow legal pad, a collection of pens and pencils and various documents. On the floor flanking the side of his chair, Manny had access to two large cartons filled with labeled files.

Behind the railing separating the trial's participants from the spectators, in the first row sat Andrea and Nick Vardas. To his right, Jane Davis, the Associated Press reporter. Filling the rest of that row and much of the other seats on the right side of the courtroom were most of the regulars and the courtroom buffs. After all, it was a first-degree murder trial starring Jon Willard for the defense, a rare occurrence for Santa Fe. The DA's parents seemed unhappy to be there.

The left side had been cordoned off for potential jurors.

As usual, at precisely 9:00 a.m. the court officer gave forth with his "Hear-ye, hear-ye . . ." and Judge Horace Baldwin took the bench.

With that, Quintana stood, all smiles, and said, "Good morning, Your Honor."

Willard stood, and said, "Good morning, Your Honor. As you know, Mr. Salazar and I are counsel and co-counsel. Between us is Mr. David Trujillo, a member of my team and staff, and of course at the end of the table is Ms. Castellano."

With his mention of Rachel, Willard was half-way back into his seat, attempting to avoid any comment or question from the judge or DA, who dropped the ball by not asking what David's job was.

The gambit worked, as the judge said, "We all know why we're here, so let's get started. Do either counsel want to be heard?"

Neither did.

"Then, Mr. Court Officer, please bring in fifty prospective jurors."

He did, seating them in the left side of the spectator section.

Jon, David, and Manny went into red alert.

There were too many potential jurors for an accurate count of how many were male or female.

"Good morning, ladies and gentlemen," the judge said to the crowd.

Some of the potential jurors mumbled greetings in return, while others remained silent.

The judge gave them the standard introductory speech about "public service" and asked for their patience because selecting a jury was a tedious task. He then said, "I am going to ask questions, and if your answer is 'yes,' please raise your hand." He made it through the age, citizenship, language, residency, conviction, and disability questions until a hand raised on the word "scheduling." A middle-aged man said he was a staff sergeant in the Air Force Reserve, and though he worked in a civilian job he could be activated and deployed at a moment's notice.

The defense held their breath when the judge asked

whether the sergeant wanted to serve, hoping they could easily replace him if need be.

"I believe in public service, sir," he said. "I'm game if you are."

"Counsel?" The judge asked.

Pending more specific questions to be asked by the lawyers later, there were no objections. Juror 1 came forward and was seated in the jury box. Again, the prosecution had dropped the ball.

The judge then introduced the DA's and Willard's teams and Rachel Castellano and asked if any of the jurors knew any of them, about any of them, or anyone who worked or had worked in the DA's office.

Two hands went up. One potential juror said he had seen Willard on TV at the Senate hearing but averred it would not affect her judgment in this case. "He was just doing his lawyer job for the government."

The second juror had seen Willard at the same hearing, and gratuitously offered that she thought he was brash, abrasive and "too loud." The judge and lawyers had seen this many times; the woman did not want to serve, and this was a way for her to be disqualified. Without waiting for an objection, the judge removed her for cause.

As to whether any prospective juror knew anything about the case because it had been all over local radio, television, and print media, the judge skipped the normal question and asked if anyone could not judge the case fairly or had already made up her or his mind. Five hands went up, and without being asked for a reason were excused for cause.

And so it went for a few hours, with the judge asking stock questions such as prior jury service, deciding only on the evidence, believing indictment equaled guilt, being a prior witness, family, law enforcement employment, and such.

Three hours later, after each side had used two peremptory challenges, the judge had seated twelve potential jurors, and four potential alternates. "We'll take a thirty-minute break, and afterwards the lawyers will take over with individualized questions."

No one had noticed that immediately after the fourth alternate had been seated a nondescript woman in the last row of the spectator section unobtrusively left the courtroom. Her briefcase contained names and other information about each potential juror and alternate. She was a Pinkerton International Detective Agency agent.

CHAPTER 58

WILLARD'S TEAM — ANDREA, DAVID, Manny, Allison, and Rachel — headed for the attorney's room. There was no food or small talk.

Jon said, "We have thirty minutes to deal with sixteen potential jurors. We've all taken copious notes and received the potential jurors' questionnaires. David is going to give you a number and name, tell you his opinion, and solicit yours. No need to speak. But say so if you disagree. Don't forget, this is *voir dire*, jury selection, subject to more questions later and strikes for cause or peremptorily."

"I have no problem," David said — "at the moment — with (1) Kaufman, (3) Esteban , (4) Benavidez, (5) Hidalgo, (6) N. Rivera, (7) E. Rivera, (8) Cruz, and (9) Lujan, all subject to more questions."

Negative comments were made about (2) Gomez, a K1 teacher and (10) Lopez, a singer, but after Jon and David pressed the point, the dissidents backed off, saying they could not explain why they objected. Gut feelings. All agreed they would watch the two during the next round.

"I am concerned about (11) Harrison, a retired college professor, and (12) Williams, a retired banker," David said, but recommended they wait for the next round before eliminating any of the four. "Also, let's hold off on the alternates until then." Unanimous consent, in a voice vote.

When the court officer knocked on the door, Jon said, "David and I are returning to the courtroom. I am leaving everyone else behind with my notes and the jury questionnaires for you to dissect, looking for anything that can help or hurt us. I will complete this round of questioning and we will rendezvous later to make our final choices."

CHAPTER 59

RETURNING TO THE COURTROOM, COUNSEL was seated. Jon's job was to ask questions, David's to take notes, size up the potential final jurors, and make judgments. They and the DA would question the prospective jurors one at a time.

The DA began, standing at the prosecution table with her notes before her. After all, what trouble could she get into with prepared questions taken from a form book, such as disbelieving police witnesses simply because they were cops? Stiff and formal, like a stereotypical female prosecutor in a Grade B television movie, none of her questions or the answers moved her juror-knowledge needle.

When Willard stood up to question the first potential witness, he unbuttoned his jacket and to the surprise of the judge and prosecutors carried no notes. Walking toward the jury box, but not close enough to crowd any of the potential jurors, he looked at Juror 1, the Air Force reservist.

Smiling, Jon said, "I was about to ask you a few questions, but realized I don't know whether to address you as 'Mr.' or 'Sergeant'."

A few chuckles around the room.

Returning the smile, the potential juror said, "Well, Mr. Willard, I'm off duty, so I guess '*Mr.*' is okay."

Rapport.

"Fine. I am going to ask softball questions, but they are profoundly serious. I'll ask one, pause, wait for your answer, get it, and move on. Okay?"

"Yes, sir."

"Do you know that this indictment, and every other one in America, is only a charge that a group of people called the 'grand jury' decided to make? A mere allegation. Proof of nothing. Not evidence."

"Yes, sir."

"Do you know at the grand jury, a soon-to-be indicted man or woman is not allowed to be present, and all that happens is secret, do you know that?"

"I did not, no, but now I do."

"Have you ever heard the expression that because of these rules, a District Attorney could 'indict a ham sandwich'?"

Most potential jurors laughed, as the sergeant said that he had not.

Willard could not believe the roll he was on and wondered whether the DA would move to strike the sergeant. There was no 'for cause', so she would have to use a peremptory challenge, not something done without a good reason. Also, it would not go down well with the remaining potential jurors because the same thing could happen to them.

Willard continued. "Do you know that the law says Ms. Castellano is *innocent*, not guilty but *innocent*, until the prosecution proves her guilty of first-degree murder, (1) beyond a reasonable doubt, (2) by a unanimous verdict of every one of you twelve jurors, (3) by proving every one of the elements that make murder in the first-degree a crime, and (4) that she has no legal defense to the shooting? I know that's a mouthful, but do you know all that?"

"I do, sir. But I didn't know that the prosecutor has to prove that Ms. Castellano has no legal defense. That she has no defense."

The DA started to stand, but Zimmerman pulled her down. The judge saw what happened and smiled to himself. Absent an objection, he would not intervene, though he knew what Willard was doing, and why.

"And do you know, Mr. Kaufman," Willard continued,

"that despite this horrendous charge, if Ms. Castellano, for any reason — for example, to deny the prosecution the satisfaction of hearing her beg when she has done nothing wrong — declines to testify, no conclusion of any kind can be drawn, nor can her declination to testify be held against her in any way?"

"Yes, sir, that's always been my understanding. The Fifth Amendment."

"Correct."

Willard asked every one of the other potential jurors, including the four alternate prospects the same questions, receiving the same answers, though some were phrased differently.

While some criminal defense lawyers and Jon's team might have thought he wasted his *voir dire* opportunity to learn more about the potential jurors, they would not have fully realized why he knew what he was doing. First, his experience picking juries in criminal cases was extensive, while they had none. Second, after the lawyers finished, the judge would give the defense time to decide about final strikes, and by then he would have the opinions of his team, and hopefully juror information from the Pinkertons.

Willard had always believed that if he could instill in potential jurors the basic defendant-protective principles of constitutional-criminal law as he had just done sixteen times, he could shape the law and facts to make a convincing case to the jury. Even if he and David made a mistake in seating one or more jurors, by the time Jon had to put on the defendant's case the Pinkertons would have given him open-source profiles on all sixteen potential jurors. Willard had been emphatic to the Pinkertons that none of the sixteen could know that they were being researched. Only open information that was available to the public at large could be accessed. Even that entailed a risk that one or more jurors might find out and take it out on Rachel. But

Willard had been in this game a long time, and decided the benefit was worth the risk.

When Willard had asked the last potential juror, an alternate, his final question, the judge admonished them not to discuss the case with *anyone* under any circumstances, including fellow jurors, and report to him if anyone approached them. He then announced, "Lunch, ninety minutes."

For the Willard team in the attorneys' room, the working lunch was spent analyzing information they had on the sixteen potential jurors. The defense's task was not easy because of Jon's tactic of asking prospective jurors only fundamental constitutional-criminal law. His questions lacked nitty-gritty details such as what TV shows they watched and what professional sports teams they followed, although some of the prosecution's questions had elicited such information.

Nonetheless, the Willard team buckled down, considered the data, and expressed their opinions. Especially David Trujillo. To Rachel's surprise, Jon seemed to rely heavily on Allison Corrales's reaction to the land grant slideshows and her belief that even though a Hispano might not know anything about what happened to the grants, once they did know their sympathy would be with the defense. Unfortunately, except for Sergeant Kaufman the team did not yet know if any other potential juror had a military connection.

In the end, with David Trujillo's concurrence, Willard decided to accept the panel as constituted, having closely observed the facial and bodily reactions to his profoundly serious constitutional-criminal law questions.

When court reconvened, the judge and counsel wrapped up some loose-end jury matters and Baldwin administered the oath to the twelve jurors and four alternates.

Following that, Judge Baldwin explained in detail what their job was, what it was not, what they could do in the jury room until they were given the case, and what they could not.

Then, the judge told the jurors that from time to time it might be necessary for he and the lawyers to confer out of the jurors' hearing. Either the attorneys would "approach the bench," or the jurors would be temporarily excused from the courtroom.

The prosecution, defense, or both, might present expert witnesses, or not. If they did, the jurors should understand that such a witness was one who by knowledge, skill, experience, training, or education has become expert in a particular subject and thus may state his or her opinion as to that subject, which a juror can accept or reject, in whole or part.

Concerning exhibits, Judge Baldwin said that "just as with oral testimony, you may give them such weight and value as you think they deserve."

He then said there were two important points necessary for him to make, and for them to understand.

First, at no time and under no circumstances were they to discuss the case with fellow jurors or anyone else until they began deliberations. No exceptions.

Second, they must decide the case solely on the evidence presented within the courtroom's four walls. No outside information of any kind whatsoever, not even looking up a word in the dictionary. No exceptions.

After an hour or so telling each other something about themselves, they were to select a foreperson by majority vote. If there was a tie, they were to keep talking until someone had a majority. When they had, they would be discharged until 9:00 the following morning.

When the jury left the courtroom, Judge Baldwin asked the DA how many witnesses the prosecution would have. Fred Zimmerman took over.

"We will present four, maybe five, Your Honor, on our direct case. Perhaps another one or two if there is a rebuttal."

"As you know, Mr. Zimmerman," the judge said, "I do not favor rebuttals."

"Understood, Your Honor."

"Mr. Willard?" the judge asked, somewhat acerbically alluding to the preliminary hearing, "do you have any witnesses this time?"

"Only two, Your Honor, maybe a third, depending on how well, or poorly, the prosecution does."

Who is he kidding? Baldwin thought. *Willard already got their entire case, witnesses and all, at the preliminary hearing. Two witnesses, maybe three? I better keep being careful.*

"Madam District Attorney," Baldwin said, "9:00 am. Tomorrow, your opening statement."

CHAPTER 60

A T DISTRICT ATTORNEY MARIA QUINTANA'S request, the court clerk had placed a podium atop the prosecution's table. It was there she stood at 9:00 a.m. with Zimmerman sitting next to her. The judge was on the bench, the jury in the box, defense counsel and their client at their table and the nearly full courtroom filled with spectators.

"Please begin, Madam District Attorney," Judge Horace Baldwin said.

"May it please the court," Quintana began. During the twenty-one minutes she spoke in her slightly high-pitched voice, the DA did little more than reiterate the testimony of the prosecution's preliminary hearing witnesses, promising the jury that they would prove the defendant lay in wait for the deceased, and when he tried to enter her home, in Quintana's own words, "mutilated him to death."

In view of what the DA deliberately omitted of the facts and law — Carranza's criminal record, his two earlier threats to kill Rachel, breaking down her door, using an axe and sledgehammer, for the third time threatening to kill her, and Rachel Castellano's defense of self-defense and justification in defense of her habitat — Quintana had flagrantly misled the jury to such an extent that it could be considered unethical conduct for which she might be sanctioned by the New Mexico Bar Association.

It was a pathetic performance. Fred Zimmerman, sitting

next to the DA, doodled on his yellow pad. He knew what a disaster his boss' opening statement had been.

Listening, Jon Willard thought of something he often encountered at trials. *Whether thinking of Aristotle who held that "A is A," things are what they are, or the common saying "chickens have come home to roost," or Ayn Rand who famously defined "justice," as "getting what one deserves in reality," Jon was witnessing the phenomenon in action. The DA never had a case, she did not have one now, and because there was nothing of substance she could say, the District Attorney of Santa Fe County, basically a young, inexperienced, incompetent, publicity-seeking lawyer ruled by her emotions, was falling flat on her face by pushing a case that never should have been brought. Maria Quintana had created a tar baby and it was now stuck to her.*

The judge was also thinking to himself. *This is not a disaster waiting to happen. It is here. It started at the preliminary hearing. Willard exposed and shredded her lack of a case then, which was bad enough. Now he is going to do it again and has an additional target, her non-opening opening statement. That means I'm going to have to deliver a directed verdict of acquittal. Or am I? Don't forget, Horace, that Willard wants to get to the jury.*

If Willard had known Judge Baldwin's thoughts, he would have agreed. The DA was not only going to experience a return engagement of her preliminary hearing, but also would watch Willard destroy her opening statement.

Willard stood, opened his jacket, and slowly walked toward the jury box, stopping at a respectable distance.

The jury had obviously been bored with the DA's opening. Willard quickly turned that around.

"Good morning, jurors. It is customary in opening statements for the lawyers to make promises. Often, they are unable to keep them."

A few smiles. Juror 12, Peter Williams, a retired banker, chuckled.

Willard continued "I am going to make three promises, ladies and gentlemen, and I am going to keep every one of them. Please hold me to those promises.

"First, through cross examination of the DA's witnesses, I am going to expose the gaping holes in the District Attorney's opening statement . . . what she did not tell you.

"Second, as she presents her witnesses, I will expose facts which will require you, in good faith, to return a verdict of not guilty.

"When you know all the facts which have been evident since the beginning of this sorry prosecution, and hear the applicable law from Judge Baldwin, especially concerning Ms. Castellano's defenses, I promise that you'll wonder, as Ms. Castellano and I have, why the District Attorney of Santa Fe County brought this fake case, charging that it was murder for her to save her own life by killing her crazed would-be killer."

That said, Willard knew he had their attention, so he continued.

"This may be a first-degree murder case, but its facts are quite simple. Please bear with me if I start four hundred years ago."

The DA jumped up, and before the judge could admonish her for interrupting Willard's opening statement, said, "May it please Your Honor, four hundred years ago has nothing to do with this case."

Before she could utter a syllable more, Judge Baldwin said coldly, "Madam District Attorney, starting right now if you say even one word during the defense's opening statement, I will hold you in contempt, remove you from this case, and file an ethics complaint with the New Mexico Bar Association. Sit down, and keep your mouth shut."

Quintana's parents in the audience were near tears.

Looking at Willard who had remained next to the jury box looking stone-faced, the judge said, "Sorry for the interruption, Mr. Willard, please begin again."

"Thank you, Your Honor."

"In the 1500s, the king of Spain granted land to adventurers who would colonize New Spain, which we know as Mexico. The authorities there gave land grants to those hardy souls who agreed to migrate to your state, a huge area that later became New Mexico. Grants were given also to Europeans, mixed race individuals, Indians, Indian villages, Hispanic villages, and others."

At the words "land grants," two jurors leaned forward, and a few others made notes.

"A major award north of here was the huge Tierra Amarilla land grant, and a small portion was given to Ms. Castellano's ancestors. As some of you may know, through government incompetence and dishonesty, and the criminal activity of lawyers, judges, politicians, and others, many of those land grants were stolen, their Hispano owners deprived of their independent livelihoods, land, and their spiritual connection with it."

The attention Willard had from the entire jury, especially the nine Hispanos, was intense.

"By now, you may be wondering, despite the DA's improper outburst, what this has to do with Ms. Castellano. Well, I'm going to tell you. Her grandfather, Tomas Castellano, was luckier than most. The then-owner of what had been Tomas's land grant was willing to give him a ninety-nine-year lease instead of evicting him, his sheep, and his cattle. Ms. Castellano raises sheep and some cattle there today, as we sit in this courthouse."

Willard let that sink in for a few moments.

"Enter a fictitious company called the New Mexico Land Investors Limited Liability Company, owned by some mysterious Mexican corporation, which in turn is owned by an even more mysterious trust in far-off Gibraltar."

Willard could see the surprise of some jurors.

"The LLC recently wanted to buy Rachel Castellano's lease. Why? To raise sheep and cattle? No, the strangers wanted to locate and then reopen silver mines that have been closed for decades, and blast, blast, blast, and dig, dig, dig, and then blast and dig some more, releasing toxicity throughout your pristine lands."

Judge Baldwin, whose family had deep roots in New Mexico, leaned forward.

Willard took a few steps back from the jury box, paused, and began again.

"The company sent the now-deceased Mr. Carranza to get Ms. Castellano's land lease, by hook or by crook. He wined and dined her, but she would not sell. Finally, Carranza turned to threatening her, but still she would not sell. Twice, he tried to smash his way into her Abiquiu home, screaming he would kill her. The third time, using an axe and sledgehammer, he succeeded in breaking down her door and crossing the threshold. To save her life, Rachel blasted him to smithereens. That is why Mr. Carranza died. That is why the DA has put Rachel Castellano on trial for first-degree murder. For saving her own life. Apparently, self-defense is now a crime in New Mexico."

Juror 1, Sergeant Kaufman, and two others shook their heads.

With that, Jon Willard, Esq. returned to his seat, noting, as did the jury, that Rachel was crying.

The twelve jurors and four alternates were mesmerized, the DA team looked stunned, many of the spectators were speechless, and the judge said to himself, *Jesus Christ, let's go home, this case is over.*

Instead, he said, "Fifteen-minute recess."

CHAPTER 61

WHEN JUDGE BALDWIN CALLED FOR the recess, the Willard team, plus Nick Vardas, headed for the attorneys' room. When all of them were present, Jon said, "We have little time, so please skip the compliments." Seeing that he was stone-cold serious, no one laughed or spoke.

"What I want to know is juror reaction."

Hurriedly, each one of the team spoke. The consensus was that almost immediately after Jon started speaking, he had the jurors' rapt attention. Some took notes, others leaned forward in their seats, one juror nodded vigorously when Jon mentioned stolen land grants, at least two were near tears or crying.

"If you could name the most effective point, what was it?"

Almost unanimously, the consensus was Carranza's third attempt to breach Rachael's front door. What one team member thought most effective was when Willard said, "That is why Mr. Carranza died. That is why my client is on trial for first-degree murder. For saving her own life."

"Last group question. What about the judge?"

Their responses used words like "engaged," "alert," "interested," "shocked," "moved," "sympathetic."

Jon looked at his watch.

"Allison, what about you?"

"If I were a juror," the beautiful young Hispanic mother said, "you would have had me in the palm of your hand from the beginning. Whatever the later evidence was, I would have voted not guilty at the end. It was obvious to me that some of the Hispanos knew about the land grants, and those who did not, were unhappy about what they were hearing."

"Nick, quickly."

"I agree with this young lady. I know a lot about juries, and about your cross-examination techniques. Whatever the prosecution's case is, and whatever the prosecution's witnesses say, as of now they are dead in the water."

CHAPTER 62

O N JON'S WAY TO THE defense table, Joan Davis, the Associated Press reporter, snared him. "That was a hell of an opening statement," she said. "Can you do all that?"

"Wait and see."

"Can I grab you later today for an interview, on and off the record?"

Willard hesitated, then said, "I'll call you."

As he sat down, the court officer intoned his "Hear-ye, hear-ye" . . . and everyone in the courtroom stood as Judge Baldwin took the bench and told them to be seated.

Given what Willard already knew about the prosecution and prosecutors, especially the DA's opening statement, he expected their case to be a replay of their preliminary hearing witnesses. He was not disappointed.

When the judge told District Attorney Quintana to call her first witness, she named Officer Andrew Scott. Because none of the prospective witnesses for either side were allowed in the courtroom before or after they testified, it took a few minutes for Scott to reach the witness box, where he took the oath and sat down.

As Willard had expected, the DA took Scott through the testimony he had given at the preliminary hearing, and then made a colossal mistake. Despite Fred Zimmerman's warning, Quintana attempted to weaken what Willard had gotten out of Scott on cross examination by repeating his answers and asking new questions.

"Officer Scott," she began, "you have previously testified in this case during Mr. Willard's cross examination that you had never encountered a crime scene, and now I am quoting, 'with a busted door and a shredded corpse next to an axe and sledgehammer.' Do you recall that testimony?"

"Yes, ma'am."

"Approximately how many crime scenes have you seen in your years in law enforcement?"

Scott paused, thinking. "At least twenty." The officer apparently liked being the center of attention, so he kept talking despite Zimmerman's evident distress. "To be honest, ma'am, I've seen lots of banged-in doors, but it's the shredded corpse next to an axe and sledgehammer that I never seen before."

"Your witness, Mr. Willard," the DA said, smiling, without a clue to what she had just done.

"Hello again, Andy," Willard said.

"Hello, sir."

"Just a couple of small clarifications.

"I may be confused about whether you had never before seen such a door, or such a corpse."

"It was the corpse, etc.," the officer said.

"Thanks Andy."

"No problema, sir."

"Just two other points," Willard said, "and we'll be finished. You testified earlier and today that as Ms. Castellano sat in the wheelchair, her leg was extended straight out and there was on her ankle some kind of a bandage. Can you be more specific? Was it like a plaster cast, or something like an Ace bandage or maybe sticky tape?"

The witness thought for a moment. "As I recall, it was like an Ace bandage, for like when you sprain a bone or something. Yes, sir, because I heard that someone had pushed her down in Walmart."

By now, Zimmerman had enough. Before Willard could

continue, the Chief Deputy District Attorney said, "I object to what Mr. Willard is doing, in front of the jury, no less."

Apparently, in the heat of battle Zimmerman had forgotten his law school course in Trial Practice 101: Never let the jury believe that you're trying to hide something from them.

Keeping his face and voice neutral, the judge asked Zimmerman, "What is Mr. Willard doing?"

"It's clear as day, Your Honor. He is replaying the witnesses' testimony from the preliminary hearing as a predicate to cross examining again. . . old testimony. What I mean . . . what I'm trying to say . . ."

The judge cut him off. "I could simply overrule your objection, Mr. Zimmerman, but I fear that it has confused the jury just as much as it has confused me, and perhaps defense counsel. What you are objecting to may occur with other witnesses, so you've forced me to clarify."

On cue, Willard, Manny, and Rachel all nodded their heads, as did several jurors.

"Here is the chronology," the judge said, making an obvious attempt not to sound as frustrated as he was.

"We had a preliminary hearing. The District Attorney called Officer Scott as a witness. Mr. Willard cross examined and clarified some of the officer's direct testimony, apparently to defense counsel's satisfaction."

Slowly, it dawned on Zimmerman that he had created a tar baby he'd be stuck with for all the prosecution's witnesses. *This damn woman I work for is cutting our throats*, he thought.

"Then, Mr. Zimmerman," the judge continued, "your first witness was Officer Scott. What did the District Attorney do? She rewound the tape, so to speak, and replayed the officer's testimony from the preliminary hearing. In so doing, she was trying to rebut what Mr. Willard had gotten out of your witnesses on cross examination. Then she said to Mr. Willard, and you were sitting next to her, 'Your witness.' Madam District Attorney was even smiling. So, tell me, Mr. Zimmerman, if you were Mr. Willard, defending Ms. Castellano in a first-degree murder case, what would you have done? This is not a rhetorical question; I want an answer. Now."

Fred Zimmerman, Chief Deputy District Attorney for the County of Santa Fe, knew he had stepped in it up to his knees, and that there was only one answer.

Taking a deep breath, he said, "I would have cross examined the witness, just as he did."

"Darn right," the judge said, emphatically.

"May it please Your Honor," Zimmerman said, having summoned as much servility as he could, "may I withdraw my objection?"

"No, you may not. Your objection is overruled. I just hope the jury is now clear on what Mr. Willard was doing, that it was not only his right but his duty, and that Chief Deputy District Attorney Zimmerman's objection was inappropriate."

As Judge Baldwin spoke, he turned to the jury and saw that they understood the entire fracas.

Turning back to Willard, the judge said, "Mr. Willard, as I recall, when Mr. Zimmerman made his ill-conceived motion, you may not have finished cross examination of Officer Scott. If you like, you may continue."

What a joke, the judge thought, *I had to make that offer but if Willard accepts it, he should be disbarred. He is one smart fella, got the prosecutors all twisted and tangled in their own incompetence and stupidity. He's going to pull this with every one of the prosecution's witnesses, and I'm going to allow it if Zimmerman makes his motion again, which I doubt.*

Willard knew what the judge was thinking, because he was thinking the same thing, and knowing how far ahead he was, he said, "Thank you, Your Honor, I think the jury has had enough of this witness, and . . ." he deliberately let others fill in the words, 'Mr. Zimmerman'. Instead, Willard said, "this subject."

Willard also knew that a crucial turning point had occurred in the case. However one expressed it — "on the horns of a dilemma," "between the devil and the deep blue sea," or "between a rock and a hard place" — the choices available to the prosecution were equally perilous, maybe even fatal. The State could continue calling witnesses they used at the preliminary hearing — the Santa Fe deputy sheriff, the crime scene tech, and the coroner — and on Willard's second cross examination of them once again he would shred the prosecution's case, or . . . or what? Without those witnesses, there were no witnesses, no case. The prosecution had no choice but to keep plowing forward, consuming itself piece by piece, just as some species of snakes.

CHAPTER 63

THE PROSECUTION'S NEXT WITNESS WAS Chief Deputy Sheriff Walter Duran, as he had been at the preliminary hearing. On direct, his questioner was again the District Attorney herself, eliciting the same facts she had obtained from him earlier. This time, she knew better than to try rebutting what Willard had already obtained from Duran.

Duran testified that he had done a two-hour interview of Rachel Castellano at the scene of the shooting, and the DA tried to introduce the tape into evidence. Once Willard had verified the chain of custody, he made no objection.

However, apparently not having learned her lesson at the preliminary hearing, when the DA offered a transcript her office had made of the tape, Willard strenuously objected because he still did not know whether it was accurate or not. His objection was immediately sustained, the judge saying the jury could hear the tape during their deliberations if they wanted to. But the home-brew transcript was inadmissible.

In answering the DA's questions, Duran also testified about Manny's first visit, complaining about Antonio Carranza, his second visit accompanied by Mr. Willard about obtaining the search warrant, and the third concerning the fruits of the search.

On cross examination, Willard was about to drop a bombshell.

"Deputy Duran, you have testified to three meetings concerning Carranza's attacks on Ms. Castellano."

"Yes, sir. Correct."

"Was there a fourth meeting?"

The hammer was about to come down on the prosecution.

"Yes, sir, with me, Mr. Salazar, Ms. Castellano, and you."

"What was the purpose of that meeting?"

"Well, a fingerprint we obtained from searching Carranza's apartment in Espanola hit paydirt."

"Paydirt?" Willard asked.

"Turned out Carranza was a felon, including arson. Under an alias, he served time in New Mexico for rape."

"Was all that documented?"

"That, and more."

"Where did you obtain it?"

"Well, some from the New Mexico State crime lab, other states' data bases, and certain sources and methods I cannot reveal."

"Okay. When you were interviewed by the DA regarding your testimony for this case, did you mention the fourth meeting?"

"Yes."

"Who was present at your interview?"

Pointing at the defense table, Duran said, "The two folks over there, and some other man."

"Did you give them a copy of the documents you had obtained about Carranza's criminal record?"

"I did, at the DA's request."

"Did anyone ask you if I, Mr. Salazar, Ms. Castellano, or anyone else had a copy, except of course your sources?"

"Yes, but I do not remember who asked."

"What was your answer?"

"No one."

"No one what?" Willard asked.

"Other than my sources and the sheriff's office, and then the DA, no one else had the Carranza documents."

With that bombshell, everyone in the courtroom knew that documentary evidence of the deceased's criminality had been obtained by the Santa Fe sheriff's office, conveyed only orally in summary fashion to the four interested parties but not in writing, and given to the District Attorney. She knew no one else had a copy, and Quintana had sat on it during her presentation to the grand jury and the pretrial runup up to the trial.

While most of the jurors looked appalled, the judge asked Willard, "Do you wish to make any motions?"

"Thank you for the invitation, Your Honor, but no. Mr. Salazar and I will deal with the prosecutor's serious ethical, legal, and constitutional problems after the jury has made its decision."

The prosecution's next witness was the crime scene tech. Having learned their lesson, the prosecution only introduced the three photographs approved by the judge at the preliminary hearing. Willard had no objection and passed on cross examination.

The last witness who had testified at the preliminary hearing was the county coroner, who now testified essentially to the same facts. This time, as before, on cross examination Willard established that it was impossible for the coroner or anyone to establish the exact time of Carranza's death, which could have been after the first round or even the fourth.

Willard was not surprised that the prosecution did not rest their case after the coroner's testimony because he knew what the DA would do next. His team did not know. No one in the defense team knew. Only Pavel Friedman in New York knew.

Once Jon signed on as trial counsel, he read every New Mexico case on Castle Doctrine self-defense and habitat-justified homicide. Among them, he found three or four that purported to deal with the question of whether invoking those defenses required that the killing occur in a residence on land that the shooter-defendant owned. If the law of New Mexico required ownership, which Willard believed it did not, the prosecution could argue that Rachel did not own the property her home was on because of the land grant transfers, and thus self-defense and justifiable homicide defenses were unavailable to her.

After the prosecution debacle at the preliminary hearing and now at the trial, Willard believed that its bare bone presentation of the *facts* could be explained because they believed they could win on the *law. She was not defending a residence on land she owned, so neither self-defense nor justification could help her.*

Jon had tasked the Friedmans to brief the issue, and their report was in one of the cartons at Manny's feet.

If Willard's analysis was mistaken, the prosecution would rest and not call another witness. Willard would not have to deal with the ownership issue. If they did call another witness, and he suspected who it would be, the defense would be in even better shape.

Judge Baldwin asked the prosecution if they were resting.

"We have one more witness," the DA announced. "Please call Israel Fernandez."

Once he was seated, the DA asked, "What is your occupation, Mr. Fernandez?"

"I am county clerk of the County of Santa Fe."

"As such, do you have access to the records of who owns what parcel of land?"

"I do."

"Who owns the land on which sits the one-family residence known as 1074 Summit Drive in Abiquiu?"

"New Mexico Land Investors, LLC."

"Not Rachel Castellano?"

"No."

"Do you have a copy of the deed?""

The witness handed the DA two copies. She in turn handed one to the court for the judge, the other to Willard, who already had a copy.

"May it please the court, I offer this deed as State's Exhibit 1."

Now comes the tricky part, Jon said to himself. *I must object enough so the DA believes I want the deed kept out of evidence, but not enough for the judge to sustain my objection and keep it out.*

Manny and Andrea, but no one else, knew that Willard was about to make a fake out move on the case's chess board, but did not know what it was.

"Objection, Your Honor. I move that the county clerk's testimony be stricken, and this deed be rejected as irrelevant."

The DA took the bait, arguing it was highly relevant to the prosecution's case because "if Mr. Willard intends to mount a Castle Doctrine, self-defense, or any other such claim, ownership is a crucial factor."

Zimmerman wore an odd expression.

Not bad, kid, Willard thought. *Thanks.*

"Mr. Willard?"

"I have nothing more to say, Your Honor."

"I agree with the District Attorney," the judge said. "Ownership is important. It is a jury question. Your motion is denied, the deed is admitted as State's exhibit 1."

Andrea, who did not know this was coming, realized immediately what a coup Jon had just pulled off. *A jury question. Thanks to the prosecution, the land grants were now in the case. And we will take to the jury the story of what happened to many of them.*

When Manny saw Andrea smiling and elbowing Nick, Manny refocused on Judge Baldwin's words. "Ownership is important." *Jon had done it*, Manny realized, *Willard had gotten the issue of stolen land grants into this case. And, better still, it was a jury question.*

I would probably have denied Willard's motion, the judge thought, *because the DA seemed correct, but what I now realize is that in one respect I was swindled. Willard acted completely out of character. No argument, no brief, zip, nada.*

He wanted that land grant ownership issue in the case and suckered the DA into helping get it in. Let's see what he does with it when he presents his side of the case.

The State rested.

The judge looked at his watch.

"Lunch, ninety minutes. Mr. Willard, your first witness, or motions, when we resume."

Willard stood. "May it please the court, the defense wonders whether the trial could suspend for this afternoon and begin with its first witness promptly at 9:00 tomorrow morning. We have a few reasons."

"Let's hear them," the judge said, thinking of all the work piled up on his desk that needed to be done.

"If we have no motions, our first two witnesses will be experts, and we could use a bit more time to prepare them. Second, I would like a clear division line between the prosecution's case and the defense's because they will be significantly different. I do not want the jury to be any more confused than they may be already. Finally, I am expecting some material later today from our investigators which might help our presentation tomorrow morning."

"Madam District Attorney," the judge said, "what say you?"

Fred Zimmerman stood quickly, and said, "As a professional courtesy, the prosecution has no objection."

Baldwin rapped his gavel twice.

"Okay, 9:00 a.m. tomorrow, Mr. Willard. First witness or motions."

CHAPTER 64

JON, ANDREA, MANNY, AND NICK walked to the Eldorado Hotel on West San Francisco Street where he had a large suite, and they headed for the restaurant. Knowing that they would spend the next few hours upstairs discussing the case, they agreed to talk about other things at lunch.

Andrea and Nick caught up on semi-personal subjects, such as her work with the Innocence Project and his semi-retirement and villa in the Virgin Islands.

After apologizing for raising a subject that might be sensitive, Manny said he could not help asking about the defamation cases in New York.

Nick said, "Well, you asked the right people."

He, Andrea, and even Jon obliged, telling the "war story," leaving little out, and managing a few times to laugh. Manny asked some questions, including what moral one could draw from the entire affair.

While Jon and Andrea thought for a moment, Nick jumped in with "Don't screw with Jon Willard, that's the moral." When Andrea added, "Amen," she kicked her fiancé under the table.

It had been a convivial lunch, much appreciated by Manny who greatly respected Jon, admired Andrea, and was in awe of Nick Vardas.

When they finished lunch and were seated comfortably in Nick's suite, Jon explained that they had to discuss an important legal tactic that might or might not be used. Nick excused himself and headed for the bedroom to make some telephone calls.

Jon began and dominated the conversation.

From what Judge Baldwin had said before lunch — "Your first witness, *or motions*, when we resume" — it was clear to Willard that His Honor expected, even invited, a defense motion for a directed verdict of acquittal.

There were three statutes to be considered.

Chapter 30, Article 2, Section 1, Murder, which provided that first-degree "is the killing of one human being by another *without lawful justification* . . . ."

Chapter 30, Article 2, Section 7, which provided that an act constituted "Homicide [and] *is justifiable,* . . when committed in the necessary defense of his life . . . *or* his property, *or* in necessarily defending against any unlawful action directed at himself . . . *or* in the lawful defense of himself. . . when there is reasonable ground to believe a design exists to commit a felony *or* to do some great personal injury . . . and there is imminent danger that the design will be accomplished."

Chapter 30, Article 2, Section 8, which provided that "Whenever any person is prosecuted for a homicide, and upon his trial the killing should be found to have been . . . justifiable, the jury shall find such person not guilty and he shall be discharged." Although the statute mentioned the *jury*, New Mexico case law had been interpreted to mean that the *judge* should grant the directed verdict of acquittal.

Jon reminded them that they did not want a directed verdict after the prosecution rested. He wanted the case to go to the jury to further their second goal – after acquitting Rachel – of exposing the tragic story of stolen land grants.

The only evidence in the case so far had been provided by the prosecution's witnesses' direct testimony and Willard's cross examination. By any measure, if the case added up to anything, it proved that Rachel Castellano had acted in self-defense and justifiably in defense of her home. Indeed, it was the prosecution's burden to prove by clear and convincing evidence and beyond a reasonable doubt that she had *not* acted in that manner. Not only did the prosecution fail to do so, but it had made no effort to do so.

So, Jon explained, if he made the motion for a directed verdict of acquittal and the judge granted it, which was likely, the case would be over too soon. If the motion was not granted, the defense would benefit because the case would then go to the jury, their primary goal.

There was another angle that Willard asked the others to consider. What if he made the motion, the judge neither granted nor denied it, but instead deferred his ruling until after the jury verdict? Or not make the motion now, and keep his powder dry awaiting further developments?

When Jon had finished explaining his thinking, the three lawyers revisited it piece by piece, sometimes asking him questions, sometimes answering his, sometimes sitting in silence. In the end, they reached a consensus decision.

Agreeing that it already been a long day, they adjourned.

Manny checked in at the library, and then with Rachel.

Nick made his calls and expected a business associate for dinner who had flown down from Denver in his private jet.

Andrea was responsible for getting the expert witnesses to court, having already rehearsed their testimony. She hosted them for dinner at La Fonda.

Jon had to meet with the Associated Press reporter, clear his mind for tomorrow's witnesses, and was expecting the Pinkerton report containing information about some of the jurors.

It would be a long night.

CHAPTER 65

JANE DAVIS ARRIVED PROMPTLY AT 6:00 p.m. The Associated Press reporter had so many questions she didn't know where to begin, so Jon started the conversation.

"You've watched lots of juries, Jane, what do you make of this one?"

"Well, I've been in this courtroom from when jury selection began to and including earlier today when the prosecution rested. So, to assess their reactions, we can't look at all that as one episode. Different segments invoked different responses. If you have the time, I'll break it all down for you."

"All the time you need, because it's evident you understand what a lot of trial lawyers don't. It will be a pleasure to hear your analysis."

"Okay, then, we begin with the view from thirty thousand feet, and then I'll get to the segments. I assume that David Trujillo, who was seated between you and Mr. Salazar when jury selection began, was a jury consultant."

Jon explained who David was, stressing that not only was he a Hispano, but as Special Forces for twenty years he knew a lot about how people reacted in stressful situations.

"The prosecutors dropped the ball on that one, swallowing your characterization that he was 'a member of my team and staff.' They should have exposed that he was helping you in jury selection, making some jurors wonder why you needed help and what of their 'deep secrets' you were trying to uncover."

"Next," the reporter said, "the prosecutors should have used a peremptory on Ernest Kaufman, the Air Force guy, so the jury would never know, or at least not think too hard about, what being an Air Force staff sergeant means. At least basic training with weapons to and including maybe even some form of combat. He was seated first, he will be elected jury foreman, and, if necessary, which I doubt, turn any 'guilty' votes into 'not guilty'. A colossal mistake by the DA and Zimmerman, both non-veterans."

"Excellent point," Willard said. We knew his being military was a big plus.

"Thanks. Okay, now the segments. First, her questioning of jurors. Canned questions, sounding like they came out of a 'how to do it' lawyer's form book, so general and vanilla that they would produce zero useful information for her."

"How did the jury react?" Jon asked.

"Bored and puzzled."

Before Jane Davis could continue, Willard asked, "By the way, what do you know about 'a lawyer's form book'?"

"Well," she replied, "it's time for a confession. I have a law degree." Seeing Willard's surprise she said, "When I worked for the newspaper in Westchester County, I went at night."

"Pace University," Willard said.

"Correct. But let's get back to business so I can ask my questions."

"Have you eaten?" he asked.

Neither of them had, so they took a break and talked about New York.

The pizza and Coronas were delivered, and they went back to work.

"Now we turn to your questioning, and its impact on the jury. You took a chance — with the prosecutors, judge . . . and jury — delivering a constitutional-criminal law lecture in the form of jury selection questions."

Willard replied, "The prosecution would have worsened

their position by complaining, and the judge had no stake in it."

"True, and I think the jury would have resented a prosecution objection. On the contrary, what I saw was appreciation and understanding, in the form of smiles, posture, nodding, confidence and comfort. Your colloquy with Kaufman was classic and underscored the saying that 'knowledge is power'. And you did it several more times."

"Thank you."

"The best comes now, with the DA's and your opening statements. By then, as at the preliminary hearing, it was clear that because the prosecution had no case, they had nothing to say in the DA's opening statement. Quintana's was a disaster, basically promising again to prove that the defendant lay in wait for the victim and 'mutilated him to death'. Most of the jurors had tuned her out from word-one, and they seemed to me more than bored, especially Juror 3, Esteban, the La Fonda Hotel manager."

"What's 'more than bored'?"

"Fatally disinterested. That was bad enough, but what came next was the coup de grâce."

"I know," Willard said, modestly. "I could feel it."

"My God," Davis said. "Four hundred years ago, Spain, New Spain, Mexico, New Mexico, stolen land grants, Tierra Amarilla . . . and tying it all into the mining company, its representative Carranza, and then Castellano and the shooting . . . bravo!"

"Thank you," Willard said again. "I have my own reaction to the jury because I was talking directly to them, not focused on cross examining a witness, but I want your reaction."

"You must have seen it, talking sometimes to all of them, and sometimes individually. Some, especially the Hispanos, seemed angry, a few livid. Even the non-Hispanos seemed bothered. But none of them looked like they tumbled to what you intend to do, nor did the judge. Certainly not those incompetents at the defense table."

Modestly, Jon asked, "What do you think I intend to do?"

"You injected the land grants into the case for at least one reason I can think of, although I believe there is more than one."

I really like this woman, Jon thought. *She's shown with her analysis real smarts and hasn't yet asked a single question.*

Davis said, "You suckered the prosecution into getting the land grants into the case, as a backup for a hung jury. You're going to put the land grand thefts on trial, and hook at least one juror. If the jury is hung, the case will never be tried again. The DA may be stupid, but even she is not that stupid. Also, I think you want to use this case to expose the wrongdoing and shattered lives caused by the stolen land grants."

Willard simply smiled, and said, "Finish your pizza and beer, and then ask your questions. But remember we have not yet agreed about what is and is not on the record."

"How are you going to present the defense case?"

"With experts, of course."

"What a surprise. That's no answer."

"I wanted to see how persistent you would be."

"Very."

"Okay. Only we are still not on the record. I have two witnesses. One may be the best land surveyor in New Mexico, and certainly is concerning the Tierra Amarilla land grant. In essence, he will testify that Rachel's home in Abiquiu is on the Tierra Amarilla land grant and her leased property is deep into it."

Thinking, Davis said, "Give me a minute to digest this."

"Take all the time you like," he said.

"Okay," she said, "let me do this out loud. Rachel Castellano's land and home are on the old Tierra Amarilla land grant. Assuming New Mexico law requires for use of the Castle Doctrine self-defense and habitat justification defenses that the shooter must own the land, the jury can decide that Castellano *does* own it because it was stolen from her ancestors. In effect, the jury can nullify the thefts that occurred hundreds of years ago. Your jury can make a statement about a colossal wrong that occurred way back in time."

"Yes, but hold it there for a minute.

"My next witness will be an academic authority on land grants in general — California, Arizona, Texas — and especially in New Mexico. His testimony will explain how the grants were stolen, when, by whom, and how at least *morally,* if not legally, the descendants of the original grantees still owned the grants."

"Let me sort this out again," Davis said, anxious to speak. "In the context of a first-degree murder case, you will have obtained a New Mexico jury's factual finding that Rachel's land — and by implication, many others' — was stolen. For at least this case, a New Mexico jury will have nullified centuries-old illegal land transfers. Jesus, Willard, that's brilliant."

"There's one more point. Remember, everything you've just understood is premised on the *assumption* that under New Mexico law the defendant must be the owner."

"Right," she said, "are you implying that's not the law?"

"I am more than implying it. I am saying that flat out, and I will prove it."

"Wow! Can you do all that?"

"Remember, it was the prosecution who introduced 'ownership', and the judge who ruled it is a fact question for the jury."

"True."

"To be honest there is something about my experts' testimony I'm not telling you because I want your fresh assessment of how the jury reacts. One piece of advance notice, however. It will not be at the beginning of their testimony, but the end."

"Okay, got it."

"Any more questions?" he asked.

"None. And this is *all* off the record. I can write my story tonight from what I know already, add to it after your witnesses' testimony, and get it to AP immediately. I thank you for the scoop, and transparency. And trust."

CHAPTER 66

JUDGE HORACE BALDWIN SAT IN his chambers looking out the window at the Santa Fe National Cemetery across the street, with its acres of white crosses and Stars of David where interred lay the fallen who served their country in all its wars, declared and undeclared, known and clandestine. He was free associating and thinking about the first-degree murder case he was trying, and defense lawyer Jon Willard.

When Espanola attorney Emmanuel Salazar initially entered his appearance as attorney for the defendant, Horace was surprised because Manny hardly practiced law. He certainly was not a trial lawyer, let alone capable of defending a first-degree murder charge.

When Salazar moved Willard's admission *pro hac vice,* the situation clarified. Manny would assist from the second seat, while Willard would represent the defendant.

And he's doing a hell of a job, Horace thought. *Not because the DA is doing such a crappy job, but because he's one of the finest lawyers I've ever seen in private practice or from the bench. Which makes me wonder what's next. The prosecution has rested, so Willard has two choices. He can call witnesses or make a motion for a directed verdict of acquittal.*

The prosecution is pathetic and is not going to get any better because it has rested. No more witnesses. If Willard makes that acquittal motion, I will have to grant it or be reversed on appeal. From the prosecution's own witnesses and Willard's cross examination, it's clear to a blind man that the shooting was in self-defense and in defense of habitation.

So, if Willard makes the motion, the case ends now. What are the consequences to me? The anti-gun crowd and others are going to be madder than hell, and I'm up for re-election in eight months.

On the other hand, if I deny Willard's motion, not only is he not hurt, but he has two more bites at the apple if he wants them. He can renew his motion for the directed acquittal at the end of the presentation of the defense case. Or even after a guilty verdict.

If at the close of the defense's case, he doesn't make the motion again, or does but I deny it again, and there is a guilty verdict, he could move to overrule the jury and I could grant the acquittal then. If I did that, I could deliver a long explanation of why I did it. Interests of justice. That sort of thing.

On the other, other hand, if there's a not guilty verdict, I will never have had to rule on any one of his three acquittal motions. Instead of my having said the defendant was not guilty, the jury would have said it.

But Willard must know all this, so why would he make any of the motions?

Because he has an ulterior motive, something else that he's trying to accomplish. Well, que sera, sera. What will be, will be.

CHAPTER 67

THE JUDGE HAD GIVEN THE court officer instructions not to seat the jury because there might be a motion to dispose of first.

When he ascended the bench and counsel were at their respective tables, Judge Baldwin asked Jon if he was going to call his first witness or would like to make a motion.

"May it please the court," Jon said, "at this time, the defense elects to move pursuant to New Mexico Statute 30, Article 2, Section 8 for a directed verdict of not guilty for the defendant Rachel Castellano. If I may, Your Honor, I would like to submit a short memorandum in support of my motion and request oral argument."

He's sending me a message. There's no way I can't accept the memo or deny argument in support of, and opposition to, his motion.

"Granted."

The court officer gave a copy to the prosecutors and handed one up to the judge.

The judge called a five-minute recess while he read the memorandum, and then reconvened.

"May it please the court," Willard began, "The directed verdict statute provides that 'When any person is prosecuted for a *homicide*, and upon his trial the killing shall be found to have been excusable or *justifiable*, the jury *shall* find such person not guilty and he shall be discharged.'"

"I have in my memorandum, and now orally, deliberately emphasized those two words, *homicide* and *justifiable*. New

Mexico cases have held the meaning of Section 8 to be that the words *homicide* and *justifiable* are the only elements necessary to trigger the statute. We certainly have a homicide here."

Some laughter from the audience.

"That leaves the one word, *justifiable*. Section 7A states that 'Homicide is *justifiable* . . . when committed in the necessary defense of his life, his family or his property or necessarily defending against any unlawful action directed against himself. . . .'"

"Section 7B states that homicide is justifiable 'When committed in the lawful defense of himself . . . and when there is a reasonable ground to believe a design exists to commit a felony or to do some great personal injury . . . and there is imminent danger that the design will be accomplished. . . .'"

"Thus, Sections 7A and B, are the classic, Castle Doctrine self-defense statute."

"The defense argues that under the facts presented by the *prosecution itself,* and those elicited on cross examination by the defense, which has not yet presented our direct case, there is more than ample evidence that the requisite criteria exist for my motion to be granted."

"Thank you, Mr. Willard. Madam District Attorney, do you wish to respond?"

Fred Zimmerman stood. "May it please the court, the prosecution believes that when the directed verdict statute provides the 'jury' shall find the defendant not guilty, it means the 'jury.'"

"Mr. Willard," the judge said, looking relieved.

"Just one brief comment, Your Honor. New Mexico case law, and this is in our memorandum, has held the word 'jury' after presentation of the State's case, or for that matter after the defense case, or for that matter after a jury guilty verdict, cannot and does not mean the *jury*. It means the *judge*, who under no circumstances can force a jury to do anything. The few New Mexico cases that have addressed the issue hold that the word jury is a 'stand-in' for the judge, who has the power to let the jury decide, or not. Thank you, Your Honor."

"Interesting motion and arguments," the judge said with a straight face. "But it is early in this trial and as Mr. Willard mentioned, so far we have only the prosecution's case as evidence. I am denying Mr. Willard's motion, subject to renewal."

Inwardly, Jon Willard, Esq. thought, *Thank heaven Baldwin denied my motion! If by some fluke, there is a guilty verdict, denial of this motion will get a reversal on appeal. Another insurance policy.*

The prosecutors, wrongly, thought they had won a major victory.

CHAPTER 68

ANNY SALAZAR, WHO HAD NOT been on his feet in a courtroom in years, said in a strong voice, "The defense calls Carlos Santiago."

A tall, deeply tanned man in corduroy pants, a denim shirt and work boots, seemingly in his early sixties, entered from the side door next to the jury box. After the witness had been sworn and was seated, Manny began his direct examination.

"Please state your name and occupation for the record."

"Carlos Santiago. I am the owner and principal of Santiago & Sons." His voice was strong, the tone authoritative.

"By the way, Mr. Santiago," Manny asked, deliberately sounding puzzled, "why are you dressed like that?"

Titters throughout the courtroom.

Acting a bit embarrassed, Santiago said, "When I finish here, I have to head out to the field. Near a swamp."

"What work does Santiago & Sons do, sir?" Manny asked.

"We are the oldest land surveying firm in New Mexico."

"By 'oldest' what do you mean?"

"My grandfather, father, and I have been land surveying since before the Territory of New Mexico became a State in 1912."

"I know it's a long time ago, but do you know how your grandfather and father became land surveyors?"

"Well, Mr. Salazar," the witness said, smiling, "there's a saying, 'be careful what you ask for . . .' I mention that because land surveying is an ancient scientific practice that dates back at least to 1,400 B.C., to the time of the Egyptians. I'm sure you don't want me to start there, so my answer is that at the turn of the Twentieth Century my grandfather learned land surveying as an apprentice to a land surveyor who learned from someone before him, far, far back into antiquity when some Egyptian figured out how to use a knotted rope to measure distances."

"Did you apprentice with your father?"

"I did, sir."

"In modern times, can one become a recognized land surveyor through an academic program, that combines apprenticeship and field work?"

"Yes, sir, my father insisted, because we don't use knotted ropes anymore."

Laughter through the courtroom.

"I have an Associate of Science degree in land surveying."

A few minutes before, Fred Zimmerman finally realized that Santiago was doing so well as both a likeable personality and expert in land surveying, that the jury would believe him if he testified that two plus two equaled five. So, Zimmerman rose and said, "Your Honor, learning about the Egyptians was very interesting, but the State will concede that Mr. Santiago is an expert in land surveying."

"Mr. Salazar?" Judge Baldwin said.

"Thank you, Mr. Zimmerman, for your concession, but with your indulgence I have just a few more questions for the record, to qualify Mr. Santiago as an expert witness in land surveying."

Zimmerman reluctantly nodded "okay."

"Mr. Santiago, are you a dues-paying member of the British Royal Society of Worldwide Chartered Surveyors and its United States equivalent?"

"Yes."

"For what task were you hired by Ms. Castellano?"

"To ascertain whether the land on which her home in

Abiquiu stands, and the land she leases for her sheep herd, was part of the original Tierra Amarilla land grant."

"Did you reach a conclusion?" Willard asked, looking at the jury, some of whose members were looking at him, not the witness.

"Absolutely."

Willard let the tension mount, slowly asking the witness, "In reaching your conclusion that Ms. Castellano's owned and leased property lies within the original boundaries of the Tierra Amarilla land grant, what tools and data did you use?"

"For tools, modern electronic and digital instruments. For other data, documents including maps that survived the period of Mexican colonization and post-Territorial land transactions."

"Can you demonstrate to the jury where the original Tierra Amarilla land grant was, how it was carved up, and where today Ms. Castellano's owned and leased property is located in relation to the land grant?"

"Yes, sir, I can, and I did. In a narrated slideshow."

With that, Jon turned to the judge and signaled to Andrea, who left the courtroom.

"May it please the court, Your Honor, the defense will now prove surveyor Santiago's expert opinion is well grounded. The defense offers as our Exhibit 1 the slideshow our expert, Mr. Santiago, has just testified he created."

As Jon spoke, Andrea reentered the courtroom accompanied by two men pushing a gurney on which there was various electronic audio-video equipment. Two other men carried a large screen.

Seeing this, the judge asked, "How long is the presentation, Mr. Willard?"

"Twenty-nine minutes."

"How long will your people take to set this up?"

"Twenty minutes, maximum. They have been scoping out

the courtroom and know exactly where to place the screen and audio-video equipment."

"Okay," the judge said, "while that's happening, we'll have a thirty-minute recess. The jury can leave the box."

"By the way, Your Honor, at the conclusion of the slideshow I will have no further direct questions for the witness."

* * *

The slideshow was a *tour de force*. With maps, overlays, directions, colorizations, arrows, and text, it included a non-technical narration by Carlos Santiago himself that laypersons could easily understand. Twenty-nine minutes after his slideshow began, no fair person could think that Rachel's owned, and leased property stood anywhere but on land that had been stolen from her ancestors.

When the lights came on, several jurors — Gomez, the K1 teacher, and Harrison, the retired history teacher — were obviously impressed.

On behalf of the defense, Manny moved that the Santiago slideshow be received in evidence, and the judge so ordered. Defendant's Exhibit 1.

Manny then turned to the prosecutor and said, "Your witness, Madam District Attorney."

The jurors stared at her with anticipation. Maria Quintana paused, and said in a barely audible voice, "No questions."

With that, Santiago's testimony had one prong of the defense nailed. Now, if the jury wanted to nullify the moral wrong of crooks stealing land grants and acquit Rachel for that reason alone, without regard to evidence or the lack of it, the last twenty minutes gave them ample justification to do so.

CHAPTER 69

"THE DEFENSE CALLS DR. FELIPE Ortiz."

After the usual formalities, the dignified witness took the stand with the aid of a cane. He was a short, thin elderly man with a trimmed white beard and hair to match. Dressed impeccably in a blue serge suit, he wore a white shirt and a paisley bow tie.

Manny said, "Good morning, doctor, please tell the jury why I refer to you as 'doctor'."

Replying in a low, raspy voice, Dr. Ortiz said, "In addition to my B.A., and Masters' degree from Stamford, I have a Ph.D. from Harvard. All are in American Southwest history."

"You have taught for many years."

"Many."

"Where have you taught in the last ten years, and where are you teaching now?"

"At the University of New Mexico, where I have an endowed chair in the history department, and where for years past I was chairman of the department."

"What is your specialization? History is a vast subject."

"Vast indeed, Mr. Salazar. I am recognized nationally as an authority on land grants throughout the United States, and the Tierra Amarilla land grants in particular."

"Have you written and published in that specialization?"

"Indeed, four books and scores, maybe hundreds, of articles, reviews, and such."

"Lectures?"

"Many, many."

"In addition to writing, have you compiled the history of land grants in New Mexico in any other format?"

"I have. In a narrated slideshow entitled 'Spanish-Mexican-American Land Grants: Centuries of Dishonor, Deprivation, and Displacement."

Willard turned to the judge, "May it please the court, Your Honor, we offer as defense Exhibit 2 the narrated land grants slideshow our expert, Dr. Ortiz, has just testified he created."

"How long is it?"

"Forty minutes, Your Honor."

"Let's see it."

Forty minutes later Willard noticed a few jurors had moist eyes, and more than a few looked angry.

Dr. Ortiz's documentary had supplied details about when, where, why, how, and by whom the land grants were made through the centuries, and the criminality and incompetence that cost countless Hispanos and their ancestors their lands, livelihoods, and faith in the United States of America. The impact of Dr. Ortiz's documentary on most of the jury and spectators, and perhaps the judge, was palpable.

Having learned its lesson with the surveyor, the prosecution had no objection to defense Exhibit 2 being accepted into evidence.

CHAPTER 70

AFTER A TWENTY-MINUTE RECESS, JUDGE Baldwin told Willard that if he had any more witnesses, he should call the next one. The defense team — Rachel and Manny at their table, and Andrea and Nick in the spectator's section — smiled. They knew what was coming next.

Willard stood, and said, "The defense calls Frederick Paul Zimmerman."

The DA and her Chief Deputy jumped to their feet and began objecting in such an incoherent babble that the judge had to intervene.

"Whoa," he said firmly. "Stop and sit."

They did.

Judge Baldwin turned to Willard, who stood, but before Jon could speak the judge said, "Mr. Willard, you are much too experienced a trial lawyer to engage in stunts, and invite me to hold you in contempt, so sit down, relax, like the prosecutors over there, and listen carefully. I am assuming you are serious and have a good reason for calling Mr. Zimmerman as a defense witness."

"Thank you, Your Honor, for the confidence. I believe I'm well within the New Mexico and New York ethical standards I agreed to observe when you admitted me *pro hac vice* to try this case."

"Okay, as the lawyers here know," the judge said to the jury, "there are two kinds of witnesses, *fact* and *expert*. For the jury's benefit, an example of a fact witness would be someone standing on a street corner who observed a motorist run a red light. Or, in this case, the deputy sheriff who testified about conversations and the crime scene. As to the other kind, expert witnesses, the defense has already called two individuals who possess specialized knowledge."

Willard was about to speak when the judge held up his hand and said, "I assume, Mr. Willard, that you are calling Mr. Zimmerman as an expert witness. If so, please explain."

"Thank you, Your Honor. The defense is calling Mr. Zimmerman as an expert on New Mexico criminal law, in response to either deliberate or ignorant misstatements of that law given by the District Attorney in her opening remarks and presentation of the prosecution's witnesses— misstatements which could have irreparably misled the jury and not be corrected by your instructions."

Well, that takes the cake, the judge thought. *Never in all my years have I heard anything like that. As I understand what Willard is saying, it's that in her opening statement the DA misstated the law, probably about his defenses of self-defense and habitat justification. So, Willard wants an expert — Quintana's Chief Deputy, no less! — to correct that misstatement with Zimmerman's expert testimony about New Mexico criminal law because the Uniform Jury Instructions I must give might not be enough to adequately make the corrections.*

As a trial judge, I have great latitude over witnesses and evidence, so I could probably get away with disallowing his attempt to correct the prosecution's misleading of the jury with the expert counter-testimony of its own prosecutor. But if there's a 'not guilty' verdict, which I expect, whatever I ruled on here will not matter.

"Madam District Attorney," the judge said, "because Mr. Zimmerman is the subject of this evidentiary dispute, I'll hear from you. If you object to Mr. Willard calling Mr. Zimmerman, please state your grounds."

Nearly tongue-tied, the best Quintana could do was a semi-coherent statement that she "Never heard of this . . .not law school . . . doesn't seem right . . . my employee . . . Fred not want to. . . ."

When she had finished, the judge said, "I am going to allow it, but if somehow Mr. Willard's examination of Mr. Zimmerman gets out of hand, I will end it."

To Fred Zimmerman's great chagrin, he heard Willard say, "The defense calls Frederick Paul Zimmerman."

Willard's first question — actually, bait — was not to Zimmerman, but to the DA. "Can we stipulate, Madam District Attorney, that the witness is an expert in New Mexico criminal law, without the need for me to establish that with my questions and Mr. Zimmerman's answers?"

Zimmerman and the judge suppressed smiles.

"Are you kidding?" the DA blurted out, causing some jurors to laugh, others to hide smiles, and the judge to scribble on his yellow legal pad.

"Of course," she said, "that's why I kept him on when I was elected DA. He's the smartest criminal lawyer in town, maybe the entire state."

Quintana was oblivious that she was digging her hole deeper and deeper.

Willard's first question to Zimmerman was, "Is it fair to say that the case of *State* v. *Bailey* in the Supreme Court of New Mexico is *a,* perhaps *the,* bedrock case on Castle Doctrine self-defense and the related, but entirely different, law of defense of habitation?"

"Yes." Zimmerman knew where this was going and was determined to play it down the middle. His future might depend on it.

"Do you know when that case was decided?"

"Early 1920s."

"How about 1921?"

"Okay, 1921."

"The two defenses — self-defense, and defense of habitation — are almost identical, are they not?"

"Yes."

"I am quoting now from the New Mexico Supreme Court's *unanimous* opinion in *State* v. *Bailey*. 'There is . . . the common principle in both [defenses] . . . *that it is the necessity of preventing the commission of a felony which justifies the killing of the assailant.*' In your expert opinion, Mr. Zimmerman, is that still good law in New Mexico?"

"Yes."

"And the *Bailey* case was followed by *State* v. *Couch* in 1946, where the New Mexico Supreme Court cited with favor a Mississippi *shotgun* homicide case. In the Mississippi case, the court wrote 'the home is one of the most important institutions of the state, and has ever been regarded as a place where a person has a right to stand his ground and repel, force by force, to the extent necessary for its protection. In early English law, it was a man's castle to which he might retire and defy the whole world.' Is that still the law in New Mexico?"

"Yes, but with certain minor exceptions. Fundamentally, yes."

"Is it true that in the *Couch* case the New Mexico Supreme Court relied heavily on the 1921 *Bailey* case, quoting extensively from it?"

"Yes."

"My last question about New Mexico case law is whether since *Bailey* in 1921, through *Couch* in 1946, and as you and I are in this courtroom today, the New Mexico law of self-defense — the so-called Castle Doctrine, and the separate, but similar, defense of habitation — has remained the same?"

"Yes, as I said, with certain minor exceptions, fundamentally, yes."

"Shifting gears, Mr. Zimmerman, do you know of any New Mexico statute or judicial decision that requires an assailant to have been *inside* the would-be victim's home in order for her or him to invoke either or both of those defenses?"

"No. there is no statutory or case law to that effect. *Bailey, Couch,* and their successors suggest the opposite."

"Is it fair to say that case law in New Mexico when discussing self-defense and defense of habitation in the context of 'ownership' randomly, interchangeably, and sloppily use the following words, depending on the facts of the case: 'occupant,' 'home,' 'dwelling,' 'owner,' 'office,' 'apartment,' and other such places?"

"I pass, Mr. Willard, on 'sloppily', but as to the rest of it, regrettably, yes."

"Last question, Mr. Zimmerman. Do you know of any New Mexico statute or judicial decision that requires that the victim of an attack, whether inside or outside of his or her residence, be the fee owner of the property in which the victim resides?"

"No, there is no such statute or judicial decision."

"Your witness, Madam District Attorney," Willard said, with evident satisfaction.

Maria Quintana quickly said, "No questions."

"You may step down, Mr. Zimmerman," Willard said, "and thank you for your candor and cooperation."

"Fifteen-minute recess," Judge Baldwin said, with relief.

Back in his chambers, Judge Horace Baldwin stared at the cemetery and thought, *I never sold Willard short, but with every gambit he's smarter than the one before. His direct examination of Zimmerman has boxed me in on the instructions I must give the jury, not that I wouldn't give the same ones myself. How in hell is Zimmerman now going to argue any New Mexico law to help the prosecution's case? Willard's direct examination made that clear.*

CHAPTER 71

"**M**R. WILLARD," THE JUDGE ASKED, "do you have another witness?"

"No, Your Honor. The defense rests."

"Counsel, please approach the bench. Mr. Court Officer, please escort the jurors into the jury room."

They filed out.

"Any motions, Mr. Willard?"

"May it please the court, the defense renews its motion for a directed verdict pursuant to New Mexico Statute 30, Article 2, Sections 7A and 8, based on all the evidence."

Silently, Willard prayed the judge would deny it as he had after the State's case.

"Same ruling as earlier. I am going to let the jury decide."

Whew. Cleared that hurdle for the second time, Willard thought. *We're going to the jury with the stolen land grants.*

"Thank you, Your Honor."

The four lawyers stood before the judge, who said, "Next order of business is my instructions to the jury. Are you ready? Have counsel been consulting to find common ground?" he asked.

As a matter of professional courtesy, and to put the prosecution on the spot, Willard remained silent as the judge looked at Quintana and Zimmerman, who spoke first. "Not yet, Your Honor, we wanted to hear the defense case first."

"Mr. Willard?"

"Your Honor, the defense is ready to go right now."

"Tell you what," the judge said, "let's send the jury

home. Each of you retire to your respective corners, consult at 3:00 pm. here in the courtroom and agree on what you can. We will reconvene at 8:30 a.m. tomorrow, I will referee disagreements, and decide who wins and who loses. Then my instructions, your closing arguments, and I give the case to the jury."

CHAPTER 72

I N ACCORDANCE WITH THE JUDGE'S directions, counsel met that afternoon and reached agreement on what instructions Judge Baldwin should give to the jury

They convened the next morning at 8:30 a.m. in the absence of the jury, and the DA reported that there was no disagreement. Both sides were in accord with the standard constitutional instructions: Presumed innocence; proof beyond a reasonable doubt; unanimous jury verdict; Rachel Castellano's right to remain silent without inferences being drawn.

Willard reported to the judge that both sides agreed on various New Mexico Uniform Jury Instructions: General criminal intent; proof beyond a reasonable doubt of every statutory requirement for murder in the first degree.

When Willard was finished, he said there two final Uniform Jury Instructions. He had saved them for last because they were the core of Rachel Castellano's defenses. The prosecution had grudgingly agreed to both. Willard would emphasize the important words.

The first one was the Uniform Jury Instruction for *conventional Castle Doctrine self-defense*:

An appearance of immediate danger or death or great bodily harm to the defendant, and the defendant was in fact put in fear by the apparent danger of immediate bodily harm and killed the assailant because of that fear, and a reasonable person in the same circumstances as the defendant would have acted as the defendant did.

Crucial to this instruction was the last sentence:

The *burden* is on the *state* to prove *beyond a reasonable doubt* that the defendant *did not* act in self-defense. If you [the jury] have a reasonable doubt as to whether the defendant acted in self-defense, you *must* find the defendant *not guilty.*

Willard's second important Uniform Jury Instruction was *defense of habitation:*

A killing is *justified* if the home was being used as the defendant's dwelling and it *appeared to the defendant* that the commission of murder was *immediately* at hand and that it was *necessary to kill the intruder* to prevent the commission of such murder, and a reasonable person in the same circumstances as the defendant would have acted as the defendant did.

Again, crucial to this instruction was the last sentence:

The *burden* is on the *state* to prove *beyond a reasonable doubt* that the defendant *did not* kill in defense of her home. If you have a *reasonable doubt* as to whether the defendant acted in self-defense, you *must* find the defendant *not guilty.*

The jury was seated promptly at 9:00 a.m.

After greeting them, Judge Baldwin said, "Ladies and gentlemen of the jury, you have heard the evidence as presented by the prosecution and the defense, and now it is my duty to instruct you as to the law you must follow in this case."

Forty minutes later, the judge had finished in accordance with what the law required, and the lawyers had agreed on.

He then said, "Ladies and gentlemen, Uniform Jury Instruction 14-104 requires me to say that it is time for the lawyers to make their closing arguments to you. Please understand that all the evidence, including exhibits, has been presented, and there will be no more. Those exhibits will be available to you during deliberations. Counsel's arguments are not evidence. Their closing statements are an opportunity for them to discuss that evidence and the

New Mexico law I have just given you. Procedurally, the prosecution goes first, then the defense, and then the prosecution may, but need not, reply."

CHAPTER 73

MARIA QUINTANA, ELECTED DISTRICT ATTORNEY for New Mexico's Santa Fe County, stood at the prosecution's table, her notes on the podium that had been placed there at her request. She was dressed as a young female lawyer was expected to look, severely cut dark pants-suit, white blouse, and modest silver necklace. Her dark brown hair was pulled back from her face, which looked worried.

In one respect, Willard was surprised to see the DA herself ready to make the prosecution's closing statement. Although the prosecution had no case, Fred Zimmerman could have made it sound as if it did. On the other hand, Willard figured that the DA was looking for glory, oblivious that her closing statement would display even more of her incompetence and that she had no case. The same worried look appeared on the faces of her parents, sitting in the second row of spectators.

In the end, the DA's closing statement was worse than her performance at the preliminary hearing and in her opening statement. Essentially, she embellished her opening, emphasizing that the defendant lay in wait for the deceased, and when he tried to enter, murdered him. Quintana used the same phrase, "mutilated him to death" as she had in her opening statement. She summarized the prosecution's witnesses' testimony, ignored Willard's cross examination and his experts, and did not once use the words "justification," "self-defense" or "defense of habitation."

If the DA's opening statement had been a disaster, her closing statement was a disaster squared, pathetic in the extreme.

Observing the debacle, a thought Willard had after the DA's opening statement crossed his mind again, something he often encountered at trials. *Whether thinking of Aristotle who held that "A is A," things are what they are, or the common saying "chickens have come home to roost," or Ayn Rand who defined "justice," as getting what one deserves, he was witnessing the phenomenon in action.*

When she finished, saying, "Thank you for your attention, ladies and gentlemen of the jury," Willard stood, unbuttoned his jacket, and moved slowly to the jury box.

The previous evening, he had discussed his closing statement with Andrea, Manny, and Rachel. He knew what he was going to say but wanted their reactions both as a courtesy and because perhaps they could add something useful.

As Willard neared the jury box, he stopped at a respectable distance and shook his head from side-to-side, as if saying "no," "no," "no."

Several jurors immediately smiled, as if in silent agreement.

"Well, ladies and gentlemen, this is the last time I'll be speaking to you, formally at least, so, I want to thank you for serving as jurors in this first-degree murder case. Today may set a record for the shortest closing statement Jon Willard, Esq. has ever made in some fifteen years."

Smiles, chuckles, and laughs.

"In my opening statement, I made you three promises."

"*One*, starting with my cross examination of the prosecution's first witness and as the trial moved forward, that you would see the huge holes and misstatements in the District Attorney's opening statement, such as it was."

"*Two*, even though the prosecution has the burden of proof as Judge Baldwin has instructed you, I promised that

279

my cross examination of the prosecution's witnesses would show you, even without any additional evidence from the defense, that Rachel Castellano's shooting of Carranza was far from murder, but self-defense of herself and in justifiable defense of her home."

"*Third*, I promised that when you knew all the facts and that Rachel Castellano was innocent, you would wonder why the District Attorney of Santa Fe County brought this fake case, charging an innocent New Mexico artist with first-degree murder because she had the courage and skill to kill her crazed would-be killer. To save her own life."

A few jurors nodded their heads, remembering.

"It is up to you now to decide whether I kept my promises."

CHAPTER 74

IMMEDIATELY AFTER WILLARD FINISHED HIS brief closing statement, Judge Baldwin addressed the jury, saying, "Ladies and gentlemen, we began this morning at 9:00 a.m. I instructed you on the law, and the prosecution and defense have made their closing statements. It is now 11:25 a.m., and the case is ready for you begin deliberations. Soon, the time for lunch will rear its head, so I want some guidance from you as to what would be most comfortable. As I see it, I can give you the case now, wait until after lunch, have lunch sent in, or handle it any other way you like. So, take a few minutes, put your heads together, and let me know what you prefer. We will stand in recess until then."

The twelve jurors and four alternates filed out of the jury box, counsel and the spectators remained in place, and the judge retired to his chambers.

Willard, Manny, and Rachel stood to stretch their legs, and looked at the spectators. The DA's parents were still in the second row, looking drawn and unhappy. Andrea and Nick were sitting together in animated conversation. Emiliano and Lorraine Romero were chatting with Tom Ramirez and Stan Horden. Manny and Rachel walked over to Pablo Gallegos. The AP reporter was off in a corner talking to David Trujillo, while Walt Duran and Rose Castellano sat together looking pensive. The courtroom buffs were well represented, and Rachel saw some familiar faces, but could not place them.

Suddenly, the court officer shouted, "All rise," and as the

judge took the bench everyone else returned to the seats, the prosecutors never having left theirs.

"I have just received a note from the jury foreperson. They want to begin deliberation now, and have lunch sent in about 1:00 p.m. I will honor that request. Thus, Mr. Court Officer, please tell them so, and ask the four alternates to return to the courtroom."

When they appeared, the judge thanked them for their service, discharged them, and made a personal request, saying, "You folks are free to go, and can talk to anyone you wish, including about this case, but I beseech you not to do so until your former colleagues have rendered their verdict, been polled, and I have discharged them. Justice will be served if you do so. Thank you again."

All four agreed and asked if they could remain in the courtroom. The judge's answer was, emphatically, "Yes, but with the other spectators."

Usually, when a case is submitted to the jury, the judge retires to his chambers and the lawyers head for various locations where they can be contacted once there is a verdict. From emanations, penumbras, facial expressions, and body language Willard had been receiving from some of the jurors, as well as having anxiously waited for other verdicts for fifteen years, Willard believed these would take an early vote to get a consensus, maybe peruse the exhibits, iron out any questions, make sure they were on solid, unanimous ground — have lunch, of course — and come in with a "not guilty" verdict about an hour later.

Accordingly, the team adjourned to the attorneys' room, and ordered their lunch. Like everyone else, they waited.

Because Willard's assessment was correct, at 3:12 p.m. the court officer began getting the spectators back into their seats. Once that was accomplished, he said, "All rise," and Judge Baldwin took the bench, saying "Mr. Court Officer, please bring in the jury."

In all trials, criminal and civil, that is the moment all eyes in the courtroom are lasered on individual jurors in an attempt to learn the verdict. Smiles, frowns, looking or not looking at the defendant and lawyers. Sometimes one can tell, sometimes not. Sometimes, the analyzers are fooled. It is a very tense time, especially in a criminal trial, let alone in a first-degree murder case.

When the jury was seated, each member conscientiously trying not to give away the verdict with facial or body movements, the judge said, "Mr. Foreperson, I understand the jury has reached a verdict."

Sergeant Ernest Kaufman, Juror 1, stood holding the verdict form.

"Yes, we have, Your Honor."

"Please hand it to Mr. Court Officer."

The judge looked at it for about twenty seconds, his face as frozen as Thomas Jefferson's on Mt. Rushmore, returned it to the court officer, who handed it to the jury foreperson.

"Please read it, Mr. Foreperson," said the judge.

"We the jury, in case number CR 9538-9076, District Court, Santa Fe County, State of New Mexico, Indictment No. 110-5978, on the charge of murder first degree, find the defendant, Rachel Castellano, not guilty."

While the defense team maintained professional restraint, in the spectators' section it was different, best described as shouts, handshakes hugs, congratulations, relief and more.

Maria Quintana was crestfallen, ruined by dysfunction.

Against the noisy background of the spectator section, Rachel and Manny wept, while embracing.

As Willard smiled knowingly, they drew him into their embrace.

Judge Baldwin still looked like Jefferson. He let the celebration continue for a few minutes so the pent-up pressure from waiting could dissipate, and then gaveled until he had what resembled quiet. He said to the jury, "You have just heard your foreperson read the 'not guilty' verdict. Please stand as I call your name, and state whether that is your uncoerced verdict."

One at a time, each juror did.

"Ms. Castellano," Judge Horace Baldwin said sincerely, "I apologize on behalf of the judicial system of Santa Fe County that you had to endure this senseless perversion of justice. Prosecutors, the caretakers of that precious bedrock of our Republic, should be more careful about how they wield the trust invested in them by the public. You are free to go, with the court's best wishes."

Baldwin continued. "Please bear with me, jurors, I have a few housekeeping tasks to attend to. First, to the jury, a job well done for the defendant, for justice, for our great state, for the United States of America. Next, the jury is discharged; any member who wishes to be removed from the jury rolls for five years should see the court clerk. Bail is cancelled and will be returned as soon as the court clerk processes the paperwork."

The judge banged his gavel twice, and said, "This court stands adjourned."

Bedlam again. Willard's team, some jurors, many spectators, were all over each other with handshakes, congratulations, tears, any way they could express their relief for the not guilty verdict. Fred Zimmerman congratulated Willard, Manny, and Rachel, and said to Jon, cryptically, "Let's have lunch one of these days."

"I wouldn't miss it. I'll call," Jon said. "And bring your shovel," Manny said, "and we'll autograph it."

The three lawyers laughed.

Willard was probably one of the few people in the courtroom who realized the judge had skipped saying something routinely complimentary about the lawyers, but Jon understood why. He also understood why during the chaos in the courtroom the court officer handed him a note from the judge, saying, "At your convenience, please stop by my chambers."

Judge Horace Baldwin wanted a postmortem.

CHAPTER 75

AFTER THE PROSECUTORS LEFT AND the congratulations subsided, Willard told the team about the judge's note. The court officer escorted him to the door next to the bench, and then to Judge Baldwin's chambers.

On the telephone, Baldwin signaled Willard to come in, pointed to a sideboard holding a coffeemaker, soft drinks, and nuts, and then a large couch.

Willard understood, helped himself to coffee and a cup full of nuts, and sat down on the couch. The judge's telephone conversation apparently had something to do with making arrangements for a massage, so Willard felt no need to tune it out.

When the judge finished, Willard jumped up, saying, "Your Honor. . . ."

Baldwin smiled, walked over, extended his right hand, and said, "No need for that, the case is over. It's 'Horace'."

"Then it's 'Jon'," Willard said, as the men shook hands.

The judge sat down in a large leather chair opposite the couch.

"I wanted to meet you off the grid, so to speak, for several reasons, Jon, and I assumed you probably have a few questions you would like to ask me."

"More than a few."

"Okay, so I'll go first. There is an indirect connection between us, although we never met. It runs through Jim."

"Jim?" Willard asked, puzzled for a moment. Then it registered. "Jim, Jim Thomason?"

"Correct," Horace said, smiling.

Jon knew how Horace had a connection with Thomason, thanks to the Pinkerton detectives' report. But not wanting to disclose anything about his investigations, he said, "Well, Jim has been a lot of places. Let me guess. I figured you and I are about the same age, so it must have been Vietnam."

"Correct, again."

Jon saw something he could not identify quickly pass across the judge's face.

Horace continued. "I was in an engineer platoon of the regiment Jim commanded. After all U.N. troops, including you two and the POWs, were evacuated from Firebase Ripper, we came in and destroyed the place."

Reluctantly, Jon asked, "What happened to the hundreds of VC and North Vietnamese dead?"

"Compost," Horace answered, without a hint of regret.

"You kept in contact with Jim all these years?"

"Off and on. If ever we found ourselves in the same place at the same time.

"Matter of fact, when he learned you were coming to Santa Fe, Jim asked me to look you up, which I never got around to doing. But I got a fax from him two days ago, nothing to do with the trial, saying he and Ava were coming out here one of these days. Wants to ask you something face to face."

"Great," Jon said with enthusiasm. "All of us should get together. The trial is over. A 'not guilty' verdict. Dinner should be no problem."

"Not at all," Horace said. "Next, I want to talk about the trial."

"So do I."

"We both knew that Castellano was never going to be convicted. Either 'not guilty', which is what happened, or a hung jury."

"If there had been a hung jury or a guilty verdict," Jon said, "you would have granted my third motion for a directed verdict of acquittal, overriding the jury."

"Yes, I could have granted it after the prosecution rested, based on its lack of direct evidence and what you elicited on cross examination. The shooting was a classic case of Castle Doctrine self-defense and justification because of defense of habitation. After all, the prosecution had the burden of proof, and had failed miserably."

"Why didn't you grant my first motion, after the prosecution rested."

"Did you want me to?"

"No comment."

They laughed.

"Well," the judge said, "it was clear the prosecution wanted to go to the jury, the defendant wanted to go to the jury, she was entitled to go to the jury, so, in the end, she did. Besides, both of your directed verdict motions were out of the jury's hearing, so you were not prejudiced by my denial. Also, on both motions I got the impression that you were not trying too hard, especially because you knew I could grant it after the jury verdict."

"True."

"What's true?"

"All of it," Jon replied.

"I thought so, and that your tactics had something to do with your strategy, which seemed to have something to do with the land grants. I say this because it was clear to me that you suckered the prosecution into allowing your only two expert witnesses — the surveyor and the historian — to show their slideshows, which was clever and very effective. What was that all about?"

"Two things. Primarily to get the land grant issue in front of the American people. Also, to give the jury, which was loaded with Hispanos, to reject a guilty verdict and thus condemn the theft of the land grants."

"Well," Horace said, "you sure exposed the land grant wrongdoing. I read Jane Davis's articles. The entire country knows the truth now."

"My turn," Jon said. "I want to ask you about that. Who the hell are Maria Quintana and Zimmerman, and what the hell was going on there?"

"Well," Horace said, "the Quintana story is not so difficult, Zimmerman's is more complicated. By the way, calling him as your expert witness on New Mexico criminal law was inspired. Not only because you taught the law, but because you locked me in on the instructions I had to give. I almost did not allow it, but you had a plausible argument, barely, so we were both adequately protected."

"How about Quintana?" Jon pressed.

"Maria Quintana's father, Ernie, barely managed to get through UNM law school. If, say, there were two hundred graduates in his class, Ernie would have been number two hundred and one. However, he was smart enough to marry an oil heiress from Carlsbad."

"So, the wife had the money."

"Correct, and the Quintana parents divided the labor in bringing up Maria. Mama's job was to spoil her daughter, indulging her every whim. Daddy's was the same and, when Maria started school, his job description was broadened to include spending money to buy friends for his daughter, and anything else required for his dream for the child. Ernest Quintana, a failed law student, would see his ordinary daughter on the New Mexico Supreme Court. She loved the idea, because then everyone would respect her, and she would have lots of friends. Arrested development."

"That's delusional," Jon said.

"Delusional or not, that was the plan. It started not with acquisition of the necessary skills — philosophy, reading, writing, history, and such — but in college, gut courses and in law school, inattention, lousy grades, and a UNM degree. After graduation, for a while she worked with her father on small-time civil litigation but had no real responsibility. Then Daddy purchased the job for her as an Assistant District Attorney."

"Did she try any important cases?" Jon asked.

"No, it was three years of small misdemeanor cases and closing plea deals negotiated by senior lawyers. Not a single felony, until this one. For murder in the first degree, no less."

"Then the politics," Jon said.

"Then," Baldwin continued, "a non-contested primary, fueled with Mommy Quintana's big bucks. Maria ran as a Democrat in a Democrat town, and twenty-seven-year-old Maria Quintana was elected District Attorney for Santa Fe County two years ago. It is a disgrace. What you saw today is what I have seen four or five times in her other cases, petty as they were."

"Why does Zimmerman stay on the job?" Jon asked.

"Simple. He is a real law-and-order guy, but moral, fair, and as you proved today, a good lawyer. He wants to be DA and realized as soon as Maria Quintana was elected that she would last only one term, if that long. So, he decided to hang in there, do nothing immoral or unethical, prevent as many disasters as possible, and primary her in the next election."

"Took guts," Jon said with admiration. "He may get his wish sooner than later. Manny Salazar and I are filing an ethics complaint against her with the Bar Association because of how she stiffed the defense on Walt Duran's file on Carranza's record. That's why I didn't ask you for sanctions or, I suppose, why you did not sanction her then and there."

"Correct. I was concerned that if I sanctioned her in court, the Bar Association might see that as sufficient punishment. Truth be told, I want her disbarred."

"Well, we'll see what happens." Willard stood, saying, "I've taken a lot of your time, so, I better get going."

Judge Horace Baldwin stood, shook hands with Jon Willard, Esq., and said, "By the way, I just remembered, Jim Thomason told me to say that he has an offer for you that he hopes you can't refuse."

EPILOGUE

ONE WEEK AFTER THE TRIAL, when things wound down Manny and Rachel announced their engagement. Andrea and Jon threw them a huge party at the Eldorado Hotel, arranged by Andrea and paid for by Nick Vardas. Three months later they were married in a traditional Jewish wedding, with Rose as maid of honor, Jon as Best Man. The guests included friends of the couple, Fred Zimmerman, one juror, and friends and acquaintances of the Willard defense team. A surprise guest, with his wife, was the Honorable Horace Baldwin.

When the newlyweds returned from their honeymoon at Nick Vardas's Caribbean villa, Manny Salazar became a local hero in Espanola because of his association with Willard, and active participation in *State* v. *Castellano.* Cases began coming to him not only for civil and criminal litigation, but as a consultant on real estate and zoning matters.

At their well-publicized wedding, their having come out publicly as conversos encouraged other New Mexicans to emulate them, and suddenly they found themselves with several new co-religionist friends.

Beset by the bad publicity about what Carranza had done on its behalf, New Mexico Land Investors, LLC, whatever that was, abandoned its silver mining plans. Instead, the company extended Rachel's lease for her lifetime at a nominal rent. The only condition was that she maintain a commercial sheep ranch on the property. The company also agreed not to attempt to search for, let alone open, any of the abandoned mines.

Pursuant to New Mexico Rules of Professional Conduct, "Special Responsibilities of a Prosecutor," Jon and Manny filed a complaint with the State Bar Association against Maria Quintana based on her failure to provide the defense with a copy of the sheriff's file on Carranza, which contained evidence that "tended to negate the guilt of the accused. . . ."

Not long after, the New Mexico Bar Association negotiated a compromise with Maria Quintana's personal lawyer, Robert McLachlan. Rather than disbarring the DA, she was disciplined by a twelve-month suspension, which conveniently ran to the end of her term.

Fred Zimmerman became Acting District Attorney.

Still delusional, at the end of her suspension when Quintana ran for the Democratic Party nomination for a second term, Fred Zimmerman challenged her, won the nomination, handily beat his Republican opponent in the general election, and became District Attorney for the County of Santa Fe.

When, in an aborted bank robbery in the plaza area of Santa Fe, sheriff Dave Foster was killed trying to rescue a hostage, the governor appointed Chief Deputy Walter Duran as acting sheriff until a special election could be held within ninety days. Walt was cross endorsed by Democrats and Republicans alike and won. An anonymous donor from New York City had made a substantial contribution to Walt's campaign.

Jane Davis won a joint journalism award sponsored by the *Albuquerque Journal* and *Santa Fe New Mexican* for her coverage of *State* v. *Castellano* and was among the top ten nominees for an Associated Press award.

Willard's research about Tijerina's cynical use of the land grant issue, especially his armed raid on the Tierra Amarilla courthouse, proved that it was merely an excuse to get the land out of the hands of the large personal and corporate owners, and back into the hands of the Hispanos. Then, he and his hard-core followers would attempt to convert northern New Mexico into Soviet-style collective farms, which is what Stalin and Khrushchev had done to murder the Kulaks of Ukraine back in the 1920s and 1930s. So, all along Tijerina had been a hypocritical crypto Communist, not believing land grants should be held either by communities or individual farmers and ranchers, but instead in collective farms as in the Soviet Union.

Not having forgotten about Jon's desire to have the truth told about Tijerina, and still incensed as he became more knowledgeable about Tijerina and what he was trying to do, Andrea, Rachel, and Manny searched Castellano's home looking for a carbon copy of Tijerina's pro-communist letter to then-President Lyndon B. Johnson. On the third day, they found it inside an old wooden file cabinet in a corner of her attic.

With that as the revealing linchpin of what Tijerina had been up to, Jon wrote a series of articles for the *Rio Grande Sun* and other New Mexico newspapers. Jane Davis prevailed on the Associated Press to syndicate the series throughout the country, and they changed a lot of minds about whom Reies Lopez Tijerina really was. A statue of him in front of the Tierra Amarilla courthouse was removed by local veterans and melted by the foundry in nearby Tesuque.

For a couple years following the Castellano trial, the subject of stolen land grants was a hot issue not only in New Mexico but in states such as Arizona, California, and Texas. Committees were formed, money raised, celebrity benefits were held, TV shows produced, National Public Radio and TV's *Sixty Minutes* became interested.

But then interest waned, other hot stories came and went.

Nothing changed.

The criminals who stole the Hispanos' land got away with it.

Because justice was delayed, justice was denied.

--The End--

OTHER BOOKS BY HENRY MARK HOLZER

FICTION

Justice Delayed is Justice Denied
A Fool for a Client?
The Paladin Curse (Co-author with Erika Holzer)

NON FICTION

The "Living Constitution" and the Right to Die
The American Constitution and Ayn Rand's "Inner Contradiction"
Best Opinions of the Supreme Court of the United States (Vol. I: Race) (E-Book)
The Supreme Court Opinions of Clarence Thomas, 1991–2011 (Second Edition)
The Supreme Court Opinions of Clarence Thomas, 1991–2006 (First Edition)
The Keeper of the Flame
"Aid and Comfort": Jane Fonda in North Vietnam (with Erika Holzer)
Fake Warriors: Identifying, Exposing, and Punishing Those Who Falsify Their Military Service (with Erika Holzer) *(Second Edition)*

*Fake Warriors: Identifying, Exposing, and
Punishing: Those Who Falsify Their Military
Service* (with Erika Holzer) *(First Edition)*
*Why Not Call It Treason? Korea, Vietnam,
Afghanistan and Today*
The Layman's Guide to Tax Evasion
Speaking Freely: The Case Against Speech Codes (ed.)
*Sweet Land of Liberty? The Supreme
Court and Individual Rights*
*Government's Money Monopoly: Its Origin
and Scope and How to Fight It (ed.)*
The Gold Clause: What it is and how to use it profitably (ed.)

ACKNOWLEDGMENTS

Copy editor Stephen England, an accomplished thriller writer in his own right, has the eyes of an eagle, and excellent editorial judgment.

Also thanks to Robert Bidinotto and Streetlight Graphics for help with publishing this book.

HENRY MARK HOLZER

Henry Mark Holzer received his B.A. degree from New York University, where he studied political science and Russian. After graduation in 1954, he served in South Korea with United States Army intelligence (G-2), holding top-secret security clearance, and was Chief Order of Battle Analyst (Chinese Communist Forces), attached to Eighth Army Headquarters in Seoul.

Following Holzer's military service, he earned his Juris Doctor degree at New York University School of Law. For some sixty years, he practiced constitutional and appellate law. His clients included owners of pre-legalized gold, veterans seeking medical benefits, Soviet dissidents and defectors, and the author Ayn Rand.

In addition to Henry Mark Holzer's law practice, for two decades (1972-1993) he was a full-time professor of law at Brooklyn Law School, where he is now professor emeritus. His courses included Constitutional Law, First Amendment, National Security, and Appellate Advocacy. He spent one semester as a visiting professor at the University of New Mexico School of Law in 1993.

Professor Holzer is the author of hundreds of articles, essays, and reviews, and for many years he frequently published commentary on current legal/political issues and events in the print and electronic media. He was often invited to provide that commentary on broadcast media.

Several of Professor Holzer's six out-of-print books—*The Gold Clause*; *Government's Money Monopoly*; *Sweet Land of Liberty? The Supreme Court and Individual Rights*; *The Layman's Guide to Tax Evasion*; *Speaking Freely: The Case Against Speech Codes*; and *Why Not Call It Treason? Korea, Vietnam, Afghanistan and Today*—may be available through his website, www.henrymarkholzer.com and from various Internet booksellers, including www.amazon.com.

With lawyer and novelist Erika Holzer, Henry Mark Holzer is co-author of *"Aid and Comfort": Jane Fonda in North Vietnam*, the seminal book that definitively answers the question of whether Fonda's trip to Hanoi during the Vietnam War, and her activities there, constituted constitutional treason. With Erika Holzer, Professor Holzer also co-authored *Fake Warriors: Identifying, Exposing, and Punishing Those Who Falsify Their Military Service*. Some of these books may be available through his website, www. henrymarkholzer.com, and all are from various Internet booksellers, including www.amazon.com.

Professor Holzer's *The Supreme Court Opinions of Justice Clarence Thomas (1991–2011): A Conservative's Perspective*, second edition, was published in 2012. McFarland and Company is a noted publisher of scholarly, reference, and academic books. See https:// www.abebooks.com/9780786463343/Supreme-Court-Opinions-Clarence-Thomas-0786463341/ plp

His most recent non-fiction books are *The Living Constitution and the Right to Die* and then *The American Constitution and Ayn Rand's "Inner Contradiction."*

Professor Holzer previously blogged at www. henrymarkholzer.blogspot.com. A selection of his essays appears there.

Printed in Great Britain
by Amazon